ATLANTIS
LOST

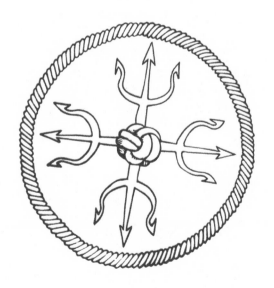

Poseidon's Children

Atlantis Lost

Orion's Hunt

The Mermaid and the Flame

Poseidon's Deep

The Island of the Last Song

The Labyrinth Under the Waves

When the Tide Comes Rising

ATLANTIS

LOST

BOOK ONE OF POSEIDON'S CHILDREN

BY PELAGIUS NEMO

It is nine hundred years since the war between the people who lived inside the Mediterranean Sea, and those who lived outside it. One side was led by Athens, the other by the kings of Atlantis.

This island was larger than Africa and Asia, but it was struck by earthquakes and floods, and in one single, terrible night, Atlantis sank beneath the sea and vanished.

This is the war which I will now describe.

Plato, approximately 360 BC

CONTENTS

1	Farewell	3
2	Poseidon's Children	24
3	An Exhilaration of Dolphins	28
4	Blood Feud of the Gods	46
5	Last Night of Safety	50
6	Atlantis	70
7	Atlantis Lost	75
8	Children of Zeus	98
9	Searching	102
10	Lords of Athens	121
11	Divers and Cavers	127
12	Peace	144
13	Deep Water, Shallow Sleep	148
14	War	165
15	Dangerous Waters	172
16	Andromeda's Curse	185
17	Decisions	192
18	The Breaking	210
19	Out to Sea	217
20	The Hiding	231
21	Nets	237
22	The First Convocation	257
23	Stormdancer	264
	Merspeech: a Short Glossary	283

My name is Pelagius Nemo, and I am a merman.

If you know anything about the war between men and mers, you know me. I was there when the flames burned on the water. I was there when the singers rose from the sea.

My sister and our friends were there when Poseidon's trident shook the seabed, and the wave swallowed Atlantis for a second time.

That is how the story ended, but you do not know how it began. You know nothing of Atlas and Perseus; you know nothing of Andromeda's Curse. You never heard the thunder that shattered the home-cave, or felt the strangling nets in the storm.

When you found me, you thought I had no history at all. That is why you called me "Nemo", which means "nobody" in your language.

But our history goes back through three thousand years of war. Mers and humans share it, and we mers have never forgotten.

Swim with me now, back through time, and I will tell it to you.

It begins with a farewell.

1
Farewell

It was time to say farewell.

The full moon had risen. The waves were still. Lights glowed on the island. Under water, the daytime fish were sleeping, hiding in crevices from the hunters of the night. And in a hidden cave, its entrance far below the waves, the spring tide was rising, bringing a new year – and a new life.

Mielikki was bubbling with impatience. Her eyes sparkled in the darkness as she stared at the pinnacle of rock.

"It's nearly there!" she exclaimed, breaking the silence. The others jumped, then laughed.

"Mielikki, there's still a fin's breadth to go," Helmi told her kindly. Helmi was Mielikki's best friend.

"Well, a fin *is* nearly," Mielikki protested. She settled back down on to the ledge, and tried to control her impatience.

The cave was shaped like a giant teardrop, upside down in the rock. The entrance was a narrow crevice twenty fathoms below the waves, but it climbed into a cavern so high that it was always half full of air, even at the highest tide. A rock spike as narrow as a needle jutted up into the middle of the dome, and on one day of the year, the tide rose so high that the tip of the needle was covered.

That day had now come.

The three merchildren waited, hearts pounding, staring across at the rising tide. To a human, the cave would have seemed utterly dark, but mer-eyes are made to pierce the depths of the ocean: they could see the water, clear as black glass, rising moment by moment.

"It's nearly there," Pel whispered after what seemed an eternity. "Nearly there..." Pel was Mielikki's little brother; he had just turned twelve.

"See?" Mielikki burst out, clapping her hands with excitement. "I told you!"

Helmi reached out and pushed her hands downwards. Mielikki had clapped right next to her ear, and her head was ringing.

They stared, quivering with tension, three pairs of eyes drilling into the dark water. There was still a tiny spike of rock sticking out, making little rings of ripples. An inch ... half an inch... Then, with a shrug as if it could not understand what all the fuss was about, the spring tide heaved up over the pinnacle, and the new year had come.

For a second there was utter silence. They had waited for so long, and the moment had come so quickly and quietly, that it was hard to believe. Then, as one, three merchildren let out a breath that they had not known they were holding.

"It's come," Pel said quietly, as if amazed. He turned to the girls, his thin face flushed with excitement. "Mielikki, it's come!"

He put his hands on the ledge, rolled forward and plunged into the water. His tail-flukes sent a shower of spray crashing over them, and he was

4

gone.

Mielikki and Helmi looked at one another. They had been waiting for this night their whole lives: now that it had come, it was almost too much to hold.

"Happy new year," Helmi said, with a crooked grin.

"Happy new year," Mielikki answered, her own grin splitting her face.

"Shall we?"

Mielikki shuffled to the edge and looked down at the water, which was still heaving where Pel had jumped.

"Let's," she said, and they dived together.

They hit the water in a fountain of spray, and arrowed downwards. Echoes volleyed around the cave, painting a sound-picture of rocks and crevices as if they were bathed in light. Helmi swooped, curving round the pillar. Mielikki swirled after her, feeling the water rush through her hair. Below them, Pel was already plunging towards the exit. The mergirls followed him, chattering excitedly.

They stopped in the cave-mouth and looked out carefully. New year or not, netmen and sharks were always a danger. But everything was still. High above, the waves shone silver. The moon's rays shivered over the cliff-face. Below, the gray sands dropped away into darkness.

- All clear, - Pel said eagerly in the underwater speech, a language of sonar clicks and whistles. - Come on! -

He pushed out into the moonlight, and laughed to see it ripple across his skin. His excitement was infectious: the others laughed too, and followed him. This was their night. This was *the* night.

After tonight, life would never be the same again.

Normally, in their night-time forays, they would have turned left or right, and gone hunting among the rocks. But this was not a normal night. They swam quickly to the surface, blinked at the netmen's lights, turned seawards and looked up at the stars. The clouds hid the Pole Star, but Orion was clearly visible, hanging low in the south-east.

"That way," Helmi said in surface language, pointing to where Orion's tail just brushed the waves. To the mers, Orion was a merman, the Wild Hunter, and the stars on his belt were trophies of his greatest kills.

The others nodded, took careful note of the direction, and dived.

They swam fast and straight, their long, deep-curved tails driving them through the water as swiftly as any dolphin. With each stroke, their excitement grew, tingling in their nerves and shining in their eyes. It was hard to keep together, hard to remember to scan for danger: the new year had come at last!

But their parents had taught them well. Automatically, they swam in a formation which gave all three the greatest protection, and at the same time allowed them to help each other along.

Helmi swam in front. Almost fourteen, she was the eldest of the three. She was slight and quick, with a fine-boned face, and her tail was as deeply-curved as a swallow's. Her eyes were the green of icy seas, and her hair was pale silver, streaked with blue. Her back and flanks were blue too, and silver ripple patterns ran across them like moonlight. She swam beautifully, graceful and balanced, but not strongly. She could sing better than anyone in the islands, but never very loud.

Pel came next, swimming half a body-length behind her and slightly to one side, so that her bow wave carried him along. He was the smallest and weakest in the school. He had been born in a time of famine, after the netmen had devastated the fishing grounds, and he had never caught up on his growth. But his hands were nimble and his eyes were bright and quick, and his mind was quicker still. He loved songs and stories, and he had the best memory of any mer in the school. His eyes were a blue so deep it was almost violet; his hair and flanks were copper, striped with bronze.

Last of the three came Mielikki. She was half a year younger than Helmi, but she looked older: strong-armed, broad-shouldered, long-tailed. She could swim as fast and dive as deep as a sixteen-year-old boy, and her tail-flukes were broad and powerful, promising that she would be even faster in time. Her eyes were amber, and shifted in color with her mood, from the brightness of evening sunlight to the smolder of kelp-stems in the fall. Her hair was the color of fire coral, deep red with white tips, and her back and flanks were blood red, shot through with tongues of gold. In daylight, she would have looked like a flame beneath the water. But the children did not come out in daylight, for then they might be seen.

She swam just behind and below the others, so that she could help them with her bow wave, without bumping into them. Mielikki often bumped into things: she always seemed to have too much strength for her body to control. When she went exploring with Helmi, Helmi would swim straight and calm, careful, controlled and quick; but Mielikki would race off, dive, pick up a shell or a stone, come back to show her, bump into her, drop the stone, apologize in confusion, try to swim straight, and then start all over again.

When she was excited, which was often, she would barge into whatever lay ahead, a fish, a rock or a fight. Viliga, one of the elder boys, sometimes said that the Atlantis Ocean was not big enough for Mielikki, and that she should move to the greatest ocean of all, Poseidon's Deep, to get more room. It was a cruel joke, because there was truth in it; there was something too big about Mielikki, something that she could never quite hide or tame.

Only when she went exploring alone did she seem to find calm. Then she would dive deeper and deeper, ignoring the pressure, swooping through the lightless depths as if they were her own. The rest of the time, she was wild and clumsy and accident prone, a difficult mer to be with. But her father said there was enough warmth in her to heat the Atlantis Ocean, and there was truth in that, too.

They swam for half an hour at a depth of six fathoms, then came up to breathe. They were now some miles offshore, and the island had slipped beneath the waves, like the last fragment of Atlantis sinking. The moon rode high in the south, but through its glow the stars twinkled clear: Atlas and Andromeda, Cassiopeia and Cepheus, Perseus and the Seven Sisters. To the children, the moon and stars were history, written across the sky: the story of Andromeda's Curse.

"How far?" Mielikki asked.

"About a mile. That way," Pel said. He knew the name and shape of every rock within twenty miles of the island, and could recite swimming directions like a song. He looked around for a moment, and then added, trying to sound casual, "Where's Thettis meeting us?"

Thettis was Helmi's elder sister, already fifteen and by far the cleverest merchild on the island. Pel regarded her with awe. Tonight, she would join them to say farewell.

"At the Gate," Helmi said, looking up at the stars. "She went to the Cleaning Station with the others."

"They're not coming too, are they?" Mielikki asked quickly. "I mean ... I don't mind Dohan, but Riakka? And *Viliga*?"

Helmi shook her head.

"It's all right. She just wanted to clean up first. She doesn't want them watching either. It's going to be difficult enough without that."

They looked at one another nervously. Tonight, they would become their own mers ... *if* they passed the test.

"Well, shall we go, then?" Pel asked. "We don't want to be late."

Helmi nodded and gave a double-click with

her tongue, Click-*clock*. It was a word from underwater language that they had adopted into surface speech; in essence, it meant, "Come on."

They dived.

They went more slowly now, for they were entering dangerous waters. Far below them, the seabed sloped slowly downwards, a waste of sand and rock. Moonbeams made shimmering pillars, straight and tall. Once, a barracuda drifted into sight, glinting like a knife; it stared at them with cold eyes, then flicked its tail and was gone.

Fear grew, stealing over their excitement like the tide over sand. The moonbeams seemed treacherous, the shadows threatening. At any moment something could come lunging out of the darkness, a deep-sea hunter like a mako or an oceanic white-tip striking into the shallows. Here, there was nowhere to hide, and a very long way to swim for safety. Mielikki heard Helmi swallow, and edged closer to her.

- It'll be all right, - she said in underwater speech, a stream of clicks so soft and tightly focused that only Helmi could hear it. Mers call it the private channel.

Helmi shot her a grateful glance.

- I know. But still... -

She fell silent.

Mielikki nodded. Whatever happened tonight would change their world. Failure would be too terrible to think of, but even success would mean not only freedom, but farewell. She looked for words, and could not find them.

- Me too, - she said finally. They swam on,

closer together.

Now the sea bed shelved more steeply, and far ahead they could sense an echoing void. There the sand and rocks poured over a cliff and down to the plains of ooze, handreds of fathoms below. ("A handred", in merspeech, means twelve dozen: one hundred and forty-four.)

For a moment, the three merchildren stopped and shivered, gazing beyond their own world; for the drop-off marked the end of the kingdom of Poseidon, lord of the sea, and the gateway to the kingdom of Hades, lord of the abyss.

Pel was the first to tear his eyes away and look up through the moonlight. He gave a happy shout.

- There she is! Thettis! - And he started to swim towards her.

Mielikki jumped and followed his gaze. There in the moonlight was a tall, slender mermaid with silver hair and blue and silver skin. She was hanging in the water a fathom or two above them, and a sense of stillness flowed from her like a warm current. As the trio swam towards her, Mielikki shifted uneasily and slowed down. Something about Thettis made her feel even more clumsy.

But she avoided any accidents, and as the four came together she saw that even Thettis' green eyes were bright with suppressed tension.

- You made it, - the elder girl said quietly. - Just in time: well done. -

- Are they here? - Pel asked eagerly, pushing forward and craning his neck to see into the darkness. Thettis smiled. She liked Pel, with his enthusiasm for songs and stories.

- Not yet, but I think I heard them, just before you called. - She glanced down at the drop-off, far below. Right underneath them, two flows of rock came together in a curious, twisted archway, ringed with jagged fangs almost like a shark's gape.

- That's the Gate, - she said quietly. - We're here. -

They fell silent, staring at the black archway so far below. The stories said that it lay seventwé - seven dozen - fathoms down, deeper than even Mielikki had ever dived. They had all heard of it, all their lives had been spent preparing for it, but they had never seen it before; children did not come this way. More than an arch, it was the Gateway: the place on the edge of the abyss where childhood ended, and a new life began.

This was the place. This was the night. Mielikki and Helmi looked at one another, and each saw her own fear mirrored in the other's eyes. Pel stared down at the arch which he had heard of in so many songs. For once his own mind was not on singing, but on the test which was to come. Thettis had withdrawn into herself, trying not to think. It was bad enough to face the test of the black waters; facing it in the sight of so many children younger than herself was too much.

But they did not have to wait for long. All of a sudden, there came a dazzling call, and the adults swept up through the moonlight like rising stars.

Heliä Solace led them, Mielikki and Pel's mother, a tall and beautiful merwoman. Her hair was long and dark, and her eyes were wise and kind. She was the most graceful swimmer the Atlantic had seen in two hundred years; Mielikki would have given anything to be that graceful herself.

Beside her was Nereus, her husband. He was smaller and darker, but his eyes were wells of laughter and his voice was beautiful and deep. His nickname, what mers call his "life-name," was Fivefingers. He had been born with five fingers on his left hand, not the usual six. He had been teased about it all through childhood, but on the day he became an adult, he had taken the name for his own, because he would not be shamed for who he was.

A little behind came Nereus' elder brother Tauno, the Red Mer. His eyes were the color of amber, and his tail-flukes flared like a banner. He was the fastest merman in a generation; all the children idolized him. But his voice was less beautiful than his brother's, and there was darkness behind his eyes. He had loved and married long ago, a merwoman from Poseidon's Deep on the other side of the world, and she had drowned in a drift-net. He had no children: he was there for his niece and nephew.

Last came Veikko Knifeblade, father of Thettis and Helmi, and his wife, Tiiu Truesinger. They looked very similar, both small and fine-boned, silver-haired and green-eyed, like siblings. But Tiiu had been born among the Blue Reefs, an ancient colony of Atlantis on the far side of the ocean. She and Veikko had met at the Convocation in the diamond waters of the far north, twenty-five years before, and they had come back to the home islands of Atlantis to marry and raise a family.

All five were smiling, glad to see their children, relieved that they had made it; but they were painfully thin. There were twelve merpeople living in these islands, struggling to find enough food as the netmen's boats thundered by, and there was never enough to go around. If it went on like this, they would starve. So tonight, the parents would swim out to sea, and leave the islands and the fishing grounds to their children. If they lived, and if they found their own life-names, in time the children would leave the islands too, and swim out to sea to rejoin their parents, and make the family complete again.

That was the way it had been for handreds of years, ever since the netmen drove the merpeople into hiding. The children had grown up believing it was how things would always be.

They were wrong.

Children and parents met at the surface in a flurry of spray. Normally their meeting would have been wild and playful, a thing of dances and leaping – a still night, a clear sky, the full moon and the stars! But this was a solemn moment, a ritual handreds of years old. They stopped, floating vertically in the water, tails beating slowly.

Black and silver, the Atlantic surrounded them, as if waiting.

Veikko and Tiiu looked at their daughters, looked at one another, and nodded.

"Thettis," they said together. The elder girl swallowed.

"Thettis, since the day you were born we have loved you. We have given and taught you all we had to give and teach. Now the last thing we can give you is the freedom to teach yourself. Are you ready to accept it?"

They all knew the words, of course; every mer knew them; they were part of growing up. But the children shivered nonetheless. It was one thing to hear them like a story, safe in the cave in the long hours of daylight; it was another to hear them in open water at night, with the Gate gaping below.

"I am," Thettis said unsteadily.

"Then swim with us out of childhood, and in at the gates of youth."

They reached out their hands. Thettis swam over and took them. Without a backwards glance, the three turned and dived, kicking straight and hard for the arch below.

Mielikki put her face in the water and watched, her heart in her mouth. It seemed as if the abyss were sucking them in, pressing them down so that they shrank: the size of a barracuda; the size of a mackerel; the size of a minnow flickering silver against the black rocks. Still they finned, closer and closer to the archway, and Mielikki realized that she was squeezing her own breath inwards in sympathy. Beside her, Helmi watched her sister go, her fists clenched, willing her to make the dive.

All of a sudden the silver shapes vanished, swallowed up into the darkness of the arch. Despite herself, Helmi grabbed Mielikki's hand. Then, suddenly, they flicked back into the light, and the watching merfolk cheered.

- There she is! - Pel.

- Well done! Oh, well done! - Heliä.

- Good girl! - Nereus.

Helmi and Mielikki said nothing. Their hearts were beating too fast.

Quickly now the silver figures rose, flickering through the moonbeams and finning fast for the air: in those days a seventwé-fathom dive was close to the limit of endurance, even for an adult. They came to the surface with a whoosh of breath and embraced, then bent their heads close together. It was a sacred moment, as the parents blessed the new merwoman. Not even the closest friend would ask what they said.

Then they swam back to join the group, and Pel, who only had eyes for Thettis, saw that her eyes were wide and her flanks heaving, but already she seemed different: older and stronger. She swam up to Helmi and gave her a quick, fierce hug, whispering something that not even Mielikki heard.

"Helmi," their parents said softly.

Helmi's fingers and Mielikki's clenched on one another, a last mute sharing of support; then Helmi pushed gently away.

"Helmi, since the day you were born we have loved you. We have given and taught you all we had to give and teach. Now the last thing we can give you is the freedom to teach yourself. Are you ready to accept it?"

Helmi cast one last glance back at her childhood friends, and swallowed.

"I am," she said, barely audible.

They held hands, breathed deeply, and dived.

This time Mielikki thrust her whole head under the water to watch, willing her friend onward with every fiber of her being. She bent forwards, her whole body tense, and she jumped as a hand touched her arm.

- Gently, daughter, - Nereus clicked on the private channel. - Don't deafen her. She'll be all right, you'll see. -

With a shock, Mielikki realized that she had been sending pulse after pulse of navigation clicks after her friend, using the echoes to follow her progress and cheer her on. It must have been horribly loud. She blushed.

- Sorry, - she whispered back. His hand squeezed her shoulder.

- Never say sorry for being a friend. Look, she's there. -

Mielikki looked down just in time to see the three shapes flick into the darkness. Her heart pounded. The seconds passed. Were they all right? Where were they? Why were they taking so long? She tensed, ready to dive to the rescue; then the three shapes blinked out into the light, and she let out a sigh of relief that burst in silver bubbles.

- Well done, - Nereus whispered. Whether referring to Helmi or herself, Mielikki could not say.

She watched in silence as Helmi surfaced, breathed and spoke with her parents; then she turned towards them. Her face was wreathed in smiles, and she took up her old place at Mielikki's side as if nothing at all had changed.

"I did it!" she whispered excitedly. "I did it!"

"You did! You were pelagic!" Mielikki whispered back. "Pelagic" literally meant "of the open sea," but it was their word for anything brave, outstanding, exciting, and Helmi's dive had been all of those. "What was it like?"

"I'll tell you when you're grown up," Helmi flashed back with a grin. "Hush, now."

There was a pause. The adults were whispering together, the moonlight bright on their wet hair. Mielikki watched, her heart pounding. When they straightened up, it would be her turn. Time to leave childhood and safety behind. Time to dive down to the gate of the abyss. Time to live on her own, until she had earned her life-name, and learned enough to find her family again. But – would she ever learn?

She swallowed. Helmi eyed her sympathetically. She knew all Mielikki's moods and secret fears. Mielikki believed Viliga's joke: she felt as if she was swimming in the wrong ocean. Helmi knew it; but she did not reach out her hand. Some things have to be faced alone.

Then, far too soon, the whispered conversation was over, and Mielikki's parents were speaking. She tried to listen, but her heart was pounding too hard. In a sudden panic, she tried to read the words on their lips, and realized that they were holding out their hands to her, and everyone else was looking at her, waiting.

"I am," she croaked in a voice that was not her own. She blundered forwards, felt her parents take her hands, and dived.

Straight down between the moonbeams she went, kicking hard and fast, but clumsily, nearly knocking her mother aside. The tension mounted in her chest. The pressure clamped on her head and ears. Now the light was fading, blackness spreading its arms out to reach her, the archway a shadow lost in a world of night. For a second she blinked, and lost it from sight. At once panic rose: where was it? Where was she? She shook her head desperately, and looked again.

- We're here, darling, - came her mother's voice close by; her mother, swimming with all the grace and freedom that Mielikki longed for, and did not have.

- You're doing well, - said her father on the other side. - Keep going. -

She gritted her teeth and, without realizing, clenched her hands tighter. The pressure was immense now, closing on her and pulling her down. At this depth, the air in her lungs was so compressed that the water could no longer support her, and her own weight dragged her down: Hades' Hand, they called it. Desperately she squeezed her stomach muscles, forcing air into her throat and ears; and all of a sudden the pain eased, and her head cleared, and she could hear the echoes of the arch right ahead of her.

She set her teeth and, without thinking, pulled her hands free of her parents' grip and kicked forwards, accelerating straight at the Gate. She heard a startled cry from her mother, a laugh from her father, a whoop from Tauno, swimming behind. The sharp-fanged archway raced closer, like a shark coming in for the kill. She let out a burst of navigation clicks that cascaded back like sparks. All of a sudden the rocks were around her, and a sharp fang of stone was coming straight at her, and she swerved and ducked and flashed past it and into the clear water beyond.

Mielikki burst through the Gate of Childhood and out into her new life like a flaming, shooting star.

- Good girl! - came her father's cry, and faintly, far above, she heard the others cheer.

Now they were rising, kicking fierce and hard for the surface. Her parents swept up beside her, ready to take her hands if she needed help. But Mielikki was climbing, the air expanding in her lungs again: Poseidon's Hand, lifting her back towards the air. Her ears squeaked with the releasing pressure, and her heart was full of a fierce excitement. She had done it! She had swum through the archway and out of childhood, alone!

She hit the surface and burst out into the moonlight, and for a second the night was so beautiful that she wanted to sing.

"You know," said her father, surfacing beside her, "most people try to keep holding hands when they're at the deepest bit."

She looked down, embarrassed, the exaltation abruptly quenched; but then she saw that he was smiling, his eyes full of pride.

"My wonderful daughter," he said, and put his hands on either side of her head, and kissed her brow.

"Well done, darling," said her mother, coming up in her turn. "You're an even better swimmer than I thought. I'm proud of you. Are you?"

Tauno surfaced, came up to them and swept

all three into a fierce, wordless hug.

They looked at one another, bright in the moonlight. Mielikki swallowed. Here, of all places, she had to tell the truth.

"I almost crashed," she admitted. "I almost swam into a rock. I almost didn't make it."

She did not know what reaction she expected; but it was not for her father to laugh.

"Who cares about almost? You *did* make it. You swam through, and made it to the far side, and you did it alone. I'm proud of you."

She looked at her mother; her eyes were very kind.

"Sweetheart, when I swam through that arch, I nearly broke my back on the last rock because I came up too soon. And your father cut his shoulder on the first pinnacle and had to spend the next week hiding in the cave, because of the blood-scent."

Mielikki stared, caught between wonder and a terrible urge to laugh.

"You just swam out of childhood. Not many people make it through that arch without a scar or two," her father told her softly. "You made it. And you deserve to be here."

She blinked back tears, heart full. There was no need to speak: they understood.

"When are you going?" she asked after a moment.

"Soon, darling. As soon as Pel has made the swim."

She nodded. Her eyes prickled.

"And when will I see you again?"

"When you're ready to come and find us.

When you know your name."

"But how will I know? I'm clumsy! I break things! *How will I know*?"

Her parents looked at her with love and compassion, and deep understanding.

"Mielikki, everymer finds their name in time. I don't know where you will find yours; perhaps you will have to go through deep waters. But I know that you are strong. You will look for it. You will find it. And you will know when your time has come," Nereus said.

"And when you know that, swim out to the ocean, and you will find us," Heliä added. "And we will be glad to see you."

They looked at each other in silence, their hands on one another's shoulders.

"This is the new year," her father said. "A new life. A new beginning. We give our islands to you, for as long as you need them. Swim and play. Grow and learn. Always keep looking, and you will find your name."

His hand squeezed her shoulder; a blessing; a farewell.

"We love you," Heliä said.

"I love you, my heart's daughter," Tauno said.

There was silence for a moment.

"Now," said Nereus after a moment, his eyes suspiciously bright. "Let's bring Pel out of childhood, and leave the islands to their new owners."

It was done. Pel had swum down, and swum up

again, slowly and painfully, but unstoppable. Again, the four youths floated together. Again, their parents faced them. Strangely, it was Tauno who spoke.

"You are the children of our hearts, and we love you. We give these seas to you. Grow wise. Grow strong. And when you are ready, we will meet, out at sea."

"We will meet, out at sea," they chorused; the ritual farewell.

For a long moment they floated there, looking at one another. Then, one by one, the adults leaned forward, swam past them so that a little wave washed over them like a blessing, turned, and headed for the open ocean. Their heads showed dark against the moonlight; their tails waved in farewell; and they were gone.

The four young merpeople stayed there, drifting, between the silver light and the black water. They had swum out of childhood and into a new world, and they were excited, exalted and exhausted, all at once.

"Come on. We're grown-ups now," Pel said, after a long, long moment. "Let's go home."

They turned their backs on the ocean, and swam towards the cave. But as they swam, each one cast a backward glance at those glittering black waters, heaving restlessly under the breeze.

One day, they would swim out to sea.

2
Poseidon's Children

Who are the merpeople? Even now, many of you humans do not know. Few of you have ever spoken with us; few have even seen us, except on a screen. For most of you, we are stories, and most of the stories are wrong.

I have read the mermaid tales you made up in the years you lived under Andromeda's Curse: sometimes I laughed, and sometimes I sighed. You say we are a cross between humans and fish, with skin on our torsos, but scales on our tails; you say we breathe water, yet talk like you. Even if you believe in magic, it is ridiculous. Fish are cold-blooded and breathe water, humans are warm-blooded and breathe air. How could a cross between the two survive?

We are not magic: we are mers.

We are your cousins. Nothing else makes sense. We have heads and hair and arms, like you; breathe air, like you; have warm blood and feed our children milk, like you; speak a language of words and poetry, like you.

But we are the cousins of the dolphins, too. We have a tail, like them; live in the sea, like them; navigate by sound, like them; speak a language of clicks and whistles, like them.

We are Poseidon's children: half human, half dolphin, wholly us. Once, in the oldest stories, we shared our secrets with you; but that was before the Curse. By the time I was born, we were the secret, and we would have died before we let you see us.

This is what we look like: a human-like head set on broad shoulders, a strong waist and a long, muscular tail. Our tails beat up and down, like a dolphin's, not side to side like a shark's. They are shaped like a marlin's, ending in deep-curved flukes. We are built for speed.

We do not have scales: our skin is smooth and sleek. Our bellies are pale, but our backs and flanks and hair are rippled with many colors, so that a band of merpeople swimming together glows like a rainbow. We do not need to wear clothes, because our skin and body fat keep us warm. Besides, anything we wore would slow us down, and a slow merman is a dead merman.

Our arms are shorter than yours; one mer fathom, the distance from fingertip to fingertip with both arms outstretched, makes one and a half human yards. But our hands are bigger, our fingers are webbed, and we have six of them, not five. Because of that, we count in twelves, not tens, and if you ever wonder why a human clock has twelve hours, and a human foot twelve inches, and a human compass three hundred and sixty degrees, it is because we taught you.

Those hands, the speed and the strength of them, are all we need to hunt. Imagine when the tide falls and the current runs wild along the rocks. At the tip of the island, the reef turns a sudden corner, and the current rushes out into the emptiness. There, a merman clings one-handed to the coral, the silver-blue ripples of his flanks blending into the moonlight, his hair drifting like weed, his free hand dangling like a frond of kelp. Nobody would notice him, least of all the school of great silver bonito drifting down the tide – until a fish brushes against him and his fingers snap shut.

25

Or picture a band of merwomen hunting snapper, in the dizzying blue far off the reef. They herd their prey into a swirling ball; then they dive into the frenzy, arms pressed close to their sides. The snapper feel the approaching bow wave and veer out of the way in panic. The merwoman feels them brush her hands; her fingers snap shut; and if she has timed her snatch right, she plunges out of the roiling tower with a fish in either hand.

Never, not even in the times of greatest hunger, would we eat the biggest fish, the titans of the open ocean like tuna and marlin and swordfish: they are far too beautiful. If you are very lucky, one day at dawn you might see a marlin jump. It breaks out in a fountain of spray. The water kindles to rainbows around it. It hangs in a shower of flying crystals, and falls, and vanishes under the waves, and you will live and die knowing that you have seen the most beautiful sight in the oceans.

When I was born, it was the time of greatest hunger. By night, we hunted among the rocks, and ate what we could catch, or starved. By day, we hid in the home-cave, and played games and told riddles and sang songs to forget our hunger, and pretended we lived in a better world - the world before the Curse.

Before the Curse! Andromeda cursed you, but we were the ones who paid for it. Once, our songs told us, we lived in great clans, millions strong, on the island of Atlantis and its colonies around the world. By the time I was born, we were reduced to little bands, twenty or thirty strong, scattered across the globe like rags of kelp after a summer storm. The only place and time we could gather safely was at midsummer in the Diamond Sea (the Arctic Ocean, you call it). There, each year, our people would gather from all across the oceans to share stories, and feed on the teeming fish, and sing, and remember who we were. There is no sight like that gathering, and no music like it: the Convocation of Mers.

When I was born, we were dying. A century before, the name-lists said that more than a hundred young merpeople had lived in our islands; now we were seven. Our people were dwindling; and if nothing had changed, within another century we would have died out.

But something did change. Something beyond our imagining. Something that turned our world and stories upside down.

Our world – and yours.

3

An Exhilaration of Dolphins

Part of learning to be free is making mistakes.

Mielikki was convinced they were making a big one.

It was the end of a summer night, nine months since they had said farewell to their parents. Behind them hung the crescent moon, a curve of molten light. Above, Arcturus glittered, a yellow beacon. Ahead, the tide of dawn was rising: green, pale yellow and the orange that brings the sun. Beneath them, the Atlantis Ocean rose and fell, dropping them into the twilight between the waves, and lifting them back up the crests towards the day.

It was the last time they would see the sun rise in peace; but they did not know that.

"Where are they?" Dohan asked impatiently, straining his eyes around the skyrim. "They should be here by now!"

Pel put his face into the waves and sent a burst of sonar towards the distant seabed.

"I *think* we're in the right place," he said when he surfaced, but he sounded uncertain.

Helmi and Mielikki exchanged nervous glances. Then, as one, they looked towards the eastern skyrim, where the orange band of dawn was growing brighter and broader by the second.

"Do you think we'll make it home before daylight?" Helmi asked.

Mielikki shook her head, and looked uncomfortably at the knotted ropes of seaweed in her hand.

We shouldn't be doing this, she thought for the handredth time.

It had all been Dohan's idea; most bad ideas were. Dohan was seventeen, his shoulders and flanks as muscular as a full-grown merman's. But his body had grown up before his mind, so that he behaved like a big, cheerful child. His best friend was Pel, so different in body and mind; the two would often go off swimming together, poking into nooks and crevices, searching for hidden treasures and laughing like little boys. Sometimes Dohan swam with the elder children, but they teased him and made him cry. Then Pel would find him, and tell him stories, and take him to play with the crabs until he laughed again.

Twice a year, a pod of goldstreak dolphins came past the islands on their long migration. By ancient tradition, the adult merpeople would go out to meet them, to ask for news – and to make sure that they did not empty the fishing grounds.

But the younger ones were strictly forbidden to follow: dolphins are unpredictable, and can be aggressive. And it was every merchild's dream to rope a dolphin and ride it. The songs said that, far to the north, there lived a race of mers who tamed the great one-horned Ghostwhales, and looped ropes around their tusks, and rode them through the ice floes. It was the children's favorite story. Every time the dolphins passed, they dared one another to try it. Every time, their parents and their own discipline told them not to.

The previous midwinter, soon after their parents left, the school had obeyed the rule. They had heard the dolphins far out to sea, but had ignored the call and stuck to the safety of the home-reefs; and it had felt like they had passed a test, and moved that much closer to adulthood. But this summer, everything seemed to have gone wrong. Fish were harder to find. There were strange tastes in the water. And on the cliff above the home-cave, the netmen were doing loud and frightening things, filling the days with the roar of thunder-machines and the clash of metal on rock.

The school slept during the day, and for a month, their sleep had been broken by the grim and grinding noise. Heads ached; tempers flared; Mielikki and her friends fought with each other, and with the older children; even Helmi and Thettis argued. And one particularly bad-tempered night they had heard the dolphins calling far out to sea, and Dohan had dared the others to go and see.

The argument was dreadful, even by the standards of that dreadful month. Riakka, the eldest of the school, had flatly rejected the idea. Dohan, in tears, had threatened to go anyway. Pel had tried to defend him. Viliga, the trouble-maker, had cuffed Pel round the head. Mielikki had tried to tail-splash Viliga, mis-timed the stroke and smacked him in the face. The elder children had turned on her. It had ended with Mielikki fleeing the cave, sobbing, while Riakka shouted that she would never be grown-up enough to find her name.

Dohan, Pel and Helmi had followed her a safe time later, and found her curled up beside a rock, staring out to sea with the tears pouring hot and furious down her face. That was when Dohan had suggested that they swim out anyway. In the blaze of her resentment, Mielikki had agreed. Now she was regretting the impulse. They were far out to sea. The sun was nearly up. There was no way they would be able to make it back to the cave before dawn. At best, that would mean another shouting match with Riakka. At worst – they might be seen by netmen. That would be catastrophic. Secrecy was safety; the end of hiding would be the end of the world.

I hope there aren't any netmen here, she thought fearfully, and glanced around the skyrim.

But her thoughts were blown away in an instant as Pel lifted his head and shouted "I hear them!"

The girls ducked their faces, staring down into water like a blue mist shot through with light. For a second there was silence; then they heard it, rising out of the depths like a flash of light: the high-pitched trill of a mother dolphin calling to her calf.

- It's them! That was them! - Helmi shouted, her face still in the water. Her own rope trailed limp and green beside her.

Another call answered, deeper and more powerful, bursting up out of the deep.

- That's Old Ukko! - Pel exclaimed. - It must be! - Ukko was the leader of the pod, a dolphin they said was a hundred years old. They had grown up hearing stories about his wisdom, his cunning and his tricks.

- It must be! - echoed Dohan, beside himself with excitement; and then, - Listen! They're going to leap! -

The clicks and squeals were rocketing out of the depths. The four young merpeople swung back to the surface to look. Even in the minute they had spent below, the light had grown stronger: now the waves were green windows rolling towards Africa, and the moon was a pale scratch in the sky. They gazed southwards, staring along the hills and valleys of water. For a second, the waves were blank, unreadable. Then:

"There!"

"Look!"

"Dolphins!"

They all shouted, they all pointed at once as a great, sleek, gray-blue shape burst out of the swell, hung curving in the diamonds of its own spray and crashed back into the water.

"Oh!"

Two more shapes, lighter and more streamlined, sailed in flamboyant arcs from one wave crest to the next.

"Look! Oh, look!"

Then the sea was boiling as the dolphins came bursting out in shoals and schools and squadrons, leaping and somersaulting and turning head over fins; cutting into the water like diving birds or crashing like dropped logs; whooping and whistling and chattering with glee.

"Come on!" Dohan burst out, and swung across the waves. Pel followed. Helmi and Mielikki hesitated for a moment. Even the smallest of those dolphins was bigger than they were, and they could be very wild... But then exhilaration seized them. It was dawn, and the dolphins were jumping! At the same moment, they laughed and sprang away, their ropes ready in their hands.

The dolphins heard them coming; dolphins always hear you coming, unless you are quieter and cleverer than an octopus, the silent burglar of the reef. They whooped and turned, bursting through the wave crests and tunneling through the troughs.

Mielikki barrel-rolled closer to Helmi, called "We're going to do it! We're actually going to do it!", dived forwards, broke through a wave and nearly crashed into a great, scarred, thick-bodied dolphin.

They swerved simultaneously. For a split second she saw his grinning mouth and winking eye as he rushed past; then she turned in her own length and flung the rope. Something huge and powerful ripped it from her grasp. Her fingers snapped shut by instinct. Every muscle in her body jolted, and the next second she was up-ended and dragged into the depths.

- Mielikki! - Helmi screamed, but she was too late: they were plunging down in a rush and roar of foam. The dolphin's cold skin, scarred with age and surging with muscle, was against her arm; bubbles streamed past her like panicking fish; the blue-black of the deep opened up below.

The water roared past her. The air squeezed her ears. Mielikki was terrified. The dolphin was bigger and stronger and wilder than she could have imagined. Somewhere behind her she heard Helmi scream. Pel gave a little yelp of distress. Her heart turned to ice. *What have we done? What have I got us into?*

All of a sudden, water swirled around her, knocked her spinning. In the same moment, the rope went limp. For a horrified second she curled in upon herself, waiting for the dolphin's attack. Then, when nothing happened, she opened one eye.

She was in deep water, so deep that the waves looked like tiny wrinkles, high above. Straight in front of her, the massive dolphin hung, the rope twined loosely around his body. His sonar swept her, so powerful that she shut her eyes in terror.

Nothing happened.

She opened one eye again.

The dolphin was still there. His beak nudged the rope, almost playfully.

She opened the other eye.

He moved his tail delicately, once, and drifted towards her.

- Rope: not good - the dolphin clicked. Dolphins and merpeople speak different languages, but the pod had been visiting these waters for generations: over the years, they had developed a set of simple phrases that both could understand.

His clicks were like a storm high overhead. Mielikki winced.

The tail beat violently, and the rope jerked into life and swirled away into the deeps. The dolphin laughed, deeply, but not unkindly.

- Catch without rope: good. Catch me! -

And with a lunge he swept past her, swirled twice around her and raced for the surface, trailing bubbles like a laugh.

The wash of his flukes sent her tumbling. When she straightened, he was already high above, a dark shape spearing up towards the waves.

Mielikki's fear vanished like wind ripples. She laughed and kicked after him, her whole body arching with the power of her tail-strokes. The dolphin was far ahead, a vanishing flicker against the waves: she kicked harder, arms pressed close to her sides, feeling her ears squeak as the pressure unclamped. She was gaining on him, she was catching him fathom by fathom, the rolling silver carpet of the waves was racing towards her...

Mielikki and the dolphin hit the surface together, burst through, curved across the sky and plunged back into the swell in an explosion of light and laughter.

"Mielikki!"

"Wonderful!"

"Me too! Me too!"

Mielikki let out a shout of joy, and the dolphin rolled, looked at her with a bright black eye and said:

- Fun! Again! -

They breathed – his breath smelt like the sea breeze – and dived. She threshed with her tail to keep pace, feeling his bow wave force her onwards. They were side by side, an arm's length apart. Dolphins swooped by. The sea was cross-stitched with bubbles. She heard a cacophony of clicks and whistles, and in the middle of it Pel's excited voice calling: - Again! Again! -

Deeper, still deeper, Hades' Hand crushing

in on them. Now they were in darkness, and the waves above looked as small as fish scales.

- Ready? - the great dolphin clicked. Mielikki tensed.

- Ready! - she clicked back.

- Now! -

They arched their backs and curved around at full speed, swooping, surging, soaring back upwards.

- Spin! - the dolphin commanded, and spiralled off to the left. Mielikki laughed and spun to her right, passing him in a rush of water. She turned further, seeing the ocean whirl by, all the way back round to meet him, and again the surface raced at them, and they exploded into the air and the light.

- Now catch! - the dolphin squealed as they knifed back through the blue, and he turned downwind and away like a skimming stone.

Mielikki tried to turn in mid-air, and fell sideways into a wave. She felt it heave her bodily upwards; then it surged past and tumbled her into the trough. She righted herself, spluttering. Another wave rose under her. She kicked out and flailed with her arms. This time she managed to lift her head above the swell. There was the dolphin, seven waves away, leaping from crest to crest. Mielikki sank back down, spat out salt, waited for the next wave, felt it lift her, kicked with all her strength – and this time she timed it just right, and the wave flung her clean out of the water like the tail-slap of a whale.

For a brief moment she saw the surface spread out below her, white-capped waves running towards the dawn; then she crash landed, kicked out and felt the swell pick her up and throw her again. Air roared in her ears as she flew. Water thundered as she dived. Leap and crash, leap and crash, she chased the dolphin down the waves.

Now he was turning, curving sideways on to the swell. Mielikki turned to cut him off, angling down into a trough, and the following wave shoved her down and rolled her under. She twisted and dove deeper, and there he was ahead of her, skimming back towards the pod a fathom below the surface.

Mielikki turned to follow. But now they were swimming against the waves, and the swell dragged and pushed her back. She gritted her teeth and went deeper. There was the great dolphin, the light rippling across his gold-streaked flanks. There were the others, not far ahead. The ropes hung twisted in the water, sinking slowly into the abyss; the dolphins were whirling around her friends like a storm. She kicked faster, faster still. She was catching him! She was actually catching him!

In the same moment he slewed sideways, coming to a stop almost in his own length. She flung her arms out desperately, and just managed to avoid crashing into him.

He half rolled, and his dark eye looked squarely at her. It was an old eye, full of years and full of wisdom. The expression on his beak did not change – dolphins cannot move their face muscles – but his glance was approving.

- I: Ukko, - he said. - This pod: my pod. You? - Mielikki gaped.

- Mielikki, - she said with an effort. *I just tried*

to rope Ukko! her mind yammered. - I: Mielikki. -

- Mielikki: good, - he replied. - Island far. Water deep. Children: good. -

I just tried to rope Ukko! Oh Poseidon, I just tried to rope Ukko...

He seemed to be waiting. She swallowed again, desperately.

- Rope: bad, - she said nervously after a moment. - I: sorry. -

He rolled over, a silent laugh, and the black eye sparkled like jet.

- Rope: normal. All mers try, - he said. - Mielikki father Nereus? Nereus try. Nereus' father Antti. Antti try. -

Mielikki gaped again. Thoughts flashed in and out of her mind like fleeing fish. *He knows Father? Of course he knows Father. But ... Father tried to rope a dolphin? Grandpa Antti did?*

- Dolphin. Not Ghostwhale, - Ukko said firmly, but there was humor in his voice. - Mers ride Ghostwhale, not goldstreak. -

She looked down at her hands, looked up again. Before she could think of what to say, he spoke again.

- Pod sing for children? -

Mielikki's jaw dropped in shock. *The pod? Sing for us? Is that even possible?*

She forced herself to be calm.

- Pod sing. Yes please! Then children sing for pod. -

It was out before she even knew she was thinking it, and she bit her lip. *The four of us, sing for a hundred dolphins? Am I mad?*

But Ukko rolled right over in surprise and laughed a laugh that bounced off the bottom of the ocean.

- Good children! Pod sing: children sing. Special children. -

He let out a long trill, and the game of catch slowed like a wave washing back down the beach. The blue water heaved up and down. The last bubbles bobbled to the surface. The ropes sank gently, gently out of sight. The dolphins hovered all around them, watching, waiting. Pel, Helmi and Dohan hung between them, faces alight with excitement.

Again Ukko whistled, and this time, straining her ears, Mielikki thought she caught words in there, like the mer-words for "sing" – and for "hunt." A chill ran through her. Surely she had misheard? There was no time to wonder. With a flick of tails, the dolphins scattered into the blue. Within seconds, the merchildren and Ukko were alone.

Helmi hurried over to Mielikki and took both her hands.

- It's all right! - she exclaimed. - We tried to rope them, but it's all right! -

Dohan turned a back-flip in pure excitement. Ukko laughed: not having arms, that is one thing that no dolphin can do underwater as well as a mer. Hearing the laugh, Dohan back-flipped again.

- There they are! - said Pel all of a sudden. He was scanning into the blue with his own sonar. - They're scattering. -

The other children turned to look. All their eyes could see was blueness, a spectrum made of one color, from blue-white at the surface to blue-black in the depths. But as they sent out streams of clicks, they picked up many echoes, swift and flickering: dolphins.

- They're all around us, - Helmi said, suddenly uneasy.

- That's how they hunt, - Dohan said.

Mielikki shivered. All the warnings came back to her. Stay away from dolphins, until you're big enough to escape them ... Never anger a dolphin (*Ropes*, she wondered. *What about ropes?*). Tales of dolphins going mad, running wild, attacking everyone they saw, even mer-children ... She glanced sidelong at Ukko (was it really Ukko?), but there was no expression on that smiling beak, that impenetrable black eye.

What have we done? Why did we come?

She swallowed and moved closer to Helmi for reassurance.

They hung there in the empty water, one dolphin and four merchildren waiting for the song. To the eye, they looked all alone, lost in an expanse of blue; to the ear, they were surrounded by a mile-wide ring of dolphins. They were circling slowly, almost silently, and sinking gradually deeper: soon they were a good twenty fathoms below.

Far out of sight, one big male whistled. At once the circle began to spin faster. In the same moment, the clicking began, a wild, menacing heartbeat from every point of the circle. The ring spun faster, and began to rise like a whirlpool.

One dolphin let out a cascade of whistles, a firework of sound.

Faster spun the circle, and faster still.

A second dolphin let out a flurry of whistles, and then a third, bursts of music like shooting stars. More joined in, until the children were blinded and deafened, their own sonar lost in the storm.

Mielikki swallowed. *This is a hunting song,* she thought urgently. *Are we the prey?* Dolphins hunt by circling shoals of smaller fish, herding them into an ever-tighter ring, trapping them against the surface and launching themselves in for the kill. For a second she knew how it must feel to be their quarry. She edged still closer to Helmi.

- There! - her friend burst out suddenly, her voice high with nervousness. Right on the edge of sight, where the water melted into blue infinity, a golden blur flicked into sight and vanished again: the flank-patch of a dolphin.

They strained their eyes, desperately trying to pierce the blue, but the dolphins hung in the shadows, out of eyeshot.

- And there! - Even Dohan sounded alarmed.

Now the circle came into sight; now the singing reached its peak. It was as if the sea had turned to rainbows, flashing and darting, melting and shifting, dazzling, bewildering, blinding.

Suddenly a dolphin broke out of the circle and shot straight towards them – a dark shape crowned with lightning bolts of sound. Mielikki let out a yelp of sheer terror, and he swirled past them and was gone. Another came soaring on a wave of music, swerved to pass them, and raced out of sight. They spun round, and this time two swept in from opposite directions, barrel-rolled to pass each other, and sped off in a trail of bubbles.

Now there were dolphins coming at them from all angles, slicing through the water barely a finger's breadth away. The merchildren hung in a storm of sound, too terrified and exalted to move.

All at once Ukko gave a deafening trill, and the ring imploded. Every dolphin spun at once and raced in towards the center. The children barely had time to flinch. All around them were racing fins and flailing tails, the water battering them in mad swirls and currents; and then, just as suddenly, it was over, and the dolphins flicked into the blue.

Mielikki and Helmi stared at each other, utterly drained. Beside them, Pel and Dohan were hanging onto Ukko's flank, speechless.

- Good song, - the old dolphin clicked calmly. - Hunt song: good song. -

- Yes. Yes! - Mielikki and Helmi replied breathlessly. - Good song! -

Ukko angled his body gently upwards, rising towards the air.

- Breathe now: children sing after, - he said. Mielikki's friends exchanged startled glances.

- Sing? - Helmi quavered privately to Mielikki.

- I promised, - she replied uncomfortably. - I'll do it on my own if you want. -

They broke the surface, and realized that it was full day: the sun was a blinding disc above the waves, and the scream of seagulls and the rumble of engines filled the air. They breathed quickly and sank back down: daytime was no time to be on the surface, with the netmen prowling.

- Day, - Ukko said. - Children: island. -

They looked at each other; the reminder of the long swim back was like a splash of icy water. Their discomfort was clear. A rapid burst of conversation passed between the dolphins, too high and fast to follow.

- Children swim: Ukko swim. Ukko swim: pod swim, - the bull said. - All safe together. -

Mielikki felt a sudden weight lift off her heart.

- Thank you, - she said. - Ukko: good. Ukko: very good. -

Again, laughter lit the bright, black eye.

- Good children. Brave children. Children: sing. -

The pod was gathering again, whistling and chattering: their hunt song had been magnificent, and they knew it. Mielikki swallowed and looked at her friends.

- What shall we sing them? - she asked. Dohan shrugged; Helmi said nothing.

- They sang a hunt song. We can sing a greeting song, - Pel suggested.

Mielikki considered it. When one band of merpeople meets another, they sing: one song if they come in peace, a second for a challenge, a third if they are passing through. It was generations since any strangers had come to Mielikki's islands, but every one of those generations had passed its songs on to the next.

- A peace song, - she decided. - A slow one. -

- So we don't make mistakes, - Helmi said nervously. Mielikki tried to smile at her.

- We won't, - she said.

- We can't, - said Pel cheerfully. - You could sing it in your sleep. -

Without waiting for the others, he started to sing. His voice was small, all but lost in the immensity of the blue, but clear and true, a slow, solemn melody like waves under the moon.

Mielikki squeezed Helmi's hand, and they joined in. At first their voices wavered; but the song was so familiar that their fears quickly vanished. Mielikki's voice was strong, but harsh: she had never been much of a singer. But Helmi's rang like a bell, and all around the dolphins came clustering in, rolling and clicking and looking at them with eager eyes.

Now Dohan joined in. Unconsciously, the four began to move with their music, tails beating, arms reaching out, hands opening to each point of the compass. To Mielikki's amazement, the dolphins began to turn with them, dozens of sleek bodies mirroring their movements, and a wave of joy swept through her so strongly that her voice broke.

Almost before they knew it, the song was done. The pod stared at them in silence.

- Good song, - said Ukko eventually. - Good children: good song. - It was like a verdict, and all at once, the pod shook back into life: with flicks of their tails they swam in closer to their leader, and an excited buzz of chatter rose.

- Now: island, - Ukko said firmly. - Day time: danger time. Island safe. -

- Island: swim, - Mielikki agreed. All of a sudden, the desire to lie down on her own sleeping ledge was overpowering. Even the thought of facing an angry Riakka did not worry her much.

- Sleep! I could sleep all day, - Helmi whispered, beside her. - Even with the racket the netmen make. But I'll never forget that. -

Ukko heard her, and clicked approvingly.

- Dolphins remember. Remember friends, - he said. - Come now. -

He sculled forwards, slowly enough that they could keep up. Above, the sun climbed over the Atlantic Ocean. Below, its rays probed the blue-black depths. All around, the pod swam, watching for danger. And in the middle, tired and happy, swam the school.

They did not look up to see the home island rise out of the waves. If they had, they might have seen the yellow digging-machines perched on the cliff above the home-cave, their steel-tipped claws raised, like Zeus' thunderbolts poised to strike.

4

Blood Feud of the Gods

What caused the Blood Feud of the Gods? What disaster led to Andromeda's Curse, so that the history of our two races ran through three thousand years of war?

This is the tale we merchildren learned, in the bitter years before Poseidon's Thunder shook the deep...

In the beginning were the sea and the sky. The world was a playground, and they played like children: the wind chased the waves, and the ocean currents chased the wind.

One day, the sky looked down at the sea, and thought: how beautiful she is! I will lift her up, and show her my kingdom. And the sky swept the water up into the air, and carried her as clouds, to show her the glory of the world. And the water wept with happiness, and the first rain fell.

And the water looked up at the sky, and thought: how handsome and kind he is! I will make treasures for him. And she sculpted frost like lace and ice like jewels, and the wind blew around them and cried out with delight.

Thus their love was born before they even knew it, quick and sudden at the gateway out of childhood. Night and day they danced and played, until all the world resounded with their joy.

Then the sky said: Come, live with me, and we can be one for ever! And he swept the water up into his embrace. But his arms could not hold her, and she fell back into the sea.

And the water said: Come, live with me, and we can be one for ever! And she reached out to catch him. But when her arms closed, he slipped through her fingers, and was gone.

And the wind wept, and the sea sobbed.

When the tempest passed, they looked at each other with new sorrow, and new love. And the ocean said: Let us make a new place, so that we can be there together. So the wind blew harder, and the waters rolled back, and out of the ocean there rose the land; and where land and sky and sea came together, their three sons were born.

They named the eldest Poseidon. The second, they called Hades. And the youngest son, but the biggest, they called Zeus.

The boys grew swiftly, until the world seemed too small to hold them; and they fought, as boys will, until the lands and the ocean shook. So their parents called them together and said: You have come to your full strength, but not to your full wisdom. Now you need room to learn wisdom, and that you must do alone. So we will go out, beyond the circle of the world, and leave it as your inheritance. Share it well, and learn wisdom, until the time comes for you to rejoin us.

And the spirits of sea and sky departed, even as the parents of the merpeople still depart, leaving their children to grow and find wisdom, if they can.

The three brothers looked at one another, suddenly bereft and uncertain. And Poseidon said: I am the eldest. I will take the seas for my inheritance, because that is the fairest and largest portion, and it is my right.

Hastily, Zeus said: I am the strongest! I will take

the land and the sky, and rule over heaven and earth, and Hades will have the abyss.

But Hades said: Not so. I am the second-born, and the second choice should be mine.

Zeus frowned, and for the first time, lightning flashed across the heavens. Poseidon leaned forward to challenge him, and the mountains trembled. Their shapes fell dark upon their brother, and it seemed as though they would crush all the world in their lust for power.

Then Hades looked from brother to brother, and he held up his hand, and the world was still.

In the silence, Hades said to Poseidon: You have taken the greatest portion. That is your right, and I accept it. And Poseidon bowed.

And Hades said to Zeus: You have demanded the sky; and I give to you the second choice which should have been mine, because you are stronger. And Zeus bowed.

And Hades laughed a laugh which silenced the wind, and said: The abyss is my share, the poorest portion, though I am not the poorest in spirit. But because you have both bowed to me, at the last I shall have power over both of you. For all living things come to the abyss in the end.

Then the sky thundered, and the waves crashed; but the laughter of Hades brought a dreadful silence.

And the brothers turned their backs on one another, and each went to his own kingdom, and filled it with life.

Poseidon, the eldest, brought forth the richest store; and there is more beauty in the oceans than all the lands and skies of the world. And he forged himself a trident, to show that he ruled the three brothers; and the power of the earthquake was in it.

And he married Thalatta, goddess of the salt waters; and they had two mighty sons, Atlas and Orion, born to be kings. And Atlas made his home on a great island ringed with reefs, which was called Atlantis, the Island of Atlas; and he married Amphitrite the Kind, she who cares for the creatures of the sea; and they had seven daughters, each greater than any queen.

But Orion the Wild Hunter vanished into the seas, and none in those days knew where he made his kingdom; and if he had children, no song of Atlantis tells.

And Zeus brought forth the birds and animals, and cloaked the land in grass and flowers, and said it was rich and great; but he knew in his heart that the sea was greater. And so he created Man, and put in him the desire to rule the waters which were not his; and he forged for himself a spear like a bolt of lightning, with a single dazzling point, to show that he ruled alone. And Zeus, too, had many children; and they hated the children of Poseidon, and there was war between them.

And Hades, the silent and the wise, took his kingdom in the uttermost depths of the sea, and made life where the fires burst from the sea bed, far from the light of day. And he had no spear, but made himself a trumpet, and it had no color, but was as clear as glass; and he will only sound it once, at the end of days. And there in the abyss he watches and waits for his time to come.

For all living things come to the abyss in their time; but the sea and the sky are for ever.

5
Last Night of Safety

The night after they sang to the dolphins was the last night they would ever be safe.

Mielikki awoke just after sunset, feeling hungry. Outside, the wind was questing through the rocks. Little waves were lapping against the cliff: *slip-slap, slip-slap*. The sounds filled the cavern with a faint glow of sonar, as if the walls were shining.

For a moment she lay there, remembering. They had come home in the full glare of morning, through seas alive with light and noise. Netboats thundered by; once a quartet of crash hulls had battered across the waves right above them, sending them plunging for the depths in a panic. But Ukko and his pod had protected them, swimming close above them so that they were invisible to anyone on the surface. They had said a swift farewell at the mouth of the home-cave, swum into the cave, crawled out onto their rocky sleeping platforms and fallen asleep after no more than a little excited whispering. Riakka and the other elder children, deep asleep, seemed not to have noticed.

For once, the netmen had not disturbed them. The young mers blessed the silence, and hoped that it meant their ordeal was over. They did not know that it was the netmen's day of rest, and that it would be followed by a greater ordeal than they could have dreamed...

Mielikki listened. She was alone: she could tell it as easily as seeing, by the gap in the pattern of sound that would have been her friends' breathing and heartbeats. That was all right: Helmi would be nearby, and Pel would be off playing with Dohan, hunting for octopus under the rocks, or sitting and listening to the music of the sea. The elder children would also be off somewhere, practicing being grown up.

She heaved herself to the lip of her sleeping ledge and sent an enquiring click downwards. The tide was more than halfway in: there was a three fathom drop to the surface. Only the faintest murmur ruffled the web of sound as she took a deep breath; then she rolled over the edge.

Crazy echoes ricocheted around the cave as she hit the water, but she raced below them, plunging into the exit tunnel. After twe-six fathoms (twelve-and-six, the merword for eighteen) it ended in a crack barely wide enough for a merman to pass, at the back of a small cave. The cave was empty, save for one enormous violet anemone in the middle of the ceiling; arrow crabs scuttled around it on red-gold stick legs, their spiked noses lifted curiously. On the far side, an even narrower passage wound downwards, turned a corner, and opened abruptly into the cool gray shadow world of the night.

She stopped just within the cave mouth, and glanced upwards. Straight over her head, the cliff reared in a crumbling wall two-three fathoms high. Waves broke against it, unnaturally white in the twilight, and beyond the surface it kept on rising in a crumbling, unstable wall. Every now and then, a rock would break off and crash into the sea, sinking with a sullen roar of bubbles; the last time it had happened, it had thrown up a cloud of foul tasting silt that had lingered all night. It was a dangerous place; but at least it meant that the humans had never tried to live there.

Not yet.

The sun was down, the moon not yet up: all was gray and misty. A few damselfish were feeding, their little bobbing shapes faint in the twilight. The brilliant blue streaks at the base of their fins showed clearly. There seemed to be nothing to fear.

A sudden movement to her left made her jump; but it was only a moray eel peering out of a crack. Its pugnacious jaws gaped wide: that is the way morays breathe.

- Good evening, - she said light-heartedly. The moray gave an offended twitch and slid back into its crevice. Eels talk, but only to other eels.

Mielikki stuck her head out of the cave and sent a low call into the darkness, ready to duck back if danger showed. Faint echoes came back from the damselfish; further off, a pair of cuttlefish scuttled between the rocks. Far off to her right, she could hear Pel and Dohan; they seemed to be hunting something, whether for fun or food she could not tell. Apart from that, nothing.

She looked out further.

- Helmi! - she called.

For a moment, there was no reply.

- Helmi! - she called again.

- Here I am! - the warm answer washed over her from directly overhead, where a narrow ledge provided a convenient resting place. Helmi could make even a call-click sound like a smile.

- Coming out? -

- Coming out! -

A watcher floating above them might have seen two shadows stretch out from the cliff-face, look up and around, and swoop together. If that watcher had had the ears to hear, they would have heard the excited chatter of two girls who have not seen each other for hours, as the friends spun round each other, arched their tails and nose-dived down the slope. But that watcher would have had to be more than silent, more than invisible, or the girls would not have come out at all.

The damselfish scattered as they curved past, then went back to feeding on floating specks. An octopus flowing across the rocks sank back into a crack, its beak outwards. A big, scarred turtle looked up warily from browsing on algae and veered off into the depths: the merchildren used to tease him by tickling his beak with bubbles to make him sneeze. Laughing and giggling, Mielikki and Helmi chased each other around boulders furred with weed, and across sand flats ribbed by the waves, towards a black spire of rock where fish clustered like birds around a tree.

This was the Cleaning Station. Here, as far back as the songs went, fish, turtles, dolphins, sharks and merpeople had come to have their skins cleaned and their teeth picked by the little cleaner-fish and shrimps; tiny, colorful animals that lived on parasites and scraps of dead skin. All day and night, fish would cluster to the tower of rock, tilt themselves head down to show that they wanted to be cleaned, and wait patiently as the little animals went to work. Mielikki had once seen a manta roll completely upside down in pleasure as a dozen red-striped shrimps scurried over its pure white belly picking off ticks; on that enormous surface they looked like ants running across a beach.

- Make way, make way! - giggled Helmi, waving her hands at a sluggish gilthead bream. The fish shook her metallic head and stuck out her huge lips critically as she flicked away.

- That's right, some of us have to breathe, - Mielikki added, pushing in close to the rock. She and Helmi hooked their fingers under a ledge and swung head down as first one cleaner wrasse hurried over, then a second. They were tiny things, no bigger than a finger, with bright green flanks, yellow stripes and a black eye-spot in the middle of their backs. They looked too vulnerable to survive; but they were the safest things in the ocean. Not even a shark would attack a cleaner-fish. They were too valuable to eat.

The girls talked happily as the fish went to work. Cleaning was one of the great social activities on the reef, as the songs said:

> *Chatter, clicks and cleaning:*
> *No ticks where talk is teeming.*

There was so much to talk about: the dolphins' dance, the songs, the brilliance of the blue in daylight, the quivering sunbeams probing the depths, the excitement of breaking a rule and getting away with it. They both talked at the same time, interrupting each other so often that it was like holding two conversations in the space of one.

- Next new moon I'm really going to do it. I'm really going to swim out! - Helmi clicked, arching her back luxuriously as the wrasse worked its way over her tail-flukes. One of the biggest tests they had to face before they were ready to follow their parents was to swim alone, at night, to the Lone Rock, an underwater mountain far away that marked the end of the inshore waters. To do it took strength, endurance, navigation and courage.

- You keep saying that! You've been saying it all summer! - Mielikki told her. Helmi stuck her tongue out. Mielikki blew a raspberry which came out in a string of silver bubbles, startling the fish.

- This time I am! Next new moon, I'm going to swim out to the rock. If you can do it, I can, - she added firmly.

Mielikki wriggled uncomfortably. She had already made the swim, by accident, that spring: she had swum out on one of her lonely expeditions, searching for caves near the drop-off, and the current had swept her so far out to sea that she lost all sense of direction. Only when she saw the Lone Rock beneath her did she realize where she was. Nomer in history had made the swim at such a young age; as Viliga said maliciously, it was just like Mielikki to do it by mistake. At the time, she had been terrified of the size and darkness and emptiness of the ocean; but there was no way she would worry Helmi by saying so.

She decided to take refuge in teasing.

- You'll be scared! - she said in her special teasing voice, the one which meant, *You know I'm lying, but it's fun, so join me.* - There are white-bellies... and assassin whales... and striped sharks...
-

Helmi gave a double-click, a sound that usually meant "Yes," but laden with so much irony that it came out as an unbelieving question, tk-*tik?*

- Oh, really? And you saw all of those, did you? -

Mielikki replied with an emphatic double-click of her own, tak-*tak!* In reality, she had not seen anything larger than a sardine.

- I did too! It was pelagic! -

- Oh, really? And how did you get away? -

- The white-belly saw the assassin whale and thought, He's whiter than me, and swam away. Then the assassin whale saw the striped shark and thought, He's got more patches than me, and he swam away. Then the patched shark saw me, and thought, She's scarier than me, and he swam away too... -

They both giggled, spurting out bubbles so that the wrasse scattered.

- Time to breathe? - Mielikki asked.

- Time to breathe, - Helmi clicked, and they curled themselves upright and drifted carefully towards the surface.

Two fathoms below the waves they stopped, feeling the surge pick them gently up and drop them back downwards. This was the danger depth, where they were vulnerable to attack from above and below, and the barrier of the surface made it hard to see threats above. First Mielikki turned in a complete circle and sent a long stream of clicks just under the surface, while Helmi scanned the depths; then they swapped.

- Ready? -

- Ready. -

They drifted up the last two fathoms and broke the surface in the trough of a wave.

The moon had not yet risen, but still it was brighter here, after the gloom below. Far to the right, the orange lights of the netmen's town gleamed angrily, spilling oily reflections into the water. Further still, their lighthouse dragged its white finger around the sky. The mess of human noise rolled heavily over the sea: grumbling motors, thumping songs, the sudden spikes of shouting.

Mielikki pulled a face.

"Do you think they know how ugly it sounds?"

"Maybe they like it that way," Helmi answered.

"Stupid mullets. They must be deaf." The boxlip mullet of the Atlantic islands feeds by scraping its food off the silt. Mers think it the second most stupid fish in the sea, after the striped bream, which sticks its snout in the sand and sucks.

"Maybe that's why they play it so loud."

Mielikki looked towards the town, her face hard. Then she turned away.

"Forget them. Come on, I'm starving."

"You're always starving."

"These days, who isn't?"

They took a deep breath, finned upwards so that they rose out of the water to the waist, pointed their flukes and let the momentum carry them under water. At once the human noise was muted and the sounds of the reef returned: clicking, crackling, grunting and scraping as a million sea creatures went about their nightly lives. At the six fathom line they levelled off and finned gently southwards, parallel to the coast.

They had only gone a few fathoms when they heard sonar approaching. Helmi groaned.

- Here comes Riakka, - she muttered apprehensively. - Can't we hide? -

Mielikki looked around, but the rocks were blank and bare.

- There's nowhere to go. -

- What if they ask about last night? We were out much too late! They must have noticed! -

Mielikki lifted her chin defiantly. - So what? We came home with dolphins! You can't get safer than that! -

- But the rules! We were out in daylight! They'll be furious! -

- The rule is don't be seen! And we weren't. - She flashed her friend an encouraging smile. - Don't worry. Leave the talking to me, and we'll be all right. -

Helmi nodded and tried to look confident, without success. None could question Mielikki's loyalty to her friends; the problem was the questionable stories she made up to protect them.

Soon they came into sight, three merchildren almost fully grown, drifting down the current towards the home-cave. Riakka was leading them, as usual: a big, black haired mergirl with a long tail and powerful shoulders. She was Dohan's twin sister, half an hour older, and expected to swim out to sea at the next spring tide. Since she acted as if she were responsible for everyone else, the younger merpeople could not wait to see her go.

Below and a little behind her came Thettis. She had grown thinner in the nine months since their parents swam out to sea; they all had. She still carried with her an air of calm, unfathomable depths, but her face was more drawn, and she spent less time with her sister and the younger ones. She expected to swim out with Riakka, and the tension of knowing that her days on the island were numbered was slowly growing upon her.

Behind them all came Viliga. He was fifteen, halfway between the younger children and the older ones in age. His body was thin and his face was sharp, and his arms seemed too long for the rest of him. He had been born at low tide in the dark of the moon, the worst time to come into the world, and both his parents had died in the famine. He was always ready with a snide comment or a sneaky attack: he teased Dohan because he was big, Pel because he was small, Helmi because she was graceful, Mielikki because she wasn't. But his ears were as sharp as his malice, and his sonar was more precise than anyone in the school.

- Where were you? - Riakka called, as soon as they came into sight. - We went looking for you before sunrise, and we couldn't hear you anywhere! -

Mielikki stifled a groan. She had known they

were taking a risk, staying out so late, but it had never occurred to her that the elder children would actually go looking for them.

- *Trrr...* - It was a hesitant trill of the tongue, the mer equivalent of a human "erm".

- That's convincing, - Helmi whispered on their private channel, with a scared giggle.

- Yes, where were you? - Viliga chimed in, always eager to stir up trouble. - We looked everywhere! You haven't been out in daylight again, have you? -

The three stopped swimming and hovered in front of them, frowning.

- We went deep, - Mielikki said resentfully

- Deep? - asked Thettis.

- Deep. We went looking for orange coral, and lost track of the time. You know how dark it is down there, - she improvised.

- All of you? - Riakka asked suspiciously. She knew that Mielikki loved deep diving, but neither Helmi nor Pel was a strong swimmer.

- All of us, - Mielikki replied stoutly. - Pel stayed a bit shallower, because they were looking for a cuttlefish. -

- So what time did you come back? Was it light? -

Mielikki hesitated. It was tempting to say that they had come back in darkness, but what if the others had been awake?

- It was just getting light when we came up to breathe, - Helmi broke in suddenly. - We were a long way offshore. Then we went back down and swam back to the cave underwater. We stayed deep the whole way. -

Everymer looked at her, Mielikki surprised, Riakka suspicious, Thettis with an expression that seemed far too knowing for comfort.

- And you weren't on the surface in daylight? Not even by mistake? I know what you're like! - Riakka said, still suspicious.

- *No!* - clicked Mielikki, a hard and furious sound. Anger and embarrassment boiled inside her. She did not know that Riakka had panicked when she realized that the younger children had not come home by dawn. She had organized the others into a search party and rushed out to find them. By the time they came up to breathe, the sun was risen: they had found themselves on the surface and close in to the shore when the humans were already stirring. Riakka's anger with Mielikki was more than half anger at herself.

The silence lengthened.

At last Viliga broke it, seeing no way of causing more trouble. – This is stupid, - he said, - Why are we wasting time? -

Riakka and Mielikki glared at one another a moment longer; then Thettis swam forwards.

- Viliga's right, - she said. - We're all here, and we're all safe. We need some peace and quiet. Let's go. -

Riakka nodded. Without another word, she leaned forward and flicked away down the tide. The others followed her. Viliga nudged Mielikki with his hip as he went by.

Mielikki stared after them, her hands working with anger and embarrassment.

- Are you all right? - Helmi asked nervously.

- No I'm not all right! How dare she talk to me like that? Just like some little baby who's broken the rules! -

Helmi twisted her fingers together. - Well, you did, - she said hesitantly.

- Did what? - Mielikki snapped, turning on her.

- Break the rules. I mean … we were out on the surface at daylight, weren't we? -

Mielikki threw a smoldering glance at her; then, gradually, the heat went out of her gaze.

- I suppose we were, - she admitted. - Anyway, we sang for the dolphins. I bet Riakka's never done anything like that. -

Helmi began to relax. Mielikki's bad moods were like a big stone dropped in a small pool: a loud splash, but it sank quickly. But then she saw the spark of mischief growing in her friend's amber eyes. Helmi watched apprehensively.

Mielikki turned to her. - Thettis was right: we need some peace and quiet. -

Helmi blinked.

- And I know where we're going to find it, - Mielikki continued.

- Not the surface again, - Helmi warned.

- The surface? Who mentioned the surface? They want us to stay away from the surface, so that's what we're going to do. We'll go as far from the surface as we can. -

Helmi groaned as realization dawned. - Mielikki… -

- Well, why not? We told them we'd gone

deep, and they didn't complain. Why don't we go deep after all? -

- Because it's cold and dark and dangerous? - Helmi suggested, without much hope: she knew Mielikki too well.

- No, it's not! It's just … deep, - Mielikki said. By her standards, that was a major concession. Mielikki loved deep water, and was always amazed when others preferred the shallows.

Helmi could not help laughing, blowing out a thread of bubbles which shone like silver mirrors in the moonlight.

- All right, then, if you want to so much. Let's go really deep, - she said.

They rose carefully to the surface, and lay there for a minute, dragging in great lungfuls of air and puffing it out again hard: deep diving starts with deep breathing. The waves heaved by as black as jet, and the moonlight laid a shining scepter southwards to the Equator.

"Ready?" Mielikki asked.

"Ready."

Together they took the deepest breaths they could, arched forwards and dived.

They finned quickly downwards, slanting steeply between the moonbeams. The pressure built up in their ears; they pinched their noses and blew against them to ease it. The moonlight faded. The surface noises died away. Below them, a long slope of sand thickened into sight. They swooped low over it and followed it deeper, out to sea.

It was utterly dark. Even straining their eyes, they could barely see the gray-black sand below them, or the silver waves high above. This was the realm of sound, not sight. Instead of light, there were echoes; instead of colors, textures. Sand gave back a soft sound, blurred and shifting like mist. Boulders echoed sharp and brilliant like lamps. A hake swimming up out of deep water to hunt gave back a surprisingly metallic echo, his smooth snout ringing like a bell. A grove of eels shrank back into their holes, making a sound like a gusting wind. As they went deeper, red and yellow fans of coral appeared, their echoes humming like a harp string. Urchins, which make rocks look sharper, made them sound softer, blurring the sound with their countless spikes.

Thirty fathoms down, the long slope stopped abruptly, pouring over a lip of broken rock into nothingness. Here, by silent consent, the two girls stopped for a moment, scanning all around. Straight beneath their tails, the cliff fell sheer handreds of fathoms deep. Ahead, the emptiness sucked away all sound.

- All right? - Mielikki asked Helmi, and heard her swallow. The abyss looked very black.

- All right, - she replied bravely.

Mielikki reached out and squeezed her hand. - We can go back, if you want. -

There was silence for a moment; then Helmi blew a raspberry like a burst of purple light, kicked forwards and nose-dived over the drop-off. Mielikki laughed and followed her.

This was real diving: head down, straight down, between the black rock wall and the black gulf of the ocean. The cliff sped past, crawling with strange life: hairy crabs and see-through shrimps, a gold-spotted moray, urchins clicking their needles in the current.

Blackness behind them, blackness below, blackness to either side. Then an echo bloomed ahead of them: a shelf of rock, wide enough for six mers to sit together. On either side, great fans of coral opened their lacy wings. Behind the shelf, a little cave opened in the cliff. On the wall above, orange corals bloomed like flowers in Hades' garden.

They sped towards it in a headlong dive, their hair whipping backwards in their wake. As they descended, a shape moved sluggishly: a fish as heavy as they were, thick-bodied and sullen-lipped, with a crest of spines along its back. It shook itself and flicked away as they approached: a giant comb-back, good to eat, but too hard to catch at this depth.

The shelf grew and grew, racing up at them; and at the last moment, when a crash seemed inevitable, they flung out their arms, flared their webbed fingers, pivoted in a rush of water, and curled their tails down with barely a puff of sand.

It was a perfect place to sit. The fan corals on either side screened them from the current; only their hair, floating above them, streamed out to one side as the tide hurried along. The sand was level and smooth, too deep for waves to sculpt it in uncomfortable ridges. Mielikki had found it that winter on one of her long, deep exploring dives. She had told Helmi about it, but this was the first time the smaller girl had dared to come there.

- This is nice, - Helmi said. There was excitement in her voice: she had dared to come here, she had dared! Mielikki laughed.

- I told you it wasn't so bad, didn't I? -

Helmi nodded. It was cold and dark, of course, but now that she was down there, neither cold nor darkness seemed too terrible. She could still use her sonar, her skin still kept her warm, and the wall behind her was protection and landmark all at the same time.

- You did, - she admitted. - Well done you. -

Mielikki leaned forwards and sent a long, low moan down into the depths. They listened for a long time, but no echo came back.

- I wonder what it's like down there, - she said. Helmi laughed.

- You always say that! Ever since we were babies, you've wanted to go deeper. -

- Well, I do, - Mielikki replied. - What's wrong with that? -

Helmi sat back and began to count on her fingers.

- Well, there was the time when you got your head stuck under a rock and we had to pull you out by the tail ... and the time you swam away when our mothers were talking, and they had to chase you all the way to the wreck ... and the time you forgot you'd need to breathe and nearly ran out of air on the way back up... -

Mielikki nudged her with an elbow. - That doesn't count! I was young then, - she said. - And anyway, I still want to know what it's like. -

- Cold and dark, - said Helmi pragmatically. - And once you break through the heat-floor... brrr! - She shuddered. In all oceans, the warmest water is at the surface, heated by the sun. It rises and sinks in a great slow cycle, carrying life through the shallows. But the sun cannot reach below a certain depth, and the warm surface waters sit on a foundation of bitter cold. The border where warm and cold divide is as clear and sharp as a wall. Humans call it the thermocline. Mers call it the heat-floor.

- But imagine what you could see down there! Giants and monsters, things nomer has ever seen... -

- Things which eat you and things which poison you? No, thank you! Give me the shallows any time: food when you want it and air when you need it. Besides, - Helmi added practically, - how would you ever get there? By the time you're seventwé fathoms down, you'd have to turn round to breathe. Remember what it was like passing the Gates? -

- I could practice, - Mielikki said defiantly. - I'm already good at going deep, and I'll get better. -

- Well, I know you will! You're pelagic at diving. But how deep do you think this wall goes? A myriad fathoms? I mean, if anyone can dive deep, it's you, but how much deeper can you go? Even if you make it a handred fathoms down, you'll be nowhere near the bottom. -

- I know, - said Mielikki irritably, - I know! I just wish... I wish... -

Helmi waited.

- I wish we could do what they did in the stories! Every song we sing, there's someone who dives to a myriad fathoms and comes back with something special. Every story we tell has someone who knows how to dive deep. And look at us! Fivetwé fathoms, and we have to start worrying about turning back! Why? Why can't we go deeper? - Helmi winced at the anger and despair in her voice.

- I know how you feel, - she said gingerly, after a moment. - But it's one of the Lost Arts, isn't it? Diving deep, lighting fire, storing songs. We used to know how to do it, but the Seven Sisters hid the secrets after Andromeda's Curse. -

- I know! But why did it have to be that way? Why do we have to live like this, always hiding, always hungry, and always more netmen, netmen, netmen! - She turned sharply to look at her friend. - I dream of the days when we didn't have to hide! When we didn't have to swim from their noise, breathe their stink, swim through that black... black *stuff* they pour out on the water. When we didn't have to flee from their thunder boats, and their rubbish, and their nets! - She turned back to stare into the darkness. - I just really, really wish that life was more like the stories. So we could live without hiding, just for one day... -

- Maybe we will, one day, - Helmi said, trying to soothe her. - It's not long now. A couple more years, and we'll find our names, and be able to leave the home-cave, and swim back to the parents, and go and live out on the deep, far away from netmen. -

- Free, and in the blue... - With an effort, Mielikki dragged her thoughts back from the darkness. - And I bet your name will be Helmi Deep-diver. Bet you anything. -

- And you'll be Mielikki the Graceful, - Helmi said, but kindly, as if she meant it.

They sat there in silence, imagining a better future. They could not know what the future really held – or how soon it would come.

After a while, Helmi looked up. The moon was at its highest now, and they could see it through the distant waves, a bright white speck like a shell on a black beach.

- Should we go? - she suggested. - I'll need to breathe soon. And I'm *starving*. -

- Me too, - agreed Mielikki. Air always gets used up quicker in deep water. - Let's breathe, and find something to eat. -

They pushed themselves off the sand, uncurled their tails and began finning back up the wall.

6

Atlantis

Where was Atlantis? How did it come to hold the empire of the oceans?

This is what the songs told us, after it was gone...

Atlantis was a mighty island, almost a continent itself. It lay off the bulge of Africa, angling north-west into the ocean, and because Atlas, who ruled the island, also ruled the seas around, that ocean has carried his name ever since: Atlantic, "the ocean of Atlas." To the north-west, the island was a narrow chain of mountains, handreds of miles long. To the south-east, it broadened out into a great plain, roughly square, shining with rivers and marshes; but the south-eastern corner rose in a curve of volcanoes, a barrier against the storms.

Its shape was like the constellation of seven stars which point towards the Pole: the one we call the Rudder of the Sky. The songs say that the seven highest peaks of Atlantis were set in the same pattern as those stars, three in the long, curving stem, four at the corners of the blade; and for that reason, we have always loved that constellation most. When we look at it burning in the midnight sky, we see our home.

Those mountains are all that are left now; the only thing the sea did not take when Poseidon's thunder broke. You have given them human names: the Canaries, the Azores, the Madeiras. But for us, they are all one group, the Gravestones, and they stand in memory of Atlantis.

And what a memory to mark! You think the reef that fringes the Isle of Red Winds like a barrier is beautiful, on the far side of the world? You never saw the reefs of Atlantis! Three myriad miles they stretched, and corals bloomed on every inch, and the ruby-fish swarmed over them like a blizzard of golden sparks. The wind brought the waves rolling down from the north, and the sea brought the deep current up out of south, and the riches of two hemispheres were poured out on the island of Atlas. The fish schooled so thick that you could not see water between them: snapper and angelfish, grouper and wrasse, barracuda in silver tornadoes a hundred fathoms deep. Every reef held a treasure. Every rock sheltered life. No boats dragged their wakes across the water, or lowered their nets into the sea. And from every cave, the merpeople sang.

The caves! Atlantis was an island of innumerable caverns, carved out of the tideline by the waves. Each reef was seamed with grottoes and swim-throughs, a lacework of water and air. At night, every family had a home to sleep in, and by day, the ocean was ours to explore. We did not need to hide: we came out in the sunshine, and sang on the shores, and reveled in the brightness of the day. And on the western shore, looking across his ocean, King Atlas had his palace.

It was the greatest marvel in the seas: a hundred caves linked by winding passageways between high tide and low. Its gate was an arch of coral set with pearls. Its walls rang with singing. Jewels shone in treasuries deep within the rocks. Deeper still, most treasured of all, lay the cave they called Poseidon's Tear. In that cave stood a rock pinnacle; and on the pinnacle lay a basket of sea-grass; and in the basket was a bed of sponge: the cradle of Atlas and

Orion, born to be kings.

But Orion was gone, nomer knew where, and the first tears Poseidon ever wept were for his vanished son.

To that palace, King Atlas, Queen Amphitrite, and their seven daughters gathered the wisest and strongest and swiftest of our peoples, to help guide them as they ruled. They were the stewards of the merpeople, as the merpeople were stewards of the sea.

Now to help the stewards in their labor, the royal family taught them three secrets; and those arts were the glory of Atlantis until its fall.

For the King taught the stewards how to make fire: red flame, that they could kindle and carry over the waves. With the King's Gift, they worked metals, until his halls shone with gold below the water, and rang with bells above. With metal tools, they worked stone, carving the caves greater and fairer, with more enchanting echoes than ever before: echoes to thrill and delight, to guard and protect, even echoes that were themselves a weapon, a shout of anger to protect the treasury of the King.

And the Queen taught them to dive deep, even to the edge of the abyss, where light and life die. The songs say the mers who received the Queen's Gift counted their dives in hours, not minutes; measured depth in miles, not fathoms; moved through the deepest water as if it were air. And because it was the Queen's Gift, no merman has ever been able to dive as deep or long as a merwoman.

And the Seven Sisters, who sang together so beautifully, taught them to capture songs in brazen vessels, and call them back again at need, so that a melody once sung might never die. And with the Sisters' Gift, the stewards spread music and learning right around the world.

For Atlantis was only the heart of our empire, and that empire was the sea. Long before you netmen first dared to face the waters, our people circled the globe. North-west we went to the Iron Seas, and danced on the racing tides. West we went to the Blue Reefs with jungles on their shores, and the Blood-Warm Bay, and the Coast of Great Rivers where strange dolphins swim. South-west we went round Black Crag Head, and saw for the first time the endless roll of Poseidon's Deep, mightiest of oceans. Day and night the explorers went out; day and night the messengers came back with news of more seas and more splendors. The ocean currents were our highways. Messages flowed across them like the music of whales, and the arts of Atlantis were carried across the Seven Seas.

For the people grew until the caves were too small to hold them; and Atlas gave them leave to swim out and found new kingdoms in new seas. One by one, six great bands set out, to settle in the Iron Seas and the Blue Reefs, down the Coast of Great Rivers and around Taniwha's Isle, among the Sporadic Islands and in the warm Marsh Bight. Each chose their kings and queens, but all bowed to Atlas and Amphitrite; and the law of Atlantis was honored by all the Seven Clans.

For Atlas and Amphitrite gave us law, as well as lordship. They made the rules that kept the peace between the countless clans. Their justice ran as far as the salt tide rises, and as deep as the edge of the abyss. They divided the sea and its riches, laying down who should hunt, and where, and when, so that the fish were never over-hunted, and no family went hungry. And the people loved them, and honored them, and obeyed them.

And to honor his heirs, Poseidon gave each a Treasure – the greatest gifts that have ever been made. To

Atlas he gave a golden trident that shone like the sun, and the songs say it had the power to shake the earth and wake the tsunami; and the symbol of Atlantis was four tridents, pointing to the four winds, to show that the King ruled all seas.

But to Amphitrite he gave a scepter of glass that glistened like the moon, and the people said that it gave her the power to command all the creatures that live in the ocean or within the sound of the breaking waves.

And to Maia, eldest of the Seven Sisters, Poseidon gave a rod of ebony, topped with a black pearl, that gleamed like the sea on a star-filled night; and our people believed it gave her the wisdom to understand any creature in the sea, such as a Queen would need. For Atlas and Amphitrite were mortal, and though Poseidon granted them a lifespan that was three times a mer's, when their days were fulfilled, they would die. One day, Maia would be Queen; and of all the gifts that a ruler needs, she longed for understanding most.

So Atlantis grew and flourished, the jewel in the center of the world, the island of the Rudder of the Sky, and the seal of the Four Tridents was set in gold above the King's gateway. The city grew beautiful, and the people grew rich and strong. We made songs, and danced, and guarded the seas. We reached across the oceans, and to the very fringes of the abyss. Our sonar scanned the deepest depths, and our music woke the heavens.

And Poseidon saw the wealth and happiness of his children and his ocean, and blessed them, and was content.

But Zeus saw it too.

7

Atlantis Lost

Helmi found food almost as soon as they had breathed. As they dropped down from the surface, she spotted a big slicer crab scurrying across a rock. Mielikki heard the sudden stream of clicks as she locked onto her target, heard the frantic scrabble of claws, and then Helmi flashed forwards and down like a striking barracuda, and curved back upwards holding the crab by the back of his shell. His legs flailed, and his claws lunged like flapping sails, searching for someone to pinch.

- What do you think? Is he big enough? - Helmi grinned. By a rule as old as Atlas, crabs were forbidden prey until they were as big as two clenched fists. This crab was twice that size.

- I don't know, - Mielikki grinned back. - You don't want to get too fat, do you? You'd never be able to sink. Floater, - she added cheekily. "Floater" is a childhood insult among merpeople, mocking those who still have so much baby fat that they cannot sink. For generations, the nursery reefs and caves of Atlantis had echoed to the childish taunt: "Float, float, got caught by a boat. "

Helmi blew a raspberry, a long, complex noise with overtones of disdain and flatulence: mers can pack more insult into a simple lip movement than a human could in a five minute speech.

- Anyway, - she added, - I haven't seen you catch your breakfast yet. You're going to look pretty silly when all you have to eat is a handful of sand-worms, and I'm tucking into my nice big crab. -

Mielikki bit her lip. Once, when she was much younger, she had explored the shifting sand waste that lay to the north, forgotten to eat first, and got lost. When her parents found her, she was crying and chewing on sand-worms. The taste still haunted her nightmares.

- Besides, - Helmi went on meditatively, - I wouldn't be a good friend if I gave him to you, would I? You might get too fat, and… float. -

- Ha! What makes you think you're a friend at all? -

- It must be a delusion, - Helmi said placidly. - Brought on by lack of food. So, were you planning to catch something tonight? -

Mielikki laughed and began to scan the rocks again. She had never managed to out-argue Helmi yet.

They went up to breathe, carefully and not too close together, because Helmi's crab was still threshing vigorously; then they drifted back down to the rocks. A big-eye peered out from under a ledge, resplendent in silver and red: too small to eat. Another crab scratched his way across the stones: too small to eat. A stingray rippled away over a spur of coral: too big to eat. A cuttlefish came dawdling across the slope, saw them and shot away backwards in a spurt of sand.

- Too fast to eat, - Helmi said. - Can you get a move on? I'm starving. -

- You think I'm not? - Mielikki scanned the rocks all around, looking for something to eat; but the sea was empty. All year the fish had been growing scarcer, as the netmen's ships plundered the inshore waters; now it seemed as if nothing was left at all.

Slowly they worked their way along the rocks, for as long as their breath held, but after an hour there was still nothing to eat. Helmi's hands were growing tired from holding the crab; he was still clubbing at the water, trying to find something to pinch.

They drifted to the surface and breathed. The moon was rising, a burning silver crescent: as it climbed higher, it would flood the deeps with light. Mielikki looked at it thoughtfully.

"How about the wreck?" she asked. "We haven't been there for ages, and by the time we get there, we'll have good light for hunting. No need to make too much noise."

Helmi shrugged.

"If you must, but after that, I'm going to eat, whether or not you find something. I'm starving."

This time, they did not stop at the five fathom line, but kept going, angling deeper and further from the shore. It was almost high tide: the current was barely noticeable, a gentle but insistent pressure.

At first the sea bed was a series of cliffs and ridges, where black urchins waved their needles from every crevice. Then it gave way to a long stretch of sand, furred with weed. In daylight it was a field of eels, sticking their heads out of the sand like question marks; now it was deserted. Faint wave patterns ribbed the wasteland. Faint moonbeams danced over it. Faint echoes rose from it. The two mermaids swam straight and fast, a few silvery bubbles marking their passage.

They heard the wreck long before they saw it: a hard, clear echo dazzling the senses in the dull sound-picture of the sands. They shifted to the right, and with every stroke the echo grew clearer: first a solid block, then two distinct parts separated by a narrow gap, and finally, rising out of the blackness like a man-made reef, the upreared bow and twisted stern of a wrecked fishing boat. Her name had been the *Reina Isabella*, an old trawler which had run for shelter in a storm. A freak wave had smashed her sideways on to the wind, and the next wave had rolled her end over end and thrust her contemptuously into the depths. She had broken up as she sank, her deckhouse peeling away, her stern burying itself deep in the sand. Now the rusty remains were covered in anemones, urchins and soft corals, so that the dead metal teemed with life.

She had taken five men down with her, fathers and brothers and sons, who had gone to sea because it was the only way to feed their families. The mermaids did not know that; they would not have cared if they did. For them, netmen were more than the enemy: they carried a curse. Andromeda had laid it upon them three thousand years before, on the day Atlantis fell, and now they must rob the seas until they starved – or gave back what was stolen.

At last the girls saw it, a darker patch that thickened against the shifting silver waves. On one side, the deckhouse tilted crazily, its door hanging open on a single hinge, windows ragged-toothed with broken glass. Damselfish swarmed over it; urchins bristled in the corners. Behind it, the knife-edged bow loomed like a metal mountain. She had been so strongly built that it was almost intact; but behind it jutted twisted wreckage. A single mast, the ship's derrick, drooped broken over the side, its tip buried in the sand. The railings were furred white with barnacles. Anemones waved their tentacles over the deck. And all around, little silversides flickered in every direction like a living cloud, their mouths gaping and closing as they fed on scraps.

The girls drifted gently downwards, until they were resting belly down on the sand. Neither moved; neither spoke. This close to the wreck, there was no sense in using sonar: they strained their eyes in the faint silver light, staring for anything that might look like food.

- There, - Helmi whispered. She pointed with her crab at the tangled girders behind the bow.

- Where? - Mielikki asked, straining her eyes.

- It just went... There! -

- Yes! - For an instant, she saw another comb-back peer out of the shadows and withdraw. She fixed her eyes on the spot. For a while, nothing moved; then a slanting beam of moonlight shone into the darkness, and she saw it, a red and white shape a fathom long.

- That's a big breakfast, - she whispered uneasily. She had never caught such a big fish before.

- He'll do for lunch too, - Helmi said innocently. Mielikki shot her a suspicious look.

- All right, Miss Fancy Fins, and how were you planning to get him out of there? -

Helmi giggled and waved the crab. - We'll give him breakfast. - And she began to whisper excitedly.

Together, they inched backwards from the wreck. It slowly faded from sight: a ship, a shadow, a ghost lost in the murk. Helmi began to send out quiet signals. Mielikki rose and swam back the way they had come in silence, using Helmi's echoes to guide her, so close to the sea bed that her tail-strokes raised little spurts of sand.

She reached the bows and began to rise, her heart in her mouth; one moment of clumsiness, and she might as well go home. As she came level with the deck, she reached out a finger and steadied herself against a railing. The silversides pulsed in alarm. She froze, and gradually their shifting dance resumed. She pulled herself forwards; they went on feeding. Another inch, and another, the moonlight casting the faintest of shadows on the deck. One more length, and she was at the broken end of the wreck, a tangled mess of shadows. Somewhere there, the comb-back lurked.

Mielikki steadied herself with two fingers on a broken railing, and hung there motionless. Even the current had stopped. It was high tide.

A movement by her arm made her start. She looked around sharply. It was a peace-fish, what humans call a sea-horse, clinging with his tail to a weed-grown bollard and swaying like a scrap of weed himself. She made herself relax and looked forwards again.

Suddenly the silversides scattered. Helmi swept in out of the darkness, touched down on the sand, put her crab down on its back and fled.

The crab's legs rippled. Its claws flailed as it tried to right itself. Gradually, the cloud of silversides reformed. Mielikki's eyes were locked on the tangled shadows below her. Was that a movement? No, just a clutch of glassfish. She resisted the temptation to emit a questing click; that would be the surest way to scare the comb-back into hiding. There? A hint of red and white. A jagged dorsal fin. There it was – and it was moving.

The night exploded. With a convulsive twitch the comb-back lunged for the crab. Mielikki hurled herself after it. It spotted her and swerved, a shadow streaking across the sand; but now Helmi's sonar flashed out of the dark, cutting off its escape. It swerved again. Mielikki rolled in mid-flight. It ducked desperately. As she shot past it, her hands flashed and snatched – and closed on the threshing tail.

- Got it! - she yelled. Helmi squealed. The massive body threshed as she kicked for the waves. Fins like sawblades rasped her fingers. She tightened her grip. The waves raced towards her. Then she broke the surface with a whoosh of released breath, and held the fish up, out of the water, fighting with every kick, until it shuddered, and went still.

Helmi surfaced in a shower of spray. "You got him! You got him!"

Mielikki was panting. "What a fish! What a fish!"

"That was amazing! I've never seen you turn

that fast!"

"I've never done it before! What a fish!"

"What a swim! I thought you'd never make it!"

"I didn't think at all," Mielikki admitted. Helmi's admiration made her glow with happiness; it was so rare to feel she had done something right. "I just went for him, and he swam right where I could grab him... Besides," she added fairly, "If it hadn't been for you and your crab, he never would have come out in the first place."

"That's true." Helmi laughed and held up the crab. "I told you he'd be breakfast for both of us, didn't I?"

Mielikki cast a long look at the crab, its claws still threshing in slow defiance.

"You know," she said slowly, "there's enough fish for both of us here. I think the crab's done enough for one night."

Helmi looked at her, and back at the crab.

"You think he's earned his freedom?" she asked uncertainly.

"Well, thanks to him we've got enough breakfast to feed the entire school. He's done enough for one day."

Helmi looked a moment longer, then laughed.

"I like fish more than crab anyway. Come on, let's put the poor old man back where we found him, and then you can give me my breakfast."

Together they swam back to the reef, dropped the crab beside a convenient crevice, watched him stagger sideways into it and made for the home-cave.

It was hard for Mielikki to navigate the passage, pushing the dead fish ahead of her, with the falling tide resisting every move; but she persevered. The going became easier once they reached the anemone-cave, and in time, they wriggled out of the entry tunnel into the vast, echoing cave.

"Here come the girls!" called Dohan cheerfully, seeing them surface.

"You missed the tide," Pel pointed out helpfully, sprawling on the ledge with his tail dangling. "And I'm not sure you can jump that far..." The water was already a body's length below the sleeping place. A narrow trail wound down from it to the water's edge, but to drag themselves up it would take a good five minutes.

Still aglow with the backwash of her happiness, Mielikki laughed, an unexpectedly bell-like sound that rang in the high arch.

"Bet you I can!" She pushed the fish into Helmi's hands, upended herself, speared down to the cavern floor, turned, tensed, hurled herself upwards, burst through the surface, flew through the air, curved towards the ledge, took the shock on her hands, rolled and came to rest on her sleeping place.

Helmi applauded. Dohan whooped. Even Pel laughed.

"See?" she asked, half dizzy with the roll, and the excitement of having got it right.

"Sorry, can you do it again?" he replied innocently. "I missed that one, I was picking my nose." Mielikki blew a raspberry.

"Breakfast?" Helmi asked meaningfully, pulling herself carefully up onto the ledge and heaving the comb-back out next to her. The boys were transfixed. It was a long time since they had eaten their fill of anything, let alone fish.

"Oh my," Dohan breathed. "Where did you get that?"

"It's big enough for the four of us. Fair shares, Helmi?" Pel pleaded.

"Mielikki caught him," Helmi answered. "So maybe you should ask her."

"Instead of teasing me," Mielikki added meaningfully, pulling herself across the ledge. Behind it, shelves and crevices gaped in the rock, some jagged, some smooth. Many were empty, but on a few, the mers kept their tools and treasures: knives, hammers, rope braided from seaweed; beautiful shells, and human things for which they had no name.

She reached up and pulled out her most prized possession, a stone knife, as long as her forearm and sharp enough to open clams. She had made it herself from a stone she had found on a wreck, chipping away with a hammer every day for a month until it was just as she wanted. Seen by moonlight, the dimpled blade glistened like waves. Seen by sound, the flat gave an echo that was blurred, as though filtered through sand; turned edge on, it was so finely hammered it gave no echo at all.

"I'll help," Dohan said quickly, reaching for his own knife, a rusty iron blade that his grandfather had found decades before.

"It's all right, I'll do it," said Mielikki. "But you can carry all the scraps out afterwards." She sent

Helmi a tiny click, the equivalent of a wink.

Pel groaned theatrically.

"Or you can just watch us eat," she added. Pel sighed.

They pulled themselves over to another niche, and dragged out a clam-shell as wide across as their arms. Unknown hands in ancient times had drilled through the thick root of the shell and hinged the two halves with wire. More wire held the lips together, so that when they were pulled closed, the shell was almost watertight. The young mers hauled it over the sand to the water's edge, heaved the fish into it and set to work.

They gutted and skinned the comb-back, making sure that the blood and scraps pooled in the shell; then they sliced the fillets off the bone and wrapped them in strips of seaweed, the delicate green strands they called Cassiopeia's Hair.

Then they fetched their plates. No two were alike. Mielikki had a huge crab-shell that she had found on the sands two dozen fathoms down. Dohan had a flat stone, slightly hollowed by the waves. Pel had a strange dish of some hard blue material, very thin and strong, perfectly round, with a curled lip. He had found it floating off a beach where the humans played; none of the mers knew what a frisbee was, but it was excellent for eating off.

Helmi's plate was the wonder of the reef: a perfectly round, shallow bowl of some transparent substance, standing on a solid black knob. She had found it half sunk in the mud one night; it had been almost invisible to the eye, but gave an echo as clear as a bell. Above it, the waters had been streaked with the rainbow stain of a thunder boat. She had no idea why netmen would throw away such a treasure, but it must have come from them. She had brought it back in triumph and used it ever since: a glass saucepan lid, dropped off a yacht as the captain was washing up after a long day's sail.

They ate the comb-back raw and wrapped in seaweed, quickly and without much conversation. Without the usual chatter, the echoes faded to a murmur, and the different tones of the wall came back clearly: here smooth, there rough; dusky echoes from the water, and cold, hard echoes from the dome; even, in the very highest corner where the angles of the wall came together, a faint double echo like a heartbeat, bip-bing, bip-bing, bip-bing.

After they had eaten, they played games with echoes, the same games that mers had been playing for generations to pass the frightened, secret daylight hours when the netmen prowled.

They played pebble-scrabble: one threw a stone, the others had to guess where it would fly and hit it with their narrowest beam of clicks. They played chords: each in turn sang a series of notes, and the winner was the one who managed to build the most complex chord before the first echo faded. It demanded self-control and a fine-tuned voice, because the trick was to make the first note the loudest and highest, and each subsequent one softer and lower. Surprisingly, Dohan was best at that game: his mind was slow, but he could control his voice remarkably well.

They told stories in the darkness, seeing in their minds' eyes seas far away, under long ago suns.

Some were of Atlantis, in the days of its splendor. Some described other seas, painting their corals and caves, their reefs and wrecks. Some - Dohan loved those - were of heroes and heroines and monsters.

They told of the Icemers and their Ghostwhales, riding through the Diamond Seas as they battled black and white assassin whales and white bears. They told of the giant mers who lived along the Coast of Great Rivers and never came out to sea, but swam higher and higher up the rivers, under the looming trees. They told of Orion the Wild Hunter and Aurikka the Charioteer, of the first Thettis and the first Nereus and the first mers to swim into Poseidon's Deep. They told of the Lost Mers of the Five Great Lakes, and the Starkmers who haunted the Southern Ocean, and the Sea-Witches who lived on the edge of the abyss, and only came up to breathe on the darkest night of the year.

In the restless summer days, when the netmen's noise was loudest, they told ghost stories to take their fear away: Discords, who clung to life through hatred; Echoes, lost between life and death; and Concords, who left such love behind them that it blessed the reefs where they had swum.

They swapped riddles, piling image on image to hide the meaning like a hermit crab inside its shell. Pel was unbeatable at that game:

"What is the storm of the snatchers of the scales of the fish of fish?"

Silence.

"A gale."

"No."

More silence.

"Gannets diving."

"No."

Still more silence.

"Give up."

"Dolphins dancing."

"What? How?"

"A shoal of sardines looks like one fish. That's the fish of fish. So one sardine is a scale of the fish of fish." Helmi groaned, suddenly seeing it. "Dolphins eat sardines, so they're the snatchers of the scales of the fish of fish. And when they dance it sounds like a thunderstorm. Get it?" Pel asked triumphantly.

"Let's play something else," Dohan muttered.

They played small-call: each in turn swam to the middle of the pool and tried to call out from exactly the right place and at exactly the right angle to make the echo come back from all six walls at once. Helmi was particularly good; Mielikki always called too loud.

They finished off by playing hide and sneak. It can only be played in safe and sheltered water, such as a cave or enclosed bay, because it involves swimming in pitch darkness without any sonar at all. One team is the guards: their job is to defend the goal, a fixed point such as a rocky outcrop. The others are the sneakers: their job is to touch the goal without being caught. Neither team is allowed to click or whistle. They have to rely on hearing alone, listening for the tiny traces of movement: tails finning, bodies turning, an arm moving stealthily through the water. At the start, that means it is harder for the sneakers, because they have to move, and therefore make noise. But as soon as the guards move to counter the threat, they make noise too. So for each side, the challenge is to work out where the other side is, without giving themselves away.

They played three games, boys against girls, and Dohan and Pel were thrilled when they won two games to one. Mielikki almost made it to the goal to win the final game, but at the last moment a clumsy tail-swish betrayed her, and Pel caught her.

Privately, Mielikki dreaded hide and sneak. It demanded grace, stealth and control, and she felt that she lacked all three. But afterwards, she treasured the memory of that game. It was the last one they ever played.

It was time to tidy up. For netmen who live by the sea, this is easy: they throw their filth into the water, until the fish swim out and the scavengers swim in. For merpeople, living in the sea, it requires more care. Dumping fish scraps in the water of the home-cave would be the surest way of attracting sharks; dumping them on land would be even worse, because that would attract humans.

They made sure that all the scraps were collected in one half of the clam-shell, then Pel heaved it closed and bound the two lips firmly together. He ran his fingers all the way round, to make sure that it was properly sealed: any leak would leave a trail of blood in the water, and that would be dangerous.

"You missed a bit," Mielikki told him, the second he had sealed it. Her sonar clicked off a patch of fish skin on the sand.

"How do you expect me to see that?" Pel asked. "It's sandy scales on scaly sand!"

"Try controlling your sound," Helmi said sweetly, and let a whisper of her own sonar bounce off it. The skin gave off a faint echo; the sand swallowed her noise entirely.

"Girls," muttered Dohan, scraping up the scrap of skin and poking it under the lip of the shell. "Just because you're better at diving, you think you know everything."

"No, I just know more than you," Helmi said complacently.

Dohan muttered something that might have been "Handswimmer," and turned back to the shell; a handswimmer is a crippled mer whose tail is too weak to swim.

He slid his arms under it carefully, lifted it with a grunt of effort, and wriggled backwards to the edge of the shelf with clumsy flaps of his tail.

"You missed another bit," Helmi said clinically.

"Well, stick it up your nose!" he snapped, and pushed off backwards. The tide was halfway down the pool: he fell five fathoms with a whoop of delight, crashed into the water tail-first and was instantly gone. Pel grinned, rolled to the edge and dived after him.

Mielikki looked at Helmi.

"Did he?"

"Did he what?"

"Miss a bit."

Helmi giggled. "How should I know?"

Together they rolled to the edge and dived headfirst into the cold, loud water.

Pel and Dohan were already in the

passageway, holding the shell by one side, letting the tide carry them out. Mielikki saw that they were being very careful; they knew that spilling the fish would put their home in danger. The girls sank down to join them. When they reached the anemone cave, they slipped past the boys and swam ahead of them to the exit.

The waves were already pale with the waning night. They looked all around, scanning the tumbled rocks. They saw nothing; they heard nothing.

- All safe, - Mielikki signaled. She was wrong, but the mistake would save their lives.

The scent of blood was already wreathing through the water; it was no time to linger. Quickly they popped out of the cave and followed the falling tide along the cliff. Dohan and Pel carried the shell; Mielikki and Helmi circled them, watching and listening for any hint of danger.

- Are we there yet? - Pel gasped after a few minutes.

- Almost, - Helmi said tensely, scanning ahead and out to sea. - Try not to make so much noise, you sound like a fish on a hook. -

- There, - Mielikki said suddenly, pointing to a patch of sand. They tried to find a different place to leave their scraps every night, so that scavengers did not gather.

- Perfect, - said Dohan hastily, angling down towards it.

- It looks small, - Helmi cautioned. - I think we should go further. -

- You carry the stinking thing, then, - and he and Pel swooped down. Mielikki grinned.

They set the shell down gently between two rocks: there was just enough room to open it. They plunged their hands into the coarse gray sand and scrubbed their faces with it, scouring away the blood. Mielikki laid her knife down on a stone; the cleaner-fish would pick over it during the day. Then they turned to the shell. The scent of blood was thickening; as Pel looked back the way they had come, he saw a white spotted octopus come flowing over the stones, drawn by the scent of food. Just by his hand, a little mugger crab stirred, shaking off its covering of sand.

- Ready? - clicked Dohan, hovering above the shell.

- Ready, - they replied, backing away.

Dohan heaved the lid upwards in a swirl of bubbles, blood and fish-scraps. The mugger crab scuttled in, snatched a morsel and darted into hiding. The octopus shot forwards. The stink of fish blood filled the water.

It was no time to linger. The reef crackled with footsteps as crabs and shrimps turned towards them. A fanged moray streamed down the rocks like a yellow ribbon. The octopus flowed through the cloud of scraps, picking the choicest.

- Let's fin, - Mielikki said. They nodded and turned away, swimming quickly back up against the current.

- I bet you're going to the cleaning rock again, like girls, - Dohan said cheerfully.

- Well, if you cleaned from time to time, maybe the water wouldn't stink so much, - Mielikki retorted.

- That's not stink, - Pel said loftily, - it's charisma. -

Mielikki and Helmi giggled.

- Anyway, - he added, - We're going to the sand flats, and I'm going to tame a cuttlefish. So you go and clean yourselves, and we'll see you at sunrise. -

Mielikki decided not to comment. Ever since he first heard tell of the Icemers and their Ghostwhales, Pel had dreamed of taming an undersea creature of his own. He had tried turtles, fish, an eel, and crabs, all without the least success. A month before, he had announced that cuttlefish, which communicate with colors and tentacle gestures, were intelligent enough to train as pets, and had set out to prove it by adopting one. He would lie on the sand in front of any cuttlefish that passed, fingers of one hand outstretched in front of him, trying to strike up a conversation in sign language. Once, a cuttlefish had actually mimicked his hand signs; the memory had kept him glowing with happiness for a week. He called it Älykki, the clever one, and went looking for it every evening, trying to tame it with little offerings of shrimps. Mielikki thought it an impossible task, but he enjoyed it so much that she did not want to spoil his fun.

- Well, good luck. Don't forget to look out for nets, - she cautioned. Pel gave her a look.

- Don't forget to breathe, - he retorted. - Come on, Dohan. -

But there would be no taming cuttlefish that night.

All of a sudden, a grinding roar shook the

ocean, as if every drop of water was clashing against the others. They screamed and clapped their hands to their ears. The rocks shuddered. Boulders smashed into the water at the foot of the cliff and tumbled downwards, growling with bubbles.

- Swim! - shouted Mielikki desperately. With one accord they turned and fled, kicking desperately out to sea as the water thundered around them.

They surfaced and looked back in terror. Dawn was pouring into the sky, as red as blood. All around, the waves were heaving and spouting. Boulders slammed into the water. Dust billowed off the clifftop in a black cloud; and half visible at the base of the cloud, three huge yellow thunder machines stood. Each one had an arm arched over its back like a sting ray's tail. Each arm ended in a silver spike. And the spikes were hammering down into cliff-top as if they would smash it apart.

Stones cracked and fell. The cliff-face trembled. Seagulls screamed. And halfway to shore, black dots appeared in the water as the elder children shot to the surface.

"What is it?" screamed Riakka.

"Get away! Just get away!" Mielikki screamed back. As one, they bolted for the open sea.

They had swum half a mile when the sound stopped. Sick and shaken, they turned as the machines lifted their stings, rocked back down onto their tracks and grumbled away. Another thunder machine, bright red and smoking, roared onto the cliff. Men climbed out of it and began unloading strange, round shapes. Too shocked even to hide, the merchildren watched as they rolled thin black lines across the rocks. They knew nothing of pneumatic diggers and trucks – nor of detonator cable and explosives.

Thettis was white, her eyes staring. "We were at the Cleaning Station," she whispered. "We were just about to finish when … the noise started, and the rocks fell…"

Mielikki reached out a shaking hand.

"We were just coming along the cliff. It … it came down right on top of us…" Tears. Her voice broke.

As if hypnotized, their eyes followed the tiny figures on the cliff-top. Dust still hung thick; in the early sunlight it looked as if the air was burning.

Somehow, without the terrible noise, other sounds took on a fearsome meaning. The wind was a threatening whine. Underwater, the crunch of settling boulders was like huge teeth grating. Every noise was a menace, and the worst menace of all was the netmen.

Unwilling to watch, but unable to stop, the merchildren stared as the men finished their work. The long reels of cable uncoiled across the cliff-top. Small blocks were placed in the drill holes. The men climbed into the red thunder machine. It jolted backwards over the rough ground, like a lobster scrambling over rocks, and rolled out of sight.

Nothing more. Mielikki took a deep breath.

"Well," she began. "Maybe we–"

Then the explosives went off.

They saw it first: a spurt of dust, then another and another, stitching a line across the cliff-top. Then the sound came, a stuttering series of thuds. And then the cliff-face slumped and slid, and the sea rose up and came at them.

"Swim!" screamed Mielikki. But they did not even manage to turn before the first wave hit. A blow like a hammer threw her backwards and rolled her over. A filthy wave broke over her head and smashed her downwards. The water bellowed like an assault, waves roaring, rocks clashing, stone grinding. Somewhere in the middle of it, she heard her friends screaming in terror.

Another wave hit, as though the whole ocean were kicking her. Desperate, she clawed upwards with her arms, like a merbaby in the water for the first time. Sand blinded her. Noise deafened her. She was lost and terrified and about to drown.

Suddenly, with no warning, her head broke the surface. She flailed with her arms, keeping herself afloat with the strength of panic, breathed in by reflex, and choked on the stink of dust. Already the shockwaves were growing weaker. The noise died. Only the gulls were screaming in a clanging, outraged cloud.

And ahead, the last home of the merpeople in the islands of Atlantis was gone.

Where the cliff had once sloped crazily down towards the water, seamed and seeded with a thousand years of plants, a sheer rockface gleamed as smooth and dead as an axe cut. No bird would nest there. No grass would grow there. There was nothing but bare stone, and, at the foot of the cliff, a million tons of shattered rock, reaching out into the sea like a newborn reef.

Mielikki gaped, unbelieving. And now the

red thunder machine came crawling back, slow and arrogant. It stopped. The men clambered out. They lifted out a high white board, and levered it upwards on long legs. Then they climbed back into their lorry and drove away, as if there were nothing left worth destroying.

The merchildren stared and stared through their tears at the meaningless markings on the great white sign:

SITE OF "LAS SIRENAS"
THE FIRST HOTEL IN THE ISLANDS TO HAVE ITS
OWN ARTIFICIAL REEF AND BEACH.
BE THE FIRST TO ENJOY THIS BLEND OF LUXURY
AND NATURE IN ALL ITS SPLENDOR!

Below, the waves were stained with black, as if in mourning.

8

Children of Zeus

*How did Atlantis and Athens meet? This is what the
songs told us, after the war was done...*

*The nature of Atlantis was this: the fairest reefs,
the best fishing-grounds and the grandest caves were all
on the south-western side, protected from the north-east
winds by the sheltering bulk of the island. So from the
beginning, Atlantis looked out to sea. From that long,
protected coast, it was natural to reach out across the
Atlantic, south-west with the wind to the Blue Reefs, or
north-west across it to the Iron Seas. Once the Atlantic
was crossed, it was natural to spread north and south
along the shores, and round the stormy cape into
Poseidon's Deep. And once in Poseidon's Deep, there was
no end to the blue waters.*

*That was where, for the first time, our peoples met:
out among the myriad islands of Poseidon's Deep, where
the sea and the sky run into one another, and the waves
roll a myriad miles before they come to shore. The first
stories that came back to Atlantis were hardly believed: a
people like us, but with too few fingers and legs like
monkeys, who sat on tree-trunks, and paddled out to sea,
and drowned. At first, we even pitied you; yes! In those
distant days we pitied you, because you were so weak, and
the sea is so strong. And, being the stewards of the sea, we
tried to help you, guiding your boats by day and,*

sometimes, rescuing you when you sank. There are humans who are only alive today because we pulled their ancestors out of the sea; and we have not forgotten it.

The last sea we came to was the Landlocked Sea, what you call the Mediterranean. That may seem strange, when it was so close to Atlantis; but few of our people lived on the storm-tossed north-east shore, and those who did loved the wildness of it, and did not want to leave. Then, too, a current runs in through the Gates of Atlas, sucking the water out of the Atlantic, so that anymer who passes that way has to fight the weight of the ocean to come back out again, or else dive a handred fathoms down into the ice-cold abyss, where a counter-current runs back into the ocean. What wonder could lie beyond the Gates to make up for such a struggle? With all the oceans before us, no wonder we viewed that sea as the least and last.

But at last our people did reach those waters, and saw the great mountains rear up on either hand like the fangs of a viperfish, and named them the Gates of Atlas. They learned the secrets of the two currents, the light and the dark; and King Atlas gave them leave to people those new shores.

The Landlocked Sea was a kindly place, with deep, clear waters and many fish, though never as many as in the ocean beyond. Slowly, our people spread, discovering new treasures: deep caverns and towering mountains, scattered across a sea as blue as the flash of a damselfish's fins.

And there we met humans: poor, simple creatures who lived by the waters or died in their depths; crab-hunters and oyster-diggers, who made boats of skin and sticks to brave the fury of the sea. At first we pitied you, and taught you our skills: how to navigate by wind and wave and stars, how to find shoals of fish and catch them. We even taught you how to weave nets, little knowing how soon you would use them to hunt us.

Most of all, we taught you peace. The humans of those times lived in little bands, and there was neither law nor love between them. It dismayed us to see how often they fought. Gradually, we taught them how to make laws and keep them; how to talk more, and kill less. In time, the chiefs and warlords agreed a law of sea and shore, which they called the King's Code, thinking that it came from Atlas. In truth, it was Queen Amphitrite who made it; but the men of those times did not listen to their women. Not all of you have learned differently, even now.

The Code ruled how mers and men should share the sea's riches. It said when, and how much, each could catch; it marked out hunting grounds and sanctuaries; it balanced the needs of fishers and fish. And no matter how much the humans fought on the land, at sea there was peace, and fair sharing, and the humans in their many tongues praised the King Over Sea.

So our peoples lived in peace. The merpeople were like the elder sister, leading the way, and the humans were like the little brother, always in a hurry to learn and to lead themselves. You looked to Zeus, as we looked to Poseidon, but we did not resent that. There was no feud between us, as far as we were concerned. The envy ran all the other way.

And still, beyond the Gates of Atlas, Atlantis flourished, and sent out new colonies across the world, so that what was happening in the Landlocked Sea seemed of small importance: for how could it compare? Atlantis had turned her back on the backwaters, and looked out to the oceans.

But it is dangerous to turn your back on a human, especially when that human is hungry; and soon the word was to come out of the Landlocked Sea that a new race of men had been found. They came out of the mountains, and they did not know the King or his Code. They sang of killing and war; they called their heroes Sacker of Cities, and Breaker of Men.

They built a city on a high rock, out of reach of the sea; and they reared up altars to Zeus and his children, the gods of hunting and war. And they forged weapons, and built ships, and ran them down into the sea.

And they called the city Athens.

9

Searching

Shock gripped the school. They could not move or think. They drifted on the surface, staring in shattered disbelief at their shattered home.

The seconds crawled by. Thunder boats growled. The dawn brightened. Still the school drifted, as if paralyzed.

Mielikki was the first to come to herself. As she hung there, sick with horror, the realization struck her like a blow to the stomach: they were on the surface, and it was day.

She turned to Helmi, and grabbed her by the arm.

"Quick! We need to hide! We have to move, right now!"

Helmi stared at her, eyes red with weeping. She did not move.

Mielikki let her go with a sob of fear, and turned to the mer next to her. It was Dohan. She shook him by the shoulder.

"Dohan! We have to hide, quick!"

Dohan shook his head dully, eyes still fixed on the cliff-face.

"Hide? There's nowhere to hide! We can't go … go home," and he started to cry.

Mielikki hissed. She pushed past him, and tried to shake the others into awareness. But it was hopeless. Even Riakka and Thettis seemed petrified; and all the while, the roar of thunder boats was growing.

She had to get them moving. Desperate, she spun round and aimed a tail-slap at the surface, right in the middle of the group.

She misjudged the stroke. Her tail-fin caught Viliga a glancing blow on the shoulder and shoved him under the water.

Mielikki opened her mouth in horror, ready to apologize; but it was too late. The elder children's heads snapped round, their own shock flipping instantly into anger.

"Have you gone mad?" Riakka shouted. "What are you trying to do, drown him?"

Mielikki flushed miserably, shrank in upon herself.

"I'm sorry, I–"

"You lump-sucker!" Viliga shouted. "That hurt, Zeus take you into silence!"

Mielikki flinched. "Zeus take you into silence" was the harshest curse in the mers' language: *silence* was another word for death.

But at least the shouting had broken through Riakka's shock. All of a sudden, the black-haired girl turned and aimed her own tail-slap into the group.

"Everybody shut up! We've got to get out of here! I'm the oldest, so I'm in charge. I'll go first. Dohan, you come behind me. You little ones, follow right behind us. Stay deep, stay close and don't get lost. Ready? I said *ready*? All right, follow me!"

She took a deep breath and dived. Thettis and Dohan followed. Viliga turned to the younger children, voice vicious with anger.

"Mielikki, why don't you swim back to the cliff? They might drop a rock on you."

Mielikki flushed; Helmi bit her lip; Pel scowled. Before any of them could answer, Viliga dived. A second later, an angry burst of clicks broke through the surface: Riakka yelling at them to hurry up.

"Come on, let's fin," Mielikki said through white lips. They dived into the blackened waves.

At first, they swam blind. The water was so thick with sand that their eyes were useless, and they had to keep their sonar to a whisper to avoid deafening themselves. Mielikki swam through it in a daze, the explosion and the shouting still ringing in her ears. Without even realizing, she began to fall behind the group.

- Come on, Mielikki, get a move on! - Riakka shouted.

Mielikki bit her lip.

Dimly, with their sonar, they could sense the elder children ahead and below, swimming fast and straight twelve fathoms down. Riakka and Dohan were behind, Viliga and Thettis half a body-length ahead, letting the leaders' slipstream push them along.

- I can't do it, - Helmi whispered to Mielikki. - They're too deep! I'll run out of air! -

Mielikki nodded dumbly, and levelled off at six fathoms. Her mind was still spinning. Helmi levelled off next to her, swimming as close as she could, for comfort. On her other side, Pel came in so close that she could feel the wash of his fins.

After a moment, he reached out and took her hand, something he had not done in years.

- Mielikki... - he whispered on the private channel, and broke off. He did not finish the sentence, but she knew what he wanted to say: *I'm scared*.

At the thought, her mind cleared. Pain, shock and doubt still roared like rip-tides through her; but the feeling of responsibility stood against them like a rock in the current. Pel was her little brother, and she had to look after him.

She squeezed his hand comfortingly.

- I'm scared too, - she whispered back. - But I won't let them hurt you. I won't let anyone hurt you, little gillfish. –

Gillfish had been her nickname for him when he was very small, and very proud of having learned to dive; he gave a little sad smile at the name.

Silently, Helmi took her other hand. They kicked for the open sea.

Gradually, the water began to clear. At first it was black and foul, tasting of sand. Slowly, like a long night ending, the black faded to gray, and phantom shapes began to appear. They swam further; shapes and echoes became clearer. Then, like a dolphin leaping through a wave, they broke out into clean water, and the sun's rays danced all around them, like silver fishing lines slanting into the blue.

Mielikki rolled slowly, searching sideways into the blue, up to the unaccustomed brightness of the waves, sideways the other way, and ahead. There was nothing dangerous close by. A school of boxlip mullet was grazing on the sands below, sleek silver fish with golden-brown stripes down their flanks; three barracuda were hanging like knives in mid-water; just under the surface, half a dozen oval shaped sea chub were swimming away. But the noise of thunder boats was growing in the distance behind them, a warning and a threat.

- Dohan's breathing, - Pel said.

Mielikki's head jerked down, and she saw a fine stream of silver bubbles rise from Dohan's mouth, the sign that he was about to breathe. After a moment, Viliga let out the telltale trail, and both boys angled up towards the surface.

- We should go up too. Shouldn't we, Mielikki? - Helmi asked anxiously. -We should stay together? -

Mielikki nodded. Somehow she had managed to lock her own pain and confusion away, and was grimly concentrated on survival. Even the fear of making mistakes was temporarily banished.

- We should, - she said. - Let's follow them. Carefully. -

They let themselves drift up towards the sunlit waves. A fathom below the surface, they stopped and made a complete scan: around in a full circle, and from the surface down into the deep. Their elders, Mielikki noted, popped straight up like seals, to hang there with their tails dangling down, beating in time with the swell.

- Floaters, - Helmi whispered with a nervous half -giggle. The others did not answer.

There was nothing in danger range, but there were echoes uncomfortably close: two hard-skinned thunder boats a few miles to the north; a third one, slower and quieter, to the east; a rising grumble of engines closer to shore.

- We'll have to be quick, - Pel said uncomfortably, and swam airwards. Helmi followed, and Mielikki came last of all, trying to calm the quaking in her heart at the thought of being on the surface in daylight.

But as soon as she broke through, she heard Riakka shouting at Pel. Helmi was behind him, looking scared.

" ...and next time, if I tell you to follow us, you follow us! I'm the leader! You do what I say!"

If Mielikki had thought, she would have realized that the elder girl was scared half out of her wits. But she did not think, not with Pel under attack. She thrust into the circle right in front of Riakka, pushing her brother behind her.

"You leave him alone! He swam at the right depth and kept his air! Leave him alone!"

There was a moment of shock; then Riakka let out a deep, drumming series of clicks, a growl of fury that made Helmi flinch.

"I told you to stay with us! Do you want every shark in the ocean to know you're swimming on your own?"

Mielikki kicked and let a wave heave her even closer, face to face.

"At least I had the sense to stay at swimming depth! I didn't waste all my air, like you!"

Riakka drew a deep breath, the prelude to a storm.

"Stop it, both of you!" screamed Thettis

suddenly, and slammed her tail down on the water between them, making them both flinch back in shock. Thettis *never* shouted.

"We've just lost our home, we're out on the surface in daylight, the netmen are waking up, and you think there's time to have an argument?"

Mielikki and Riakka stared at her, then at each other.

"Thettis is right," rumbled Dohan. Pel nodded, white-faced.

"You should both say sorry," Thettis went on. "And then we need a plan."

They held their glares for a moment longer; then, at the same moment, both dropped their eyes.

"Sorry," muttered Mielikki.

"I'm sorry too," said Riakka through gritted teeth.

There was a short silence.

"So what *is* the plan?" asked Dohan. He was recovering his composure better than any of them; he was slow to think, but also slow to fear.

Everyone looked at Riakka. Riakka looked down. The silence lengthened. Mielikki took a deep breath.

"I think we should leave!" she said, louder than she meant to. Riakka's head snapped up. "Swim out to sea, where we belong. Find our parents. Live out on the ocean." She looked around, hoping for support. "Shouldn't we?"

Riakka's shoulders tensed. "No we shouldn't! Swim out to sea, when none of us is ready? That's suicide!"

Mielikki swallowed, but somehow managed

to hold her ground. All at once, the ideas were pouring into her head like a rising tide, too fast to hold back.

"But don't you see? We've got nowhere to live, and nowhere to hide. That island..." She swallowed. Sudden tears pricked her eyes. She forced herself to go on. "The island isn't our home any more. We've spent our whole lives getting ready to leave. We should get away now, while we still can. Far from the island and the netmen!"

She looked around the group again, willing them to understand, but only Pel and Helmi met her gaze. Pel's eyes were shining, the thought of the open ocean over-riding all else; Helmi looked afraid.

"And right where the sharks and assassin whales and netmen will be waiting for us! We're not ready!" Riakka stormed. In her heart she meant: *I'm not ready*. She had been carrying a terrible fear within her since the spring, when she realized that she would have to leave home soon: the fear of failing. All summer, Viliga had been teasing her, calling her a "barnacle, " – one who is afraid to ever leave the home-cave; and Riakka had gone to hide and weep, because she feared it was true.

"Stop!" Thettis said, quietly but intensely, but with a tremor of fear in her voice.

Riakka subsided. She was the leader, but it was Thettis who had the ideas.

In the distance, engines thudded.

"Right," Thettis said, and the tremor grew, as if she dreaded what she was about to say. "Mielikki, we can't swim out to sea just like that. We're not ready. None of us has even found our life-name yet.

109

How can we hope to find our way across the ocean? And it's too late in the year. We should have left in the spring. If we swim out now, we'll have to go all the way to the Diamond Seas to find the parents. Can *you* swim that far?"

Mielikki felt cold. She had not thought of that. All she wanted to do was find her parents in the warm blue seas, and be safe; but their parents would already have left.

"We have to stay," Thettis went on painfully. "We're not ready, and it's the wrong time. So, we need to find somewhere to hide until we *are* ready." She gave Riakka a meaningful look.

"We need a new cave!" the elder girl exclaimed as light dawned; she had been so intent on getting away from the cliffs that she had not even thought where to go. But Thettis was a planner, and her brain had begun darting between ideas even as they swam.

"A new cave?" Dohan said doubtfully. "But where..."

"A new cave!" Now that Riakka had the idea, she clung to it as if it could keep her afloat. "Come on, you all know the island. There must be lots of other caves there. We can find somewhere to hide ... get out of the daylight ... stay there until spring, and get ready."

Mielikki, who had explored more of the caves than any of them, opened her mouth, then hesitated; the last thing she wanted was another fight. Pel spoke instead.

"What about the netmen?" he asked.

Again, their eyes turned to Riakka; again,

hers turned to Thettis.

"We'll have to be careful," the slender girl said. "But we can avoid them."

Riakka nodded. "We stay deep. Listen for their boats. Stay away from their places. We can hide. We always have."

There was a mutter of agreement around the circle. Only Mielikki stayed unhappily silent. *Those caves are dangerous,* she thought. *And there's no air.*

But the others were afraid.

"All right," she said at last, reluctantly. "Let's go back."

And she took a deep breath and ducked back under the water.

Everymer was tense as they began the swim back towards the island. Rods of sunlight danced in the blue, but they flinched at the brightness of it. In this clear water, light was a danger: a human on a boat would only have to look down to shatter the secret that had kept them safe ever since Atlantis fell.

All the same, Riakka stayed shallower than before: she knew that Mielikki had been right. She leveled off at six fathoms, and took them fast and straight back towards land. They scanned and rolled constantly, jumping at the slightest flicker of movement. The two boats that they had seen earlier almost seemed to be tracking them, heading towards the island. Further away, the gut-shaking rumble of a thunder ship trembled on the edge of hearing. Ahead, the inshore waters were snarling with motors.

- This is dangerous. This is so dangerous, - Mielikki send unhappily to Helmi on their private channel. Helmi gave her a scared look and did not answer.

Slowly the island came into range. Already they could taste the dusty flavor of stirred-up sand. Riakka slowed down, swung her head to left and right indecisively; then she turned to face the school.

- All right, we're going to go up and breathe here, all together. It looks clear enough, and that will give us enough air to get home... I mean, get to the cliffs. -

- Where are we going? - Helmi asked, a tremor in her voice. - Home's *gone*. -

Mielikki saw Thettis nod encouragingly at Riakka, and realized that the two must have been having their own private conversation as they swam.

- We'll start by the Cleaning Station and go downtide from there, - was the answer. - There are lots of rocks and caves there: we should be able to find one with air. -

Mielikki opened her mouth to say contradict her, and hesitated.

- We'll need a full breath, then, - she said instead. - It'll be too far otherwise. -

Riakka nodded and looked up.

- Kiss-breathe, - Thettis added, as they all swung their bodies vertical. - Let's not ask for trouble. -

They drifted up together, tails pulsing cautiously. A fathom below the waves, they stopped and scanned.

- Nothing too close, - whispered Riakka.

- Lots of boats, though, - muttered Viliga.

- Makes it more interesting, - Dohan said cheerfully, and was met with a battery of glares.

- Air, - Riakka said, and kicked the final fathom airwards.

They rose together, tilting their heads back until their faces were parallel with the surface. The underbelly of the waves spread out to meet them like a silver skin; then their lips broke water. At once they breathed out. As the air whooshed out they began to sink, and kicked upwards to compensate. With their lips just above the water, they dragged in a full lung's worth of air, pointed their tails down, and thrust themselves back underwater with an upwards sweep of the arms. Two fathoms down, they rolled forwards, brought their tails up, and began to swim down deeper. The whole exercise had only taken a few seconds, and only their lips had broken the surface: kiss-breathing.

- Well done, - Riakka told them, relief in her voice. - Let's go and find a cave. -

They swam close together, their nerves jumping. Soon they could see and hear the sand in the water, as well as taste it: a vast, dark plume, billowing along the current. The sea bed was rising swiftly now, but the boulders and pillars came and went as if hidden in mist.

- This should make it easier to hide, - Viliga said.

- And easier to get lost! Stay together, and stay quiet! - Riakka snapped. This close to the shore and the humans, her fear was almost overpowering.

But at first, luck seemed to be with them. Even the thunder boats seemed scared of the black water, and the din of the explosions had killed or scattered anything big enough to be a threat. Nothing larger than a damselfish – the sparrows of the sea, small and quick and eager, always clustering and pecking at floating specks – moved near them, and they kicked on with growing confidence, looking for familiar sights.

- There, - said Thettis all at once, pointing. - It's the Cleaning Station. -

- But look! - said Helmi, a catch in her voice. - They've broken it! -

It was true. There was the familiar rock pillar, thick with anemones and corals; but its well-known outlines were mutilated. The coral arms were shattered, broken by the shockwaves of the explosion; the anemones were clogged with silt; the brilliant colors were doused in sand.

- And look! - said Pel, diving closer. He sounded sick.

They followed his pointing finger. Here and there, half-buried in the sand, they could see shapes: a grouper, two gilt-head bream, the little green-edged strips of cleaner wrasse, all the fish that had been on the Cleaning Station when the shockwave hit, killed and buried in the same instant.

Mielikki felt tears spring hot in her eyes, mingling with the cold salt water.

- Told you cleaning was bad for you, - said Dohan, but even his voice was shaken.

- We should keep going, - said Pel after a moment. - There's no air to waste. -

Riakka pulled herself together with an effort.

- Follow me, - she said, and swam closer to shore.

It was a miserable search. They had known and loved this part of the sea since they had learned to swim, and now it lay in ruins: broken corals, tumbled rocks, shattered gardens, choking sand. The slope which had once led up to the home-cave was buried under a million tons of rock. Every fin-stroke drove the grief deeper. Mielikki heard Dohan swearing, and realized that her own fists were clenched in hate and rage. This was her home, and the netmen had destroyed it ... Helmi was weeping, Pel was white to the lips as he scanned this way and that. Ahead, Riakka was swimming faster, as if by hurrying, she might escape some of the pain.

- There's the first cave, - she said suddenly, pointing off to the right.

- No good, - Viliga said behind her. - I've been in there. There's no air. -

- There's more further on, though, deeper down. - That was Dohan. Riakka nodded.

- Has anyone explored all of them? - No answer. - Mielikki, have you? - It was almost a peace offering: in that black water, their fights seemed a lifetime ago.

Mielikki accepted the offering. - Only the deepest ones, - she said honestly. - They get shallower as you go in, but I never went far. - She had been in with Helmi, who had balked at the danger, but Mielikki chose not to say so. - We can look now. -

- Let's look. -

Together, they swam left along the reef, diving for deeper water. The stone blocks were bigger here, more regular, rough cubes and rectangles like bricks tumbled out of a wall. Before the explosion, it had been thick with life: shrimps and crabs, urchins and anemones, morays and sting-rays. Now it seemed deserted, the animals dead or in hiding.

Twenty fathoms down, the slope tumbled over a shallow cliff with a black crack at its base. Riakka ducked into the crack and sent a pulse of sonar in; a few glassy-eyed sentry-fish scattered past her in a flash of silver and red. A gray-backed stingray, its wings as big as a boat, pushed upwards in a cloud of sand and finned away, its frilled tail swinging from side to side.

- Nothing big in there, - she reported. - Come on. -

- Be careful, - Mielikki said hurriedly, anxious to keep the peace. - When I went in there before, the sand was really thick and light. If you kick it up, you'll be blind. -

Riakka paused, one hand on the cliff wall. She was obviously thinking fast.

- Then... we shouldn't all go in. Just one of us – no, two. One to look for the way in, and one to remember the way out. The rest can wait here and keep watch. - There was a general click of approval.

Riakka swallowed and looked around the school. She looked scared, but determined.

- I'm the oldest, so I'll go in. Will you come with me, Mielikki? -

Mielikki jumped; she had been expecting to

be left outside with the "little ones."

- You're the best of us in caves, - Riakka added beseechingly, taking her silence for refusal.

Mielikki hesitated, caught between the fear of causing an accident and the fear of starting another fight by saying no. The fear of the fight won.

- All right, - she said.

They swam into the cave.

The crack opened into a narrow, high-ceilinged chamber, running deep into the rock. Sunlight reflected through the entrance and rippled like sea-grass on the walls. They were thick with urchins: the light struck violet gleams between their waving black spines.

The mergirls finned cautiously into the cavern, staying close to the ceiling to avoid kicking up the sand. Mielikki felt fear tighten her chest: *We're deep under water, and there's no way to the surface. Thalatta, help us!*

Goddess, help me not cause another accident!

Then she looked across at Riakka, and saw the fear in the elder girl's face. Again her own terror seemed to shrink, as if something deep inside her had decided there was no time to be scared: if she did not get them through this, nobody would.

- It's all right, - she clicked quietly. - It's a big cave, and you can see the way out. -

Riakka shot her a quick look of blended anger, embarrassment and gratitude.

At the back of the cave, there was an irregular oval crack in the ceiling; a giant pink anemone clung to it, waving. They finned over and looked in, lighting it up with their sonar: its sides were surprisingly smooth, curving quickly out of sight, and they were crawling with urchins. They flinched as the clicks washed over them, rattling their spines.

- I'll go first, - Mielikki whispered. - It's not far. -

Riakka nodded. - I'll make sure you're all right, - she said firmly.

Mielikki eased into the gap, took a long look upwards and then tail-kicked carefully. She rose quickly, the air popping in her ears; too quickly, because she scraped her arm on an urchin. Then she curved around the corner, and came out into a much larger cave. It was pitch dark, but the rock walls gave back brilliant echoes.

- I'm through! - she called back. - But come carefully, I scratched myself on an urchin. -

- All right, - Riakka called. Mielikki heard the soft swirl of her fins, and then the girl was there, rising up out of the hole and looking warily around.

- Funny place, - she said after a moment. - I never knew caves could be this square. - And indeed, the walls were eerily regular, as if they had been smoothed by giant hands.

- But no air, - Mielikki said. - There's a crack there, higher up, but I don't know where it leads. -

- Let's look, then, - Riakka said.

The crack was high in a corner of the cave, a broad slot angling upwards. Mielikki swam over and sent a questing stream of clicks upwards. The echo was so loud she jumped.

- Anything? - Riakka asked, hovering above the exit like a marker buoy.

- Nothing, - said Mielikki, disappointed. - It

sounds like a dead end. -

- Are you sure? - Riakka asked, coming over.

- Yes! - she replied with a flash of irritation. The elder mergirl swam past her anyway and sent her own sonar into the slot. Mielikki noticed that she did it very quietly, to avoid a deafening echo; the realization that Riakka had thought of that when she herself had not did not improve her mood.

- You're right, - said Riakka, turning round. - It's a dead end. Come on, let's go. -

Mielikki pulled a face at her as the elder girl led the way back through the urchin-lined tunnel into the lower chamber; it seemed very bright after the blackness of the upper one. They ducked under the entrance and back into open water, and blinked at the sudden wash of light and sound. The school came crowding round them with clicks and whistles of relief.

- No luck, - Riakka told them shortly. - Two chambers, no air. -

- What do we do now? - asked Helmi.

- Go on looking, - Riakka said. - The next caves are past the Reeking Cove: we'll need to go deep to get around it. -

- There haven't been any thunder boats close, but we heard them, north and south. We'll need to be careful, - Pel said, trying to make amends for their fight. It did not work.

- I know! - snapped Riakka; it was bad enough having to lead the school, without the whole school trying to lead her. - Everyone be careful, look before you breathe, now come on! -

Again they approached the surface, stopped,

looked, breathed and descended. Again their luck held: there were no humans nearby.

They set off southwards with the falling tide, angling further away from shore, searching for deep water, and for somewhere to hide.

10
Lords of Athens

What was the first meeting between Athens and Atlantis? What led to that evil day?

This is what the songs told us, in the days when we were still in hiding from the heirs of Athens...

It began as a rumor, spreading among the human settlements of the Landlocked Sea like foam blown by the wind: a new race of men with heavy ships and heavy spears, who wore helmets and breastplates of bronze. They came out of the East, out of the mountains, and where they passed the dawn was red with the flames of burning villages and the blood of murdered men.

They had many names: Hellenoi, Danaans, Achaeans, Argives. They worshipped Zeus, lord of the thunder, and his children: Ares, god of battle, and Athene, goddess of war. Some said that they came in numbers so great their ships obscured the sea; others that they were few in number, but that every man was as strong as ten. But all the humans agreed: they lived over the skyrim, beyond the most distant wave, and there was no danger that they would come to the West.

At first, we paid little attention to the rumors: we knew that humans were always fighting, and the stories seemed nothing new. Maybe even then, some of our people said: What does it matter if they kill each other? We were tired of your passion for war. Was there ever a time when you were not in love with killing?

But then the refugees began to come: men, women and children with wild eyes and ragged clothes, their skiffs piled high with belongings. They all had the same story, no longer rumors but terribly real: black-hulled ships coming ashore in the dawn, and men with shields like towers, and spears and swords and murder. Sometimes the humans we had befriended – the people of the Code – took the refugees in, and cared for them. Sometimes they drove them out. Sometimes the refugees fought the people of the Code, and took their lands.

We did not join those battles; we only ever fought from need. Enough creatures in the sea try to kill us, without adding to their number. So we stood aside from the fighting, and cared for those that we could, guiding their skiffs, and sharing our fishing-grounds, and feeding the starving, and helping them on their way.

And sometimes, though we did not know it, some of the "refugees" would turn back eastwards after they had seen us, and vanish the way they had come, having spied out our seas. But we only learned that later.

Now, once the tide of refugees began to rise, the news of these changes was too great for the Landlocked Sea to contain, and messengers sped down the waves to the courts of the King; and the coming of that news to Atlantis was like the falling of the sea before the tsunami. And the King saw that these events could not be ignored, happening as they did so close upwind of Atlantis; so he sent his chief advisor, Protteänni, whom you call Proteus the Old Man of the Sea, to find the truth.

And Protteänni, being truly wise, judged that any decision based on rumor would be a bad one; and so, with only six companions, he set out back down the trail of refugees, East and ever East, further into that fatal sea than any merman had gone before.

And at dawn on the twelfth day, they saw black ships approaching.

I have always wondered: how did they feel, as they saw those long black shapes for the first time, crawling over the bright water to the beat of a drum? Did they realize that it was their doom, and our doom? When I hear the songs, I am there with them in the waves, watching through shaded eyes as the oars flash and fall, and the water breaks over the sharp beaks. And the hair crawls on my scalp, and my breath comes fast, to know what that meeting will bring.

But they did not know. So they swam towards the ships, closer and closer, smelling the stink of tar and unwashed humans, seeing the rough, black, splintered wood, hearing the thud of the drums and the creak and splash of the oars. They had never seen such ships, as long as a young whale and as broad in the belly as a hunchback shark. Surely they must have fallen silent; surely, they must have felt the cold current of fear, as the long black shadows stole the sunlight from the water.

The songs say that they ducked down, and looked through the shadows of the hulls to the bright water beyond; and there they saw the carrion-sharks, oceanic white-tips that feed on the weak and dying. The sharks veered off at the first click of sonar, vanishing back into the blue; but they always returned. Everywhere the black ships went, the sharks swam in their wake. Right from the first day, the men of Athens were the heralds of death.

But Prottěänni was as brave as he was wise. He led his companions aside, out of the track of those heavy hulls; and as the humans threshed slowly past, the mermen rose to their waists out of the water, and spread out their arms, and sang the men a peace song.

For a moment, it seemed as if the humans were deaf; better for us all if they had been! Then the oars jerked upwards in confusion; heads stared over the side; harsh voices shouted; the sun flashed on the tips of spears and arrows. Even then, Protteänni and his companions sang on; and that must be the bravest thing any merman has ever done.

Then a man clambered onto the side, and leapt down outside the ship, and stood balanced on an oar as if he were walking on the water; and the songs say that his hair was as black as the ship, but his eyes were blacker still. So, for the first time our people met Perseus, the fisherman's son who claimed to be son of Zeus; Perseus the accursed, whose name lives for ever in the stars.

He smiled like a shark, but spread his hands, and they were empty, and he called a greeting across the water. Now one of Protteänni's six companions, Thettis, was born and bred to the Landlocked Sea, and she had learned many human languages. She was the first mer ever to speak with the Athenians; and her name lives on in your legends – Thetis, the Nymph of the Sea. So she answered, and Perseus laughed harshly and spoke again. And it is the greatest irony of all our history that, of all the netmen, he was the first to meet us, and his first words were of peace.

For he spoke fairly, and said that he was an emissary of his king, Cepheus the Young. He said that Cepheus was camped on an island not far away, eager to learn of Atlantis and the Code. And he offered to take the emissaries to meet the human king.

Protteänni thought of the sharks, and the spears,

and the refugees' tales; and he bade Thettis ask Perseus what their stories meant. At that, Perseus smiled, while his black eyes looked murder, and said that they were simply stories, and not something that any wise man would heed.

Then Prottëänni felt fear in his heart, but he felt also that he had no choice; and so the ships turned slowly round, with the mers swimming alongside them, and together they sailed towards a shining isle, where the smoke of fires stained the sky, and the blood of cattle stained the beach. And there King Cepheus waited.

When they met, Prottëänni was astonished: for the king was a man in the prime of life, but his hair was already white, and his face was the face of a child, eager and open and free of thought. He seemed too weak to stand, but leaned on his wife Cassiopeia, who was tall and graceful; and still more on his daughter Andromeda, who was young and kind; but most of all, he leaned on Perseus.

And they met on the edge of the sea, the man bending to the water, the merpeople swimming to the end of the waves; and Cepheus was delighted, so that his words tumbled over one another in an uncontrolled stream. And he spoke of friendship, and of sharing the seas.

Again, Thettis asked, What are these stories of war? Cepheus held up his hands in horror, and swore that no man under his command would do such a thing. And all his men nodded and cried out that it was so; but it seemed to Prottëänni that Perseus smiled into his beard.

Then Cepheus bent down, so eagerly that his crown fell off and tumbled into the waves, which men remembered after. And he offered to make a bond of peace and friendship between his people and Prottëänni's people; to share the land and sea, and to live by the Code. And he *suggested that the two kings meet there on the island at the next new moon, to sanctify the peace. And Protteänni accepted, although there was a nameless fear within him; and he swam swiftly back to his Queen and King to tell them the news.*

Atlas and Amphitrite listened in silence, and it seemed to Protteänni that they heard more than just his voice. And when he had spoken, the Queen reached out and took the King's hand, and they exchanged a look of grieving knowledge that he did not understand.

But the King only sighed, and said, "So be it;" and so it was arranged. He left Amphitrite to rule the people, and set out for the Landlocked Sea.

And at the appointed time, the king of Athens and the King of Atlantis sat face to face where land and sea came together, Cepheus holding the rod of kingship, Atlas holding his trident; and Atlas spoke for his people, and Cepheus said what his wise men told him. And after long talks, and many arguments, they agreed to the Great Peace. It set out how the two races would share the seas and sands, the coasts and cliffs; it governed the shallow waters and the deep pools, the river-mouths and reefs. And on the longest day of summer, the two kings swore friendship and alliance, the merman on the altar of Poseidon, the man on the altar of Zeus. And the seven daughters of King Atlas sang a song of peace, and Queen Cassiopeia and Princess Andromeda sang a song of rejoicing, and friendship grew quickly between them.

But behind them stood Perseus, like a shadow; and he leaned on his spear and would not join the celebrations; and his eyes were dark.

11
Divers and Cavers

A mile to the south, the Reeking Cove jutted out from the shore, its massive walls like a crab's pincers enclosing a harbor full of pontoons and yachts. The songs said that the netmen had built it in the time of Mielikki's great-grandfather, Ahtto. She had never believed it before, thinking that the rocks were too huge for anyone to shift; but now she had seen for herself what netmen could do.

The harbor clung to the coast like a leech, slowly draining the life from it. Every time the tide rose, it turned the narrow entrance into a trap, sweeping in fish and lobsters, and anything too weak to swim away. On a falling tide, the water flooded out laden with waste and streaked with oil. Often, it bore clouds of pale, billowing things that tumbled back and forth across the sand like jellyfish until they drowned themselves – or something else. And every evening and morning, the harbor was a bellowing madhouse as thunder boat after thunder boat shuddered in and out between the claws.

This was the most dangerous place on the coast. As the children approached, they sank deeper, seeing the sunlight grow fainter and the colors fade to green. At twe-six fathoms, they levelled off over a rocky slope, and headed south as fast as they could fin, angling against the current that was trying to sweep them out to sea.

The noise of boats was continuous, a throbbing growl that jumped and faded and jumped again. All of a sudden, a long, dark shape swept by overhead. They froze, and an instant later it was gone, leaving a seething line of bubbles. Huddling closer together, they swam on. Another boat crashed by, then another much slower, its engine a deliberate thud-thud-thud. Rainbow streaks of oil followed it.

- Drown the lot of them, - Viliga muttered, - there won't be a fish to catch for miles after this. -

- You wouldn't want to eat it if there were, - Thettis told him. - Have you tasted the water? -

He smacked his lips. There was a bitter taste to the sea, faint but foul, the taint of generations of oil and refuse dumped into the water.

Dohan spat. - Disgusting! You'd think the tide would clear it out. -

- It does. Then it comes back in, - Thettis said drily.

Riakka rolled for a long look up, sideways and back.

- Careful now, - she called. - We're coming to the tide-run. Keep together. -

Ahead, the rocks grew more scattered, then stopped entirely. They re-started twain fathoms further on, but in between was a sandy trench, choked with the litter of the port. A twelve-volt battery lay almost buried, one sharp black corner poking out of the sand, its acid long since leached into the water. Bottles and cans lay tumbled in the silt, home to crabs and worms, little cave-dwelling blennies and the thunderclap shrimps that always lived with them. Further up the slope, a blue plastic fisherman's crate lay upside down. Weed trailed over it, and tiny fish darted in and out of its shade: a box designed to hold dead fish, now protecting live ones.

Another boat roared overhead, making them flinch. This was the danger point: as they crossed the pale sand, their silhouettes would be clearly visible to anyone glancing down from above.

Riakka drifted down between two rocks and looked across the gap. The trench faded into blue distance, too far to see across, but with her sonar she could sense the other side. The current was running fast: her hair billowed sideways, downtide.

- All right, - she said. - We'll go one at a time, as fast as we can fin. I'll go first. When I get to the other side, I'll call. You come after me one by one. The rest, hide in the rocks. - Her eyes scanned the group. - Thettis, you come last. -

Thettis nodded, pale-faced. Riakka looked up and down the trench, braced herself and kicked forwards, belly low. As soon as she was clear of the rocks, the full force of the tide hit her: they saw her stagger sideways, angle her body upstream and kick harder. Once there was a flurry beneath her as a wide-eyed flounder rocketed out of the sand; then she disappeared from sight. Tensely, they watched with sonar as she battled her way to the other side; when she made it, everymer sagged with relief.

- Made it! - Riakka called. - Watch out for the current, it'll push you out to sea if you let it. Dohan, come over. -

The big boy mimicked her, looking left, right

and up, then thrusting forward. His strokes were powerful, and he seemed to cross the gap in no time.

- Made it! - he called cheerfully. - Pity I missed the flounder, I'm hungry. -

With two of the school safely over, their mood began to rise: maybe their luck really was turning. Quickly, Viliga swam off, keeping close to the bottom to avoid the worst of the current. Soon he was in safety.

- You next, Pel! - Riakka called.

Mielikki watched anxiously as her brother crept to the edge. He had never been as strong or as fast as the others, and the tide looked fierce. Like the others, he looked round cautiously, then kicked out into the current.

At once he wavered, spinning off to the left. Mielikki braced herself to go and help; but he angled downwards and kicked hard, driving himself closer to the sand, where the current would be weakest. With one hand he steadied himself against the bottom, and began to fight his way determinedly across, kicking with his tail and pulling with his arms.

He had just reached halfway when Helmi screamed.

- Divers! Upstream! -

Every head jerked into the current. Every throat let out a storm of sonar. Out in the middle of the naked sands, Pel shot a panicked glance over his shoulder and began finning desperately, kicking up spurts of sand at every stroke.

First they heard the bubbles, jangling and clanging as they jostled towards the surface. Then they saw them, tall plumes of wasted air glinting like mirrors. They were sweeping down the current with terrible speed – and below them, they knew, must be the netmen. Any second now they would come into sight, and Pel was out in the open with nowhere to hide.

- Move, Pel! - shrieked Riakka. He thrashed frantically towards the rocks, casting terrified glances over his shoulder.

- Come on, Pel, - Mielikki muttered to herself, fists clenched in anguish. - Come on... -

She saw her brother falter and look towards the towering bubble-stacks. Already the netmen were coming into sight, a thickening darkness in the water. Any second now...

- He's not going to make it! - Helmi moaned....

And Pel kicked upwards, turned sharply to the left, and shot off down the current like a diving penguin.

Mielikki gasped. Thettis swore. Pel's form blinked out of sight in the blue distance. Before any of them had time to move, the humans came into view.

There were five of them, big and dark and clumsy, sweeping almost sideways as the current pushed them. Their skins were black with strange blue patches (the merpeople knew nothing of wetsuits), their faces blank masks spewing bubbles every few seconds. On their backs were bright yellow cylinders which gave off bell-clear echoes. Their legs were long and spindly, and their fins were astonishing colors.

One with vivid yellow fins came in front,

slow and stately, hands folded regally across its belly, for all the world like the slowest, fattest merman in the world. Its breaths were slow and deliberate: every few seconds it let out a long, loud blast of bubbles, a sign of confidence, or contempt.

Two more came side by side behind it, and even in her fear for Pel, Mielikki could not help staring: she had never seen anything so uncoordinated in her life. The one closest to her seemed to have no idea how to use its fins (which were bright green): instead, it was paddling with its hands, leaning over to one side and letting out bubbles in an almost continuous stream. Its partner swam like a shrimp, kicking, shooting up and forwards a few tail-spans, curving back down, thumping onto the seabed, and pushing off again with both hands, leaving a trail of dust clouds behind it.

The last two were holding hands; but it looked less like affection than a desperate attempt to stay in control. One was drifting feet first towards the surface, while the other one was almost crawling along the trench: it was hard to tell whether green-fins was holding pink-fins down, or pink-fins was pulling green-fins up.

The children watched in fascination as the humans – an instructor and four students on their first deep dive, if they had known it – swept by under their bubble-trees. Nothing in all the oceans looks as ridiculous as a human learning to dive. The children clung close to the rocks, ready to duck the moment the terrible blank faces swung their way; but the divers held on their course without glancing to left or right. In less than two minutes, they were lost in the blue. The jangle of bubbles faded slowly behind them.

- Pel! We've got to find Pel! – Mielikki exclaimed, bursting out of her hiding place and lunging forwards. But just at that moment a cheery shout came from the far side, and they saw his sonar-shape come battling up the current, pulling himself from rock to rock.

Discipline vanished. Mielikki charged across the gully, Helmi half a length behind, and even Thettis laughed and came after them. They swept across the sand, curving down the streaming tide, and came together in an excited huddle in the shelter of the rocks. Pel's face was shining with pride.

- The tide was so strong! I knew I couldn't make it. I really thought they were going to catch me. And then I thought, If I go *with* the current, I can be gone before they see me! It'll be on my side, not theirs. So I swam downcurrent as fast as I could, got out of sight, turned into the rocks, and … well, here I am. -

Mielikki gave him a hug. - Brilliant! - she exclaimed. - Pel, that was pelagic! -

- Good thinking, - said Thettis approvingly; her highest compliment.

They all jumped as Riakka sent a long squirt of sonar downstream.

- They're stopping, - she said warningly. - I think they're coming back. Pel, well done! Now let's find those caves. -

They found the first cave quickly, but it was no more than a gap between two giant blocks: no air, and barely any shelter. Half a mile and another cautious breath later, they came across three more. The first two were shallow caverns, but the third, a narrow, sharp-edged crack, gave out a complex echo, as if there were multiple chambers inside, catching and sending back the sound.

They looked at one another hopefully: the home-cave had sounded like that. It was now close to midday, and they had never felt so tired. Their heads ached, their nerves were stretched tight with fear, the grumble of thunder boats sawed at their ears; and having seen the divers, they knew that not even being underwater was a refuge any more.

Riakka hesitated in the cave mouth, looking at the group. Mielikki had the odd feeling that she was measuring them with something other than sonar. Of course: she must be wondering whom to take with her this time. Well, it would not be Mielikki, that was certain. Not after she had scratched herself on the urchin; not after she had made such a noise, probing that last cave with her sonar. She looked away and tried not to bump anyone with her tail. The excitement of Pel's escape had worn off, and she felt close to tears.

- Mielikki? Will you come with me? - Riakka asked.

Mielikki jumped, and bumped into Helmi.

- M-me? You want me to come? -

- No, she's joking, - Viliga said irritably. - Of *course* she wants you to come, you demersal bottom-

134

feeder! - Demersal is the opposite of pelagic, and refers to species that live in or near the sea-bed. Pelagic species despise them.

Mielikki flushed at the insult, and seemed to shrink in on herself.

- Shut up, Viliga! – Riakka snapped, without even looking at him. And then she spoke to Mielikki on the private channel, something she had never done before. - You're the best of us in caves. -

- But ... I bumped into the wall... - she replied. - And I made too much noise... -

Riakka shook her head, and there was a fear in her voice that Mielikki had never heard before. - You didn't panic! And I ... I nearly did. –

There was a long, long pause.

- I need you in there. I can't do it on my own, - Riakka said, in no more than a whisper.

Mielikki held her eyes for one moment more. Somehow her heart was racing, as if she were about to dive into a shark-filled sea. Then she swallowed, and nodded dumbly.

- Thank you, - Riakka said quietly. Together, they ducked into the cave.

It was a jagged and irregular chamber, a crack broken in the cliff-wall by some ancient earthquake. The ground was thick with sand, the walls dark with urchins. It narrowed as they made their way back into the rock, then widened suddenly into a much wider chamber, almost square and smooth-floored.

They swept the chamber with sonar, spotting three separate passages onwards. The first was a dead end. The second, a narrow crack, led into an almost-vertical chimney: Mielikki took her courage in

135

both hands and swam up as far as she could, but there was no sign of air above.

The third led into yet another cavern. Three of its walls were as smooth as the one they had just left – strangely square, even for one used to the geometric shapes of fractured basalt. But the fourth was a slope of tumbled rock. At the top was a tiny crack, with more echoes behind it; but only an eel or an octopus would have been able to get through there.

- Nothing, - said Riakka discontentedly, and turned back.

Unwilling to give up on the hope of air and sleep, Mielikki swam closer and sent her sonar upwards. It was a vain hope: the gap was far too small for anymer to pass. But near the top of the tumbled heap, there was a sudden unexpected echo, like a diamond glinting in clay. As Riakka turned impatiently, she bent closer and saw a shell as big as her fist, tightly curved and ending in a smooth-lipped bell. In the sonar-picture it shone like sunlight, and the echoes from inside were the most complex she had ever heard.

- Come on! - Riakka called.

Without knowing why, she brushed off the sand and picked it up slowly: it was cold and smooth and oddly heavy.

- Come *on*! -

Mielikki turned towards the exit and followed Riakka back out.

- What were you playing at in there? - the elder girl snapped as they rejoined the school in the daylight.

- Picking up this, - she answered defiantly, and held out one hand. There on her palm lay the shell in a tight-coiled spiral, shining like polished bronze.

There was a short silence, and then, - What is that? - everymer asked at once.

- I don't know, - she said, - But I found it, up there among the rocks. And listen, - she pointed the wide end at them, - Listen to the sound. -

Helmi sent a questing click of sonar at it, and the echo that came out hummed and sparkled with life. When a white light shines through a crystal, it comes out as a rainbow: this was the same, but in sound.

- Pelagic, - breathed Pel, exhaustion forgotten. - Can I have a go? - He sent a high, loud note into the shell's flared end, and back came a scatter of flickering notes like fish darting out of a cave.

They stared. There was nothing remotely like it in any of the songs they knew.

- Are you going to keep it? - Helmi asked.

- Of course I'm going to keep it! But right now, what I want is to sleep. –

The words were out before she even thought about them. Immediately, the shell was forgotten. Every head swung to look at Riakka, desperate, hopeful, pressing.

- We can't sleep out here, it would be suicide! There are netmen up there! - Riakka snapped at once. She was so tired that she could feel herself losing control; and she was terrified what might happen if she did.

- Look, just one more cave, all right? I'm tired

too, but just think: if we can find a cave to sleep in, we can sleep properly, and not have to worry about sharks and netmen. -

They stared at her, mute and mutinous. She tried again, desperately.

- One more cave, all right? Mielikki? -

Mielikki's heart sank. All she wanted to do was sleep; but she knew she had to keep going, for the school's sake.

- One more, - she agreed. - And after that, we sleep. -

Silently, she handed the shell to Helmi, who tucked it into her silver hair; then Mielikki swam towards the mouth of the third cave.

It was almost like the second: a narrow entrance, a smooth-walled cavern, tunnels leading up and back, and more chambers deeper inside. But there was much more sand here, as if it had poured down from high above: once Mielikki kicked too hard and saw a waft of blackness rise up around her tail, threatening to blind and deafen them. After that, they stuck as close to the ceiling as they could.

- This whole cliff must be full of caves, - Riakka muttered as they probed deeper.

- And every one of them square, - Mielikki said. - I've never seen anything like it. -

- Me neither. - Riakka sounded genuinely puzzled. - It's almost like netmen's stuff, but they'd never build this deep. -

- Maybe they built it up there and it fell into the sea, - Mielikki suggested.

- I wish the rest of them would, then! – Riakka led the way up deeper into the caves.

They came out into a third chamber, high up and deep in the rock. Again, one wall had collapsed in a jumble of rubble and sand; but this time there was a larger gap at the top of the fall, and it sounded as if there was a chamber beyond.

Riakka swam upwards, lighting her way with her clicks.

- Anything? - Mielikki asked, below her.

- Not sure, - was the answer, as she swam to the top of the rockfall. The crack looked just that, a jagged tear in the ceiling. It was much narrower than the tunnels they had taken so far, and thoroughly uninviting. Even Mielikki felt a qualm looking at it.

Riakka hung there in front of it for a moment, her fists clenching and unclenching; then she came to a decision.

- Wait here, - she said, and without waiting for an answer, she wriggled into the crack like an eel into its hole, vanishing inch by inch until only her tail-flukes were sticking out; then they disappeared. Mielikki had once seen a stonefish swallowing a wrasse that was too big for it: little by little it had gulped the fish in, starting with the head, so that the tail hung out of its mouth, threshing. This was like that, but much worse.

- It's a tunnel. It looks like it turns a corner, - Riakka's voice came faintly down. - I think there's a space beyond... -

- Take care! - Mielikki called back nervously.

- It's all right, I think I can get there. - Skin scraped on rock. - If I can just get one arm through... -

All of a sudden there was the scrape of

shifting rock.

Riakka screamed.

Black sand came gushing out of the crack.

Mielikki flinched, banged her head on the ceiling, forced herself forwards and shouted - Riakka! *Riakka!* -

There was no answer. The sand poured down in a roaring column and cascaded over the stones.

- Riakka! -

Without thinking, Mielikki rammed her hands into the tunnel and pulled herself upwards. The sand beat down on her, blinding and deafening. Her ears squeezed, and she realized that she was sinking. She lashed out with her tail, driving herself upwards, and her reaching fingers touched something soft. Without warning it kicked, slamming her head against the wall; but in the same moment her other hand brushed Riakka's tail-flukes. She grabbed them by reflex, and screamed, - *Riakka!* -

- Mielikki! I can't see! -

The sound was almost lost in the thunder of the sands.

- *Hold my hand!* - she bellowed, reaching higher, and felt Riakka's fingers lock in a bone-grinding grip.

- Come on! -

She pulled with a strength she had not known she possessed. Riakka wriggled savagely, but could not break free. Mielikki swept one hand around the walls, and found a lump of rock. She shoved against it. Riakka screamed, and with shocking suddenness she ripped back out. The two mergirls shot out of the crack in a confusion of arms and tails, slammed into the stones, rolled downwards, and found themselves in clear water, staring at the thunderous black cascade.

- Quick! The way out! - Mielikki called, dragging Riakka towards it.

- I can't see! -

- You don't need to! Hold onto me! -

Mielikki hurled herself at the exit, fought through the sand that was already spilling into it, dashed across the lower cave, sobbed in relief at the glow of daylight, forced Riakka bodily through the exit ahead of her, tore across the entry cave and bolted for the surface past the astonished school.

They broke the surface together with cries of relief. Spray fountained in the sunshine. A gull shrieked and flopped away. The sun stabbed their eyes as they dragged in shuddering lungfuls of air.

Riakka was crying openly, her hair and face clotted with sand. "I thought I could get round that corner. Then a rock moved, and I couldn't get out..." Her voice broke.

The others popped up around them, pale and scared. Viliga took one look at Riakka and turned on Mielikki.

"What have you *done?*"

Riakka was still holding Mielikki's hand, a grip so tight it cut off the blood. "She ... she got me out of there. I..."

She started sobbing again. For merpeople, the nightmare beyond all nightmares is to be trapped under the sea.

"We found a new cave," Mielikki said in a trembling voice, still caught in the horror of it.

"Riakka went into a tunnel. Something went wrong, and the sand ... the sand..." Her voice cracked, and her own tears started to flow.

There was a long silence, broken only by their crying. The school stared at them, leaderless and lost. Even Thettis seemed paralyzed, too shocked to think, too shocked to decide, too shocked to get them moving. Somewhere near, gulls were calling. Boats were growling. Danger was everywhere, and they had nowhere to go.

At last Riakka took a deep, shuddering breath and ducked her face in the water. She stayed down for a long time, and when she came up again, the water seemed to have washed away the sand – and the despair. Her eyes were red with crying, but her face was pale and set. She looked around the circle, their faces horrified and helpless, and straightened her shoulders with a desperate jerk.

"Come on, we can't stay here. Mielikki, are you all right?"

Mielikki flinched and looked away. Her friends were staring at her. She could sense their terror and exhaustion.

They can't go on like this, a voice said inside her. It terrified her. She wanted to hide from it. She wanted her parents to be there.

I want this not to be happening.

But her eyes met Riakka's, and the chill understanding passed between them.

The others can't do this. We've got to.

Mielikki gulped down the last of her tears, wiped one arm across her face and nodded shakily.

"All right."

"Then let's go. Out to sea, to sleep."

A minute later, the gull curved back down and carved his place to rest on the empty waves. He looked around cautiously, wary of another scare; but there was only a faint stain of black sand, slowly spreading down the tide, to show where the school had been.

12

Peace

How did our peoples live together, in the last good days before the war? This is what the songs tell us of the last beauty of Atlantis, like the flame of sunset before the night...

The heart of the Great Peace was this: that all salt waters, up to the rising of the highest tide, were the realm of King Atlas, and there his word was law. But above that point, the writ of Athens ran, and there the humans could build their cities and plant their crops, fell trees and clear fields; and so long as they did not foul the rivers or pour their dirt into the sea, no merman would interfere.

At first, all went well. The people of Cepheus spread along the coast of the Landlocked Sea, building shining cities and temples to Zeus. They fished, but never too much. They splashed in the shallow waters for pearls, but never too many. They felled trees and worked metal and went their own way, and they greeted us when they saw us. And we, seeing how fast and far they spread, praised the King and his counsellor for making such a peace.

But still the sharks swam behind the black-hulled ships; and still the rumors came of pirates in the East; and still Cepheus, ever innocent, laughed his child's laugh in a man's voice and said it could not be his men; and Perseus smiled and showed his teeth.

In time, trade grew up between our peoples. The

men marveled at the treasures of the sea, and they paid for them with treasures of their own: copper and silver and bronze. We made for King Cepheus a throne set with pearls and coral; and the craftsmen of Athens made for King Atlas a throne of cedar and gold. And as the trade grew, many merpeople learned the speech of Athens, so simple and flat compared with our own; but few humans learned ours.

And to fasten the love between Athens and Atlantis, Maia, the eldest daughter of King Atlas, gave to the Princess Andromeda the gift that Poseidon had given her: the rod of the Black Pearl, the gift of understanding. And Andromeda gave it to her father, knowing that he needed it most; but Cepheus laughed to see it sparkle in the sun, and declared it the symbol of all kings of Athens thenceforth.

And in the High City of Athens, by the temple of Athene daughter of Zeus, the people raised up a temple to Poseidon, and gave thanks for his wisdom, and the friendship of his children. And some said that Poseidon had brought more blessings to the kingdom than Athene had ever brought, and would have renamed the city "Poseidonia;" but they found little support.

And the two kings often met on rocky islands and sandy shores, for the good of their two peoples, and the pleasure of the meeting; and Andromeda swam and sang with Maia and her sisters, and their friendship blossomed and was strong.

And thirty years after the Great Peace was made, the kings came together on the island where they had made it, and repeated their vows; for King Cepheus loved Atlas like a father, and Atlas loved Cepheus like a child. But Cepheus now was old, his face as aged as the white hair *above it; and Cassiopeia was too old to sing. Yet Andromeda was grown glorious in her grace and beauty, and she sang with Maia and Thettis and the sisters, and their songs mirrored one another and made one another more beautiful, as the ocean mirrors the stars.*

And the two Kings sought for a way to bring their peoples still closer together; and King Atlas thought of the island Atlantis, where no human had ever set foot; and he said to Cepheus, Let us fasten our friendship for all time, so that we become one people in our hearts. Send some of your people to Atlantis, and raise a new city there; and I shall send some of my people to your shores; and we will live for ever in peace.

And King Cepheus said: Your people are welcome wherever they swim. But the ocean is too great for our ships, and the wind and waves too fierce: how will we come there?

And Prottëanni laughed and said: Leave that to us.

So it was agreed. And in the calm of late summer, the ships of Athens passed through the Gates of Atlas and felt for the first time the heave and roll of the true ocean, and their captains and crews cried out in fear. But our people spoke to them, and comforted them, and showed them the way; and after a day and a night of voyaging, they came to a sheltered bay on the eastern shore of Atlantis, and went up onto the land, and looked across the shining plain to the snow-capped mountains beyond.

So the friendship between our peoples reached its last flowering; for you humans found gold on Atlantis, there were diamonds and emeralds and rubies, and you learned how to cut them and make them shine, and both Athens and Atlantis were made still more beautiful and full of light.

And King Atlas returned to his home-cave and watched his people grow and flourish; and his messengers went out across the Seven Seas, carrying jewels as gifts, so the light of Atlantis glittered on many a distant reef. And still Atlantis looked to the sea, and still our people sang; and they waved at the humans when they saw them, and thought it would last for ever.

And King Cepheus returned to his city, dreaming of the past; for he was old, and longed for rest. And when the rumors came, as still they came, of raiding and fighting and the breaking of the Peace, he would laugh his childish laugh and look to his captains; and they would look to Perseus; and Perseus would smile the smile that showed his teeth, and reply with soothing words and smoothing excuses, and the King would go back to his dreaming.

And from out of Atlantis the treasures rolled, so that the island was a legend of wealth. And the humans listened to the legend, and longed to take that wealth for themselves.

13

Deep Water, Shallow Sleep

The tide had turned. Away from the sheltering rocks, the current was running northwards, back the way they had come. They followed it in silence. The caves vanished quickly behind them, a darkness that dimmed and faded and melted into the blue.

A boat roared by overhead, then another, crashing from wave to wave. They ignored them, and followed Riakka. They were too tired to think, almost too tired to be afraid. Every head ached with the unaccustomed light; every stomach, with hunger.

They came to the trench below the Reeking Cove. The tide was running back in now, sucking the ocean towards those narrow jaws. The surface churned with white wakes; one by one, with many a nervous glance overhead, they crossed the sands and held on their way. They passed the first cave Mielikki and Riakka had investigated; the gray-backed stingray looked out at them suspiciously. Their sonar picked up the first dim echoes of the Cleaning Station.

- I'm hungry, - grumbled Dohan to Pel. As ever, the two friends were finning close together, Dohan using his strength and weight to make it easier for Pel to swim.

-Are you? I'm *starving*, - Pel replied.

- I could eat a barracuda, teeth and all. -

- I'd settle for a handful of mussels, - said Pel wistfully, gazing up at the sand-choked rocks. It had been a good place to pick up mussels, before the explosions.

Dohan grunted. - Don't be a bream, we haven't even got a knife. How would you get the demersal things open? -

- I know. I know. I just… Oh! - Suddenly Pel's head, which had been drooping with exhaustion, came up.

- What? -

- Mielikki! Riakka! Wait a minute! - He back-paddled frantically, almost flipping head over fins. Their heads snapped round in alarm.

- What? What? -

- I'll just … wait! - He looked left and right, swung his body vertical and shot up towards the shallows.

- Come back! - shrieked Riakka, all composure gone. Mielikki swore and turned to swim after her brother. Pel did not stop. He raced up to the ten fathom mark, turned right, ducked down between the rocks and came up again with a whoop of triumph.

Mielikki gaped, and then she caught the echo of what he was holding.

- My knife! It's my knife! -

The school looked at her in bewilderment.

- Your knife? - Riakka asked faintly as Pel nose-dived back towards them.

- My knife! - She turned to Helmi. - Don't you remember? -

Light dawned in Helmi's eyes. - We cleaned

the fish ... and we cleared out the pieces and dumped them... -

- And we left your knife to be cleaned! Of course! - Dohan burst out, glowing with pride at his friend's idea. - Pel, you genius! -

The elder children looked at them, and Pel, and the long stone blade he was waving triumphantly.

- Mielikki, it's your knife! - he said. - I remembered where you put it, look! Now we can get food! -

He basked in their admiring clicks, dead tired, but thrilled. Mielikki laughed.

- Pel, that's brilliant! - He grinned and held it out to her, hilt first.

Mielikki reached out for the familiar grip, then hesitated.

- You remembered it, - she said. - You should carry it. For all of us. -

- Really? - His face lit up like seafire, the brilliant green sparks of phosphorescence that cascade through tropical water at night.

- You've earned it, - Riakka chimed in, so relieved that she even forgot to shout at him. She had been worrying how they would eat, and Pel had solved the problem.

So Pel strapped the knife to his forearm with the seaweed cords around its sheath, and they set off again. Riakka turned her tail to the island and led them straight out into the blue. The rocks and sands sank quickly away, dissolving out of sight, until they swam suspended in water, surrounded by light.

- Where are we going? - asked Viliga after a

while.

- Out, - replied Riakka curtly, sending a long stream of clicks down into the depths.

- I can see that, but where? - he retorted waspishly. Viliga was like a jellyfish: he seemed soft, but every word stung.

- Out there. Into the blue. Somewhere far away, where we can sleep. -

- So you don't know where we're going? - he asked. At that, the younger children's heads swung to look at Riakka.

She swam on for a few moments; then all at once she whirled round, and Viliga flinched to find himself face to face with her.

- Listen to me! We have to sleep, and there's nowhere safe to do it. So we'll have to sleep somewhere that *isn't* safe, all right? If we were grown-ups, we'd sleep right out in the blue, and never come back. We can't do that, because we can't swim like them and we can't hunt like them. We haven't even got our names yet! But thanks to Pel, we can eat in the shallows: shells and crabs at least. So we'll sleep out, and when night falls we'll come back to shore and feed. And we'll keep on looking until we find a cave we can live in! -

Mielikki groaned inwardly: the idea of exploring still more caves sent shivers all the way to her tail. But she swallowed her dismay. She and Riakka had to keep the rest alive, and if that meant looking for a cave to sleep in, so be it.

- We'll find one, - she echoed, before Viliga could come back with another poisonous answer. - We managed it once; we can do it again. And we'll sleep out, too. -

They all looked at her, surprised.

- Oh yes? How? - asked Viliga sharply. - Seven mers, all asleep on the surface at the same time? Why don't we just call the sharks and have done with it? -

Mielikki made to snap back at him, and stopped abruptly. She had no idea how a whole school could sleep out safely. All their training had been how to survive alone, unseen, unheard, silent but listening for danger: the skill they would need on the long swim to find their parents. But many mers together were a different problem: impossible to hide, they would have to be guarded. She knew there must be a way - their parents did it every day - but she had always assumed that they would teach her when she joined them. She could tell by the elder children's faces that they had done the same. The very heart of childhood is knowing that your parents will do things for you.

- See? - said Viliga triumphantly. - I told you! You've got no idea, have you? -

Then suddenly, Pel chimed in, singing a lullaby as if to himself.

> - Sleep on the deep is sweetest
> Where darkest depths are deepest.
> One in water, watching,
> Second sweet air is snatching.
> Others are dreaming, drifting,
> Safe where seas are shifting.

- That's how we do it, isn't it? One keeps

watch on the surface, one down below, and all the others sleep. That must be what the song's about, - he said, satisfied, as if he had solved a problem. They stared at him. - Remember? Our mother used to sing it while we were falling asleep, back in the home-cave. -

Mielikki gaped. She half remembered the words, they were part of the sayings and songs that they had all grown up with; but how had Pel thought of them now?

- Pel, that's pelagic! - Thettis said, and meant it. - How did you remember that? -

He beamed; he had never managed to impress Thettis twice in one day before.

- I don't know. I was trying to work out how we'd sleep. The song just came into my head, and it seemed to fit. -

Thettis almost laughed. - It does! It solves the problem! One above, one below, the rest sleep, and we take it in turns. -

- Right! - said Riakka, suddenly animated now that there was something to organize, and she could see how to do it. - There are seven of us. We'll need two watches to make it to nightfall. That means we need four watchers, and the little ones can sleep. -

Mielikki found herself nodding. It made sense. The four elder children were bigger and stronger, more used to going without sleep. But Riakka hesitated, looking around the group. It was as if she were weighing them up. For a moment she turned to Thettis, and a rapid conversation passed between them on their private channel. Thettis looked dubious, but nodded reluctantly.

- That's right, talk about us, not to us, - Viliga muttered, loud enough to be heard. Riakka ignored him, and turned back to the group.

- All right, we'll do it this way. We'll make two long watches. It's a long stretch, but it's the best way. Viliga and Thettis, you sleep first. You'll take the second watch together. -

They looked at each other with distaste, but Riakka had been telling both what to do since they were born: they did not bother to argue.

Riakka looked around the group again. Her eyes rested on Dohan for a moment. She seemed to be bracing herself. Then:

- I'll take the first watch. Mielikki, you watch with me. -

At once there was uproar.

-What about me? - Dohan.

- Why her? She's too clumsy! - Viliga.

- I want to watch! It was my idea! - Pel.

Astonished, Mielikki looked down at her hands. She did not know whether to be proud of being chosen, or scared of getting something wrong.

Riakka's tail lashed in frustration.

- Because I say so! She's the best diver of any of us! She can stay down longer than you, Dohan! And if I say she can do it, she can do it! Now *shut up*!
-

There was a short silence. Riakka had *never* defended Mielikki before.

- What about me? - Pel asked again.

Thettis jumped in before anyone could slap him down. - You're the one who remembers things. We need you to have a proper sleep, so you can keep on remembering tomorrow. -

Pel looked unconvinced, but said nothing.

- Right, - said Riakka briskly. - We'll swim out another breath, until it gets really deep. We'll find a bit where there aren't any humans close. Mielikki and I will watch first. Thettis and Viliga, we'll wake you when it's your turn. -

Viliga looked as if he wanted to protest, but Thettis sent him a quick sound-nudge, and he stayed quiet.

- Come on. Let's fin, - Riakka said, and turned away.

It was hard to tell that they were moving. All around them, the water was blue and brilliant, streaked with swaying rays of light. Above them, the surface was so pale it was almost white. Below, the depths were so dark they were almost black. Once, a pair of hunting trevally flashed by below them, blunt-browed as whales, sharp as harpoons. Apart from them, there was nothing to show whether the school was swimming forwards or going slowly backwards on the tide. Even sonar was of little help, above the featureless sands. The only clue was their breathing: a young mer can swim six sea-miles to a breath, half an hour of finning.

At last Riakka stopped them, and they surfaced carefully. It was past midday. The sun sparkled on the waves. The sky was a brilliant blue, utterly different from the star-filled blackness they were used to. The island had sunk below the skyrim. Nothing moved above the surface; nothing moved below. If it had not been for the endless grumble of motors, they might have been all alone in the world.

- This will do, - Riakka said. - All of you, make a circle and hold hands. That way we won't lose anyone. Mielikki will watch for boats. I'll watch for sharks. -

A day before, Dohan would probably have resisted the idea of holding hands; Viliga certainly would. But now they were too tired even to squabble. They shuffled into a circle, hands clasped, their faces just tilted out of the waves. Nothing on the surface would see them unless it sailed right over them. From below, they stood out clearly, seven tails swaying in the swell; but any hunter would have to evade their sonar – and their guards.

Pel's eyes closed almost instantly: only his determination not to seem weaker than the others had kept him going so long. Helmi managed to send Mielikki an encouraging smile before she, too, fell asleep. Dohan and Viliga stared at the waves through darkened eyes, manfully trying to spot danger until their lids drooped. Thettis gazed up at the sky, seeming to draw peace from it, and quickly fell asleep.

"All right, Mielikki?" Riakka asked. "You stay on the surface, and watch out for thunder boats: if anything comes close, wake the others and dive. I'll be six fathoms down. If I need you, I'll scream. When I come up to breathe, you dive, and we'll take it in turns."

"Pelagic," answered Mielikki, trying to sound grown-up and matter-of-fact, rather than exhausted and terrified. As soon as she said it she knew it sounded neither, but Riakka let it pass.

"Good girl," she said. She heaved in a great,

throat-swelling breath, and dived.

Even with her dark eyelid lowered - every mer has a third eyelid, a dark and transparent membrane that protects their eyes against the sun - the daylight was painfully bright. She screwed up her eyes and squinted across the glittering waves. Far away on the skyrim, she saw the white speck of a sail. Her eyes locked on it and followed its course. It seemed to fade, and with a start she realized that her eyes were closing. She jerked up her head and pinched herself hard.

"Pelagic," she repeated to herself absently; her voice croaked with tiredness. Paddling with her hands, she turned in a slow circle, scanning the skyrim. Nothing moved; even the sail was gone. There was nothing to be seen except the faces of the school, the waves just washing over them as they floated in a ring.

She found herself staring at Helmi. Her friend had been so scared of sleeping out, and yet here she was, asleep over the echoing depths. Helmi had been brave today. Riakka had been brave too, she had to admit it; the girl might be bossy, and treat the rest like babies, but it had taken courage to keep exploring those caves. And Pel... Her gaze shifted to Pel, all the worries smoothed out of his face in sleep. He had thought faster than any of them when the divers came down the trench, and again when he remembered the knife – and the songs. Songs like ... like...

"Come on, Mielikki!" she muttered angrily; she had almost fallen asleep again. She turned her back on the school and stared resolutely towards the skyrim, almost willing there to be a boat, a shark, anything to break the endless monotony of the waves.

The sun beat down, burning on her face. Without thinking, she ducked her head under water. At once she felt better; but the cool darkness was an invitation to sleep. She lifted her head again, and felt the stab of the light. Her eyes ached. Her skin prickled. Salt from the waves stiffened white in her hair. A black-and-white bird with sharp wing-tips, an Arctic tern, flew overhead, banked in surprise, then sped off in a straight line to the north. It was an omen, a spy-bird, although she did not know it.

The sun drilled down. The sky was a blue dome flecked with clouds; the sea, a blue floor flecked with waves. Far away, a thunder boat dragged its wake across the sea; far above, a thunder bird dragged its wake across the sky. Mielikki turned south towards the sun: the waves twinkled with blinding light. She turned her back on it: the blue was so intense it swamped every other color. A little clump of bladder-wrack floated past, trailing a tiny wake of bubbles. She watched it drift and drift, until it caught in Thettis' hair.

All of a sudden, Riakka was there in a burst of spray. "What's the matter with you?" she asked angrily. "Didn't you hear me call?"

Mielikki started guiltily: she had forgotten her job, distracted by a piece of seaweed.

"I'm sorry ... I..."

Riakka's gaze softened. Mielikki's face was flushed and drawn, her hair glittering with salt-dust. She looked on the verge of collapse.

"It's all right," she said. "You go down for a while. It'll do you good to get out of the sun. I checked how we're drifting: we're going north, but not fast."

"The tide should be turning soon," Mielikki said, glad to be able to say something that sounded intelligent; she felt stupid and embarrassed. The elder girl nodded.

"We won't drift far, anyway. Did you see anything up here?"

"One sail, far away. And a bird."

Riakka nodded, and reached out absently to twitch the bladder-wrack out of Thettis' hair. She put it down on a wave, and both girls watched it drift slowly away.

"Right," Riakka said with a sudden start. Mielikki jumped, then realized that, this time, the elder girl had almost fallen asleep. It made her feel a little better.

"Down you go. See you soon."

"See you," Mielikki croaked, and dived.

The relief to be out of the sun! The relief to see cool blue light again, and feel the water soothing her skin, and hear properly! She shot straight down twelve fathoms in sheer exuberance, remembered herself and tried her best to look sensible as she came back up to the six fathom mark. She sent a long stream of sonar down towards the sea bed: it came back faint and diffuse, but clear enough to show that Riakka had been right: they had drifted north, but not far. She rolled and looked up: there was the ring of tails hanging down above her, with Riakka a little way upcurrent, looking west towards the island.

Mielikki turned slowly to the four points of the compass, probing for any danger; but nothing moved.

It was much easier to keep watch down here: cool, dark, familiar. She let her dark eyelid slip down and felt the cold water bathe her eyes. All around her shone the blue, so clear and cool that it was if the sky itself had turned to water.

She turned and scanned carefully, taking her time. Quickly it became automatic; then it became boring. She looked up, and wondered how long it would be before she could surface and have a sleep. Riakka's hands were paddling gently, turning her in a circle, apparently without a care in the world.

Turn, scan, turn, scan...

For the first time, she had time to think about all that had happened: the netmen, the explosion, the divers, the cave, the falling sands. She shuddered at that last thought and spun a little faster.

Turn, scan, turn, scan...

The strange bronze shell that she had picked up. Unconsciously, her eyes lifted to Helmi, who had wound it in her hair. What was it? Where had it come from? She had never seen an animal like that. Was there some sort of copper cave-snail hiding among the rocks?

Turn, scan, turn, scan...

Maybe Pel would know. Maybe there was something in the songs which he would remember and explain it all, just as he had explained how to sleep out safely. He had amazed her that day – not by remembering the song, but by understanding it when it was needed. She had always treated Pel as, well, her little brother: there to be played with, protected, laughed at or ignored, but always less good at things than she was. She had never thought that he could be better than her at something...

Her lungs were burning, her stomach clenching: it was time to breathe. She took a last careful look around, and finned up to the surface.

She was shocked at Riakka's face. The girl's skin was flushed almost scarlet. There were deep bags under her eyes and lines of fatigue on her cheeks, and the salt had settled in them like white quartz. Her eyes were red.

"Your turn," Mielikki said. Riakka nodded, too tired even to speak: a dangerous state for a creature who lives and dies by its ability to control sound. She dived, and left Mielikki alone.

The sun barely seemed to have moved, pouring its heat and light down on the sea. In seconds, the comfort of being underwater was forgotten. In minutes, it felt as if she had been doing this for ever. Once more, her eyes began to burn. Once more, her head began to ache. Her tail-muscles burned with too much swimming. Each time she looked at the glittering waves, they left a red haze across her sight. She could feel her strength failing. She tried to sing, to keep her spirits up, but the sound was frightening in the emptiness of the sea.

Maybe if I just close my eyes for a second, she thought. But another voice inside said: *No! You promised to watch over them!* She jerked her head up and forced herself to stare at the skyrim.

Gradually another thought crept in, like an eel wriggling out of deep water: *Maybe they don't need me to watch them anyway. They can all hear in their sleep, can't they? It can't hurt just to see if I could sleep there too...* She edged closer to the group, guiltily. Pel's hand had slipped out of Helmi's as they slept. She fixed her eyes on the gap between them, and shifted closer.

After all, nothing's happened, she told herself. *There's nothing here, no ships, no sharks, not even a bird. I'm sure it'll be all right if I have a sleep. Besides, they'll need me to be fit when we go to look for another cave. I* ought *to sleep. It's for the good of all of us.*

She was already reaching out to join the circle of sleepers when she thought: *Riakka will see.* With a guilty start, she put her face in the water and looked down. There was the girl, six fathoms down, turning gently with the sunlight rippling in waves across her back.

Riakka'll see! And she'll tell everyone, and they'll know I failed! She could have cried with frustration. *Drown Riakka! It isn't fair!* But she knew, all the same, that she could not try to sleep.

At least the cold water on her face made her feel one degree less wretched. She let it soothe her eyes for as long as she dared, then looked up again at the hot sky and the blinding sea. She reached out carefully, took Pel's hand, and put it carefully back in Helmi's so that the circle was complete, without her. Pel's head lolled back and he muttered something from his dreams; she thought she caught her own name. Then she turned her back, almost weeping with fatigue, and began the slow, painful watching again.

It seemed that her ordeal would never end.

The heat, the pain, the exhaustion had become part of existence; she could not even imagine any other. And then, suddenly Riakka popped out of the water beside her, and it was over, and she had stayed awake to the end.

"Well done," Riakka said, her voice barely a croak of exhaustion. "Very well done."

Mielikki nodded dumbly, too tired even to reply.

"Let's wake Thettis and Viliga." Riakka turned to the ring and took her friend by the shoulder. Thettis groaned and tried feebly to brush the hand away. Mielikki edged over to Viliga and shook his shoulder; he shrugged her hand off, grumbling like a humpback whale, and promptly fell asleep again.

Mielikki tried again, and this time he did wake up, bleary and disoriented. Behind them there was a splash and splutter as Thettis stuck her face in the water.

"It's your turn," Riakka said across the circle. "One on the surface. One six fathoms down. Swap after half a breath, it's too hot to stay for longer. If something comes, scream."

They nodded, and finned reluctantly out of the circle. Mielikki and Riakka took their places.

"Watch out for thunder boats," Riakka reminded the guards. Thettis gave a nod which turned halfway into a colossal yawn.

"Don't do that, you'll set me … off…" Viliga protested, and yawned a yawn that seemed to go all the way round to the back of his neck, like the mouth of a scorpion-fish.

Mielikki started to laugh. Halfway through, it turned into a yawn. Halfway through the yawn, her eyes closed; and by the time her mouth was shut, she was asleep.

14

War

How did the war between Athens and Atlantis begin? This is what the songs told us, three myriad years later…

It started with a messenger, breathless and battered by the midwinter storms, swimming up to the gates of Atlantis and demanding to see the King with news that could not wait. The guards woke their captain, and he woke Prottëänni; and Prottëänni, wise in his old age, did not waste more time, but himself went to wake the King.

He found him alone in the darkness of the innermost shrine, staring at the reed basket that had cradled him and his brother so many years before; and the songs say that when Prottëänni came to him, Atlas was already waiting, and said simply, "It has come," and turned towards the door.

And the messenger told the King and Queen his news, and all who heard it cried out in horror, save the King himself; and he closed his eyes and sighed, as one who hears a tale that he already knows.

Perseus of the shark-like eyes, who called himself the son of Zeus, had proclaimed himself king of Athens, and lord of the land and sea; and he had killed Cepheus the King.

He had done it at the great gathering of midwinter on the Acropolis, the High City of Athens, when all the people came together to pay homage to their gods. In the very midst of the celebration, when Medusa the high priestess of Poseidon was leading the song of praise, Perseus marched onto the plateau in armor of black, his sword in his hand and his towering shield on his arm, a hundred armed men behind him; and he strode to where Cepheus sat on the pearl-studded throne with Cassiopeia standing beside him, and demanded his place as king.

It seemed that Cepheus was slow to understand at first, because he stared, and laughed weakly, and plucked at his beard. Medusa was before him; and she lifted up her hand to curse Perseus for breaking the ceremony and breaking his vows; and Perseus turned, and drew his sword, and with one terrible blow struck off her head, there in the sight of the king and all the people. They said that at the sight, a cry went up that shook the mountain of Athens; but King Cepheus stared as one turned to stone; and he slumped slowly sideways, and the Black Rod fell from his hand and clattered on the stones, and he tumbled from his throne, and his lips moved soundlessly in words that never quite found utterance; and Perseus' men dragged him away.

He was never seen again.

But Queen Cassiopeia whirled and sat on the throne before Perseus or any of his men could stop her, and clutched the arm-rests so hard that her fingers sank into the coral; and on this, the last day of her reign and her life, she showed herself more queenly than in any of the long years before. For when Perseus ordered her to step down, she laughed in his face, a terrible laugh of grief and rage, and dared him to pull her down himself. And he who had not hesitated to slaughter the priestess of Poseidon faltered at the thought of pulling down the Queen; and she saw *him falter, and her laughter gashed him like knives.*

Then Perseus called his warriors, pirates and war-captains who had followed him through the years. And at his bidding they levered up the throne on the shafts of their spears, and carried it to the edge of the rock, while the Queen mocked them as cowards and traitors, and none dared to so much as meet her eyes; and they threw the throne and the Queen out into the abyss, and still she mocked them as she fell.

So died Cassiopeia, in her death the greatest of all the queens of Athens; and the stars closest to the Pole are named in her honor, and they never set, but show her in the moment of tragedy and triumph, falling, ever falling, with her throne above her. And beside her is her husband Cepheus, forever plucking at his white beard.

But Andromeda stooped swiftly, and took up the Black Rod that Maia had given her, and dared Perseus to take it from her. And he would not, for he knew that the people loved her, and would not stand to see her defiled. So he bade his men chain her to a rock by the sea, and swore she would have neither food nor fire, shelter nor sleep, until she gave up the rod of kingship, and agreed to marry him and cement his claim to the throne; but Andromeda had her mother's spirit, and refused him with scorn, and endured the dark days and bitter nights unbroken.

Then the Seven Sisters left Atlantis in haste, and crossed the seas like a storm-wind; and in the dark of the night they came to Andromeda, and broke her chains, and carried her away.

They say that in later years, Perseus was ashamed to have been so outwitted. He spread the tale that it was Andromeda's own parents who chained her to the rock, and he who rescued her; but that was a lie to cover his defeat...

Then Perseus called his ships, and ordered them to scour the sea until they found the princess and the rod of the king. But no human, then or ever, was a match for the Seven Sisters. They kept her safe, and carried her across the sea, even to the courts of King Atlas, her father's friend. And the King made her welcome, but his eyes were sad; and he ordered our people to prepare for war.

Sure enough, when summer came, it brought the black ships with it, the ships with the sharks in their wake: messengers from Perseus, claiming the kingship of both Athens and Atlantis, as the birthright of his father, Zeus; and he demanded the Rod and Trident and Scepter; and he demanded the princess.

But King Atlas told the messenger: "The Princess makes her own choices, and no pirate will make them for her! Perseus has killed Cepheus and Cassiopeia, my friends, your true king and queen; he has broken the oaths he swore to them, and the Code that they agreed with me. He must make a choice: the land or the water, peace or war. If he chooses the land, I shall leave him in peace, and let others punish him for his crime if they can. But if he comes to my seas in war, he shall lose all: peace," and he lifted up the scepter of glass, "and kingship," and he lifted up the rod of ebony, "and life", and he took up the trident of gold. "As for Zeus, this island is Poseidon's gift, and it is his to hold – or to take back into the deep."

And the messenger bowed against his own will, seeing the power and glory of the King Over Seas; but he only said, "So be it. Our answer will be written in blood."

And he went his way in a fury.

That summer, the black ships came.

They came out of the East on a burning wind that

drove the storm-waves against the cliffs and turned the Gates of Atlas into a tumbling hell of water. And they came to kill. Spears they had, and long harpoons with tips of jagged bronze; ropes and nets set with spikes and venom; fire that poured onto the water and clung there, burning. They swept through the settlements of the merpeople of the Landlocked Seas, killing, fouling the fishing-grounds, burning the rocks themselves so they are black to this day, and everywhere they went, the carrion-sharks followed. Hour after hour the messengers came into Atlantis with more tales of grief and suffering, and our hearts grew hot within us, and for the only time in our history the Seven Sisters led us out to war.

Three myriad years have passed since then, and still we remember those days, when our people fought against the black ships of the usurper; fought, and had no fear! We turned their own weapons against them, bronze and rope and fire; we bored into their ships by night and burned them by day; we picked their steersmen off with casts of spear and slingstone; we drove them deaf and mad with singing, drove them wild with fear, led them out into storm and reef and let the waves do our work for us. A thousand ships, Perseus boasted that he would send out against us; and in storm and battle and sudden strike we sank and broke and burned them, until the abyss was littered with bones.

So the wave of human fury recoiled, and we drove them back from the cliffs and coves, back into the deep central basin of the Landlocked Sea, and made the western waters free from war again.

But freedom from war is not the same as peace. The Code had been broken and blood had been shed, and there would never be peace again. Like the tide the attackers fled, and like the tide they rose again. Their black ships scoured the seas with nets and harpoons, burning and looting and killing; and those of our people who survived their attacks turned their backs on the Landlocked Sea, and turned their faces to the open ocean.

So darkness came to that sheltered sea, and the music of our people died. And the next year the humans came again, and again, and again, so that it seemed that no matter how many we sank or slew, there were always more to replace them. And the fire in the hearts of our people grew cold.

But still we held the Gates of Atlas; and we fortified the Pillars, the great rocks on either side, making them strongholds and fortresses below the water, seamed and riddled with caves and passageways so a myriad mermen could wait in ambush, and surge out to defend the narrows against attacking ships. And many times the ships came; and many times we burned them, or sent them down into the bitter cold currents; and in all those years of war, not one of Perseus' ships passed through the Gates or felt the Atlantic heave beneath its keel, save only those that sank into the black depths, and were carried out by the Dark Current on their way to Hades.

And our people thought: We hold the Seven Seas, and no human can touch us there; why should we fight for the Landlocked Sea, when there are all the riches of the ocean to choose from? And the King gave those who had fled from the sea new homes and new treasures, and told the watchers at the Gates to double their vigilance; and gradually we began to look forward to peace, and turned our backs on the humans and their war.

But the humans still sailed the sheltered waters; and they looked out through the Gates of Atlas, the Gates *that they could not pass, and anger and greed and longing filled their hearts. And through the gates they saw the ocean; and over the ocean, they saw the mountains of Atlantis gleam.*

15

Dangerous Waters

When Mielikki awoke, it was cool and dark. The sun had set. In the west, the skyrim was barred with gold. Above it the light faded to yellow, then green, then a luminous blue. The stars were coming out: Orion the Wild Hunter swimming high in the darkness; the Rudder of the Sky swinging across the night; Andromeda lifting her arm from the sea as she wrought her Curse.

"Mielikki," Helmi's voice was saying. "Mielikki, come on, it's time to wake up."

She looked around, and realized that the others had woken up and broken the circle. They were swimming around not far away: they looked very dark against the shining sky.

"How..." She broke off with an enormous yawn. "Oh, I'm sleepy! Where are we?"

"All at sea," Pel said instantly, before the moment could pass, and turned a back-flip in delight. He had slept for seven hours without a break, and the shock and terror seemed like a dream.

"About a mile south of Reeking Cove, they think. The tide turned, and we drifted south," Helmi said, and yawned herself. "Oh, I needed it! And did you really keep watch? Was it all right?"

Mielikki stretched, still trying to clear the fog

of sleep from her mind. Memories were coming back slowly: the light, the heat, the sun-spears dancing in the blue.

"It was all right," she said finally, with an effort. "Hot. Bright." Another yawn. "Blue."

Helmi looked at her hungrily, hoping for something more. "And what did you see? Did you see anything?"

Mielikki blinked, trying to order her memories. "Waves. Seaweed." A long pause. "One sail, far away. And seagulls, flying."

Helmi looked at her admiringly. "You kept watch over all of us ... I'll do it next time, I will!"

Mielikki nodded. "I know you will."

She looked around. As the sunset faded, the stars grew brighter. Venus appeared in the west. Below them, the skyrim shone with a faint white glow like the rising of the moon. It grew stronger, faded, grew stronger again: the loom of the netmen's lighthouse. She had often gathered mussels from the rocks beneath it.

All of a sudden, she realized how hungry she was: just the thought of the thin-lipped black shells made her mouth water.

"I'm starving," she said. "When do we eat?"

Helmi laughed merrily for the first time since the cliff had fallen.

"As soon as we can. We're going to swim back to the rocks to collect mussels – thanks to Pel! He did so well yesterday, I'm really proud of him," she added.

"Me too," Mielikki said fervently. "Me too!"

"After we've eaten, we'll keep looking for a

cave. Riakka thinks we'll find one further south of where we looked. There were lots of openings there. Maybe one of them will have air."

Mielikki nodded dubiously. The thought of going back into those echoing, airless holes struck fear deep inside her, but there was no point in scaring Helmi by saying so. She stayed quiet.

"I suppose," Helmi went on hesitantly after a moment, as if she had been waiting for Mielikki to say something, "I suppose we do *need* a cave?"

"What?" Mielikki's head swung round in surprise.

"Well, we have slept out all day, haven't we? And we did survive. And you know, it's not like we were planning to live in a cave for ever, were we?"

Mielikki stared.

"I just mean … maybe we could keep on doing this. You know, sleeping out during the day, coming in to feed during the night. Couldn't we?"

Mielikki opened her mouth, closed it, opened again and, most unusually, found herself lost for words. She had always thought of herself as the adventurous one, and here was Helmi – Helmi! – shyly proposing something that would have struck them all dumb with amazement just one day before.

Riakka clicked before she had time to collect her thoughts; a sharp sound, cutting through the fog of sleep, a call to attention. The elder girl had been talking with Thettis, a little uptide of the rest of the school. When she spoke, her voice was hoarse, but determined.

"We're going to swim back to the island and feed on the mussel-beds. Thanks to Pel," every head turned towards the youngest member of the school, "we can eat properly. So we'll drop down to six fathoms, like before, and stick together. Remember, sharks hunt at night."

Viliga let out a little click of annoyance, just loud enough for all of them to hear it. Riakka flushed, caught stating the obvious.

"Anyway," she hurried on, "We'll feed on the mussel-beds, then work our way downtide to the caves. Mielikki and I will look there, and see what we find. When dawn comes, if we haven't found anything, we'll swim back out here. All right?"

There was a general, impatient murmuring. They had not eaten in twenty-four hours, and they were aching to get moving.

"So let's fin." She dived, and the others followed.

Pel edged over to Mielikki as they swam, and held out a hand.

- Here, - he said, - It's your knife. I carried it for you. -

She looked at it, then at her brother; the cold water had washed all sleepiness away, as if she had left it on the surface. She felt very alert, and very hungry.

- You keep it, - she said. - I told you to keep it. You earned it. -

Pel's grin lit up the water.

It was a pleasure to be underwater at night. Gone was the terror of daytime, gone the panic every time a thunder boat came near. Night was their time, and water their element: they swam purposefully, their bodies outlined in flying green sparks of seafire.

Once an oceanic white-tip shark swam into sonar range, decided they were too many to tackle, and drifted away; once a manta finned by overhead, scattering gusts of light with every wing-beat.

- No, Dohan, - Mielikki clicked sharply, without even bothering to look. The elder boy could never resist chasing mantas, grabbing hold and riding on their backs; the placid giants, even bigger and stronger and slower than he was, did not seem to mind.

- I wasn't going to! - His clicks sounded wounded.

They swam on, sensing the sea bed rising out of the abyss beneath. The tide was slackening. The black water was awash with light. Pillars of moonlight shifted and rippled. Phosphorescence outlined their tails; but here, sound was king, and they saw with their ears as the vague forms of rocks grew sharper and clearer, outlined in brilliant echoes.

Helmi was swimming close to Mielikki, finning forward eagerly. Mielikki looked across at her and noticed the little lump at the nape of her neck, tucked in among the hair. She started; she had completely forgotten the bronze shell.

- Have you looked at that shell? - she asked.

Helmi rolled to face her, her eyes suddenly alight.

- I forgot to tell you! I was looking at it before we set off - you know, when you were still asleep. I mean, you did ask me to hold it, and I'd been carrying it all day... -

She looked nervous for a second: Mielikki's tantrums when the other children took her things had been a legend ever since she was old enough to say "Mine!"

- Don't worry, - Mielikki replied quickly. - You carried it that far, you keep hold of it. -

- Are you sure? I mean, you found it… -

- I'll find another, - Mielikki said. It was prophetic, though she did not know it. - Besides, I need to keep my hands free. We're going into more caves tonight. So, what did you think of it? -

Helmi looked around conspiratorially.

- You know, at first I just put it to my ear. Like you do, you know? –

Mielikki nodded. Listening to shells was a game every merchild had played.

- The sounds were really strange, as if half the echoes were getting lost in there. Like they got stuck sometimes, and then came out all at the same time. -

Mielikki creased her brow. She had never heard of anything like that before.

- Then I tried singing into the wide end, and you know what? It sang back! I mean, the echoes were still all jumbled, but it was like there were my words and notes in there too, all mixed together. And all the time I had the feeling there was something else there, like the shell was trying to sing a song of its own. -

Mielikki shook her head. - That sounds … impossible. -

- The sounds are impossible! It's like there's a different voice in there, and the sounds you put in aren't the same ones that come out! You should try it when we stop, - she added, seeing that her friend still

177

looked skeptical. – It's like nothing I've ever heard before. -

– I will, - Mielikki promised her. - I will. -

They came to shore on a rocky reef far from the lights of the netmen's town. The mussels grew thick and fat there, and with the help of Pel's knife, they ate their fill for the first time in what seemed like an eternity. But it was an uncomfortable meal. A human road ran not far from the rocks, and every few minutes they had to duck and hide as the lights of a mutter-car swept past. It was a relief when Dohan, always the biggest eater, proclaimed himself full, and they could go back to the search.

Riakka led them south along the coast, skirting a harbor, sheering off from two narrow beaches where they heard human feet splashing in the water. They let the tide do most of the work, finning gently and watching the sea bed swirl by beneath them; but a new mood had taken hold of them. It was not the desperate searching of the night before, nor yet the happy confidence of childhood. It was as if these waters were no longer theirs: they had become strange and perilous, and there was nothing between them and death but their own eyes and ears. Mielikki thought with a pang of the days when she had still thought of these waters as home. That had collapsed with the fall of the home-cave. These were dangerous waters.

They scanned constantly, without needing to discuss it, so that the water around them was a web of sonar clicks. Out to sea, they saw the manta cruising, gliding in graceful circles just below the surface, but Dohan did not swing a hair's breadth in its direction. Below, a cuttlefish spurted across a patch of sand: Pel watched it wistfully, wondering what had become of Älykki, but only for a second, and then he turned to scan the depths again.

At last, a cave came into sight. They drifted down to the entrance and hovered there, looking around. For some reason, there were far more crabs about than normal; every rock seemed to be sprouting eye-stalks and claws, and all scurrying steadily northwards, towards the ruins of the cliff. Crabs eat carrion. The cataclysm was a feast for them.

- Right, - Riakka said. - We'll start here. Mielikki and I will go in. Thettis will be in charge out here. Keep a close look out, and if anything comes too near, scare it away. We'll need a clear run to the surface once we come out. -

- Why does it have to be you two? - Viliga asked.

- Because I'm the oldest and she's the best in caves, - was the blunt answer. - This isn't a game. We're trying to find somewhere to live. -

- Well, why don't more of us search? It's boring, waiting for you out here, - Dohan complained.

- The more people, the more sand we kick up. And if we all go off caving, who's going to come and rescue anyone who gets stuck? Now keep together, and keep safe! - And she turned and swam determinedly for the cave mouth. Mielikki hurried after her, trying to swallow a sudden rush of fear.

They saw at once that this cave was different. Instead of the broad, shallow chambers that they had seen before, it started with a passage that was so smooth it might have been made by hand, leading straight back into the rockface. Only a few fathoms inside, they came to a chamber, its walls as smooth as the tunnel had been. Two passageways led out of it, to left and right, and both gave off multiple echoes. The girls looked at one another nervously.

- Left or right? - Mielikki asked.

- Either way, we're not going to explore this in one breath. We'll have to make sure we leave ourselves time to get out and up. -

Mielikki nodded, trying not to think of the tons of rock above their heads. Something about the echoes coming out of this cave made her feel afraid. She sent a longing look back towards the moonlit entry way, and braced herself.

- Let's go left. I'm smaller, I'll go first, - she said, and kicked ahead.

The tunnel was strangely empty. Sand lay thick upon the floor, but there were none of the normal tracks upon it, no signs that sea-slugs or crabs had come that way. The smooth walls offered nowhere for eels or shrimps to hide; only a few anemones clung here and there, waving their fronds. Mielikki found herself flinching at the sound of her own echoes: it was too empty to be natural.

Surely netmen can't have built this deep?

The tunnel led ahead, ducked down, turned a sudden corner, bent upwards, and brought them out into the widest chamber they had ever seen.

- Poseidon, - muttered Riakka as she saw it, and sent a volley of clicks ringing out into the darkness. - Tak! Tak! Tak! -

Back came the echoes flashing off the walls,

Takatakatak, Takatakatak! In their light, the girls saw that they were in a vast round cave. From one side to the other it must have been three times as wide as the home-cave; and the water-filled dome, crowned with a rock like a giant anemone, was higher still.

They stared. Never in all their lives had they imagined a place like this. The darkness was complete, with not even the faintest glow to mark the exit. In silent unison they swam upwards into the middle of the enormous space, and stopped, overwhelmed.

- Just think, - breathed Mielikki after a moment, - All the time, this was here, and we never knew it... -

- Nobody knew, - Riakka answered, pivoting slowly as she took it all in. - Handreds of years, and not even the songs talked about it... You could hide every mer in the Atlantic here! -

- If they'd come, - Mielikki said nervously. It was not just the size of the place: something in the sounds rang a warning, as if there were other voices within the sonar clicks that came back – menacing voices.

She looked around. The rock walls were broken into odd, uneven shapes, some smooth, some jagged, some pocked with holes, so that they seemed to stifle sound. The echoes from the different angles and textures shifted and blurred, overlapping one another in bewildering patterns. Mielikki shook her head: the echoes were almost like a whale song, layer and layer of sound building up to a pattern she did not understand.

- This is... - she began, and stopped, lost for

words. Riakka nodded.

- Too big, - the elder girl said quietly. - I've never heard of anywhere this big. It's not ... not *real*.
-

They stared around, lost in the rainbow of overlapping sounds. Suddenly Riakka shivered.

- Well, big or not, there's no air, and we can't sleep here. I'll need to breathe soon. One more tunnel, and then we're going out. All right? -

- All right, - Mielikki agreed, relieved. There was something about that huge, black, echoing cavern which made her afraid, as if it held a secret that was too big and terrible to know.

They flipped forwards and finned together to where a low crack opened in the left-hand wall. One glance was enough to show that there was no point going in: it was blocked just a few fathoms inside. But higher up on the same side was a second opening, wider and more regular, and it gave out a muted double echo, as if another cave opened farther in. Mielikki sent a burst of sonar in, and flinched: the echo that came back was sharp and somehow threatening.

They looked at one another.

- Try it? - asked Riakka nervously.

Mielikki cast another longing look back towards the exit, but she did not want to seem less brave than Riakka. She swallowed.

- All right, - she said, trying to sound cheerful.

Together, they finned into the gap. It was narrow and slanted, so that they had to roll onto their sides, and the roof and floor came closer and closer together, until there was barely room to swim. Mielikki felt her throat constrict in fear. She was deep under water and deep under the rocks. Every tail-stroke was taking her further away from the air, and at every tail-stroke, the echoes from ahead grew angrier.

Suddenly Riakka bumped into her, and she had to bite her lip to keep from screaming. The tunnel was little more than a crack, but still the threatening echoes came from further ahead. *Just a bit further*, she told herself. *Then there'll be a cave, and air, and safety.*

But another voice inside her replied: *You know there won't. You've looked and looked, and not found anything. This is a waste of time. Why not turn back now, while you still can?*

She shook her head stubbornly, but the voice would not be silenced. Deep inside her, there was a part of her that longed to listen to it. *Come on*, it urged softly. *This is madness. You should get out of here while you still can.*

She looked behind her longingly, and in the same moment felt Riakka stop. Ahead, the crack had narrowed down to a sharp-lipped mouth, fanged with rocks. Beyond was the sound of an open space; but Riakka was hanging in front of the gap, and shivering.

- I can't, - she said desperately. - I can't go through there. -

Mielikki looked at the shark-toothed entrance, and shuddered. Her sonar came back off it so distorted and twisted that it sounded like an angry snarl. The thought of trying to push through

183

there made her lungs clench in panic.

Fighting with every nerve, she pulled herself closer. She had to click, it was the only way to see; but with every click the echo grew more frightening. Another inch, silent, silent, but the darkness was pressing in, she had to click, she could not avoid it any longer – and all at once she clicked, and the echo that came back was so loud and angry it was like a bellow of pure terror.

With one movement, the two girls pushed themselves downwards, away from that dreadful mouth. They flailed backwards until the tunnel was wide enough to turn round in: then they fled. They raced across the gigantic cave. They dived through the exit, shoulders scraping the rocks. The moonlight exploded around them as they arrowed back into open water. Then they were finning desperately for the surface, leaving the school gaping in amazement behind them.

16

Andromeda's Curse

How did Atlantis fall, and the richest island in the ocean vanish beneath the waves? How did Andromeda curse her own people, so that for three myriad years none of us would know peace?

This is what the songs told us, in the days before we learned the truth...

For three years, the uneasy peace continued. The netmen launched their raids against the Gates of Atlas, and we drove them back, or sank them. Andromeda sat in the courts of Atlas, and sang laments for her parents. And the people tried to sing as they had before; but the sun shone less brightly, and the wind blew colder, and the waves heaved restlessly and tasted of bitter tears; and the mountains of Atlantis grumbled and shook out smoke and fire.

The blow fell in the fourth year, and it came without any warning. All those years, as we found out afterwards, Perseus' people had been driving a path across the brown lands that you call Iberia; and in time they crested the hills, and found a river leading westwards to the ocean; and they followed it, and felled the trees that grew about it, and built new ships, long and high-prowed to face the ocean swells; and they sent an army to man them.

Then they launched them at the dark of the moon,

sweeping down the wind towards the mountains of Atlantis; and some songs say that the mountains glowed bright with fire, brighter than any beacon, and some say that the humans who lived on Atlantis lit fires to guide the pirates in. And they found the island, and rounded the northern cape, and came down the long west coast, and came into sight of the city; and Perseus laughed into his beard.

They came without warning as the tide rose; and by ill luck they came as the Queen was swimming out to sea, with few friends around her. What befell her we will never know, for none of those who saw it lived to see the dawn; but Queen Amphitrite never came back to Atlantis.

The ships came to our city with the spear and the flame, and burned their way across the reefs. Our people fought with the strength of despair, and some grappled the black ships and clung to them in death, turning them over so that men and merpeople rode down into the abyss together. And some leapt clear out of the water, and landed on the blood-stained decks, and grappled barehanded with the enemy until they were overwhelmed; and some called out in anger, so loud that the humans were stricken deaf and blind; and some lunged and lashed and forced the ships against the reefs, so that the wooden hulls split.

But always, more ships came.

Last of all came the ship of Perseus, and it was the biggest vessel that had ever floated; and its prow was carved with the head of Medusa, to strike fear into our hearts. And with him came a thousand men in canoes and little skiffs, and they waded over the reefs, and launched their boats on the lagoons beyond, and spread death and destruction right to the threshold of the King's halls.

Then Protteänni saw Perseus, and his ancient

heart blazed with fury, and he jumped from the water higher than a dolphin, higher than a marlin, higher than anymer has ever leapt before or since; and he flew straight at the usurper. But at the last moment Perseus saw him and sprang aside, and Prottëänni fell on the steersman beside him, and struck him dead. And before he could turn, Perseus struck in his turn, stabbing him in the back with a great spear; and so Prottëänni died, and killed a hundred of his enemies in his death. For as the steersman fell his hand jerked the steering oar, and the great ship turned and split upon the rocks, and the bronze-clad spearmen tumbled into the water and sank like stones, and the head of Medusa toppled and fell into the depths; and of all that giant ship, only Perseus managed to drag himself ashore.

And he stood on the reef facing the gate of the King, with the flames lashing and dancing around him, and lifted up the golden staff that he used to guide his ship, and called out in a voice as loud as the storm, "Son of Poseidon, come out now, for Zeus' son rules here! Come out and give me your crown, or I will ruin this place around you!"

And King Atlas came to the entry of his palace, and rose out of the water proud and strong, there in the archway where the seal of the Four Tridents pointed to the four winds in burning gold. And he lifted up the sign of royalty, the golden trident of his father, and his voice was as loud as the wave that thunders to the shore.

"Son of Zeus, get back to your hills! This is Poseidon's island and Poseidon's sea, and they are his to give or take back!"

But as he spoke, lightning flashed across the midnight clouds, and thunder crackled, Zeus urging on his son. And at that sign, Perseus laughed his white-

*toothed laugh, and lifted up his gilded staff, and behold!
The tip glistened with a blade of naked bronze. And before
the King was aware of the danger, Perseus flung the spear
across the flame-lit water; and it struck the King in the
heart, and killed him there on his own threshold, under the
very symbol of his rule; and his blood poured into the cold
Atlantic; and the trident fell into the waves.*

*A cry of horror went up from all the merpeople
who saw it; and the sea recoiled; and far, far away, at the
other end of the oceans, Poseidon felt the death of his son,
and grief and anger swept through him; and he took up the
black trident of wrath.*

*Out of the abyss came a long roll of thunder. The
rocks shook. The mountains spat fire. The bed of the ocean
heaved; and far out at sea, beyond sight and hearing, it
birthed the greatest wave that has ever been, a wall of
water three myriad miles long.*

*But Perseus was looking to the land, and he
laughed again, and shouted, "Now I am king of land and
sea! Bring out the treasures of Atlantis! And bring out
Andromeda to be my wife and my queen, so that my sons
will be kings after me!"*

*But a cry answered him, and Andromeda stood on
the highest cliff. Her white robes shone red with the fires
below, and her golden hair streamed behind her on the
wind, and she held the ebony rod of kingship that Perseus
had sought across the seas.*

*And Andromeda lifted up her hand, and standing
on the edge of the heaving cliffs she cursed Perseus, calling
him oath-breaker and murderer, coward and renegade; and
even the flames were hushed as she poured down her anger
and grief; and Perseus stood, and stared, and was still.*

"You have killed the King of the Seven Seas and

betrayed his people out of greed! So I place this curse on you, and on all those who come after you: your hunger and greed will be as deep as the ocean, and not even the ocean will be able to fill you up. No matter how much you take, you will always want more; and your hands will be empty in the moment you thought them full; and you will be a blight on the land and a poison on the sea. You will pray to the ocean to give you your food, and the ocean will be empty before you. You will never find rest until you give back what you stole, and the time of the merpeople comes again!

"Behold!" she cried, and Zeus' lightning split the sky behind her. "My own race has betrayed me! I will have no more of the netmen and their lands. I go to the friends of my heart, Poseidon's children. Whenever the merpeople call on me, I will come, and I will be a spear in the heart of the human race until our time comes again!"

And with that she leapt from the cliff, and plunged into the sea, and perished; and Perseus reached out helpless arms as if to stop her. Still in the stars you can see them there, Andromeda falling, falling through the night skies, while Perseus reaches out in vain.

Then the Seven Sisters cried out as one, a cry that struck ice into the bones of every netman who heard it; and they turned and dived into the bloody waters, taking the bodies of their dead with them; and all the merpeople who still could, turned and fled for the ocean. And Perseus laughed like a man who has nothing but death to live for, and stepped forward to the edge of the reef as if the water would give back before him.

And the waters gave back, a long, slow groan as if of grief. The tide fell and fell, and sank back from the rocks, and left the caverns and palaces of Atlas bare as they had not been since the world was made; and Perseus laughed and marched across the dripping rocks, and into the palace of the King; for he thought in his madness that the sea was pulling back for him.

And his men raged through the secret places of Atlantis. They brought burning torches, and red light flamed in the caves, and hard hands tore the diamonds and pearls, the gold and copper from the walls, and piled it in heaps upon the rocks.

And Perseus followed the narrow channels, deeper and deeper into the rock, his hands and feet stained with blood, the red torch casting eerie lights off the black puddles and the black walls; and in an evil hour he found his way into the innermost sanctum, and saw ahead of him the great Pillar of the King, and on it the cradle that had held the sons of Poseidon, far, far above his head; and Perseus laughed, a cold sound that filled the cave with echoes of evil; and he threw his torch into the cradle and watched it burn.

And Poseidon's wave broke over Atlantis.

There was no warning; the gods do not give warning. In the same moment the flames crackled and rose from the cradle, there came a noise like thunder out of the sea, and the wind roared, and the rocks shook, and the pirates of Perseus stopped in the midst of their looting, and looked at one another with white faces and wide eyes.

And out of the night came such a wave as has never been seen before or since, higher than trees, higher than mountains, higher than the Pillars of Atlas themselves. Its front was a wall of green. Its crest foamed as high and white as the clouds. The abyss opened up at its feet. It drove the gale before it.

The mountains of Atlantis erupted in fire, and the

wave crashed down upon them.

They say that the noise of the explosion echoed around the world. The mountains burst. The plains erupted. Rocks and flames tore the air. A cloud as thick as midnight was blasted into the sky. The world reeled in darkness for fivetwé nights and days. And when the steams cleared and the echoes died, Atlantis was no more, and the bitter seas rolled where it had been, and only the snow-capped mountains stood in a grieving ocean to mark its grave. Atlas was dead, and Perseus was gone, his broken bones and shattered armor rolled beneath the contemptuous waves; and Andromeda had sealed her curse in her blood.

And from that day on, the war never ceased between your people and ours. Andromeda's Curse drove you, so that you never found satisfaction in the sea, but only a hunger that bit ever deeper as the years went by. And the more you took from us, the more your own emptiness grew, and you made boats that were bigger, and faster, and greedier, with wider nets, and you spread your filth and poison to every sea there is; and still there was no filling your hunger.

And we hid, and watched, and waited, until our time should come again.

17
Decisions

The school stared as their two leaders shot out of the cave and raced for the surface. They had been hanging between the moonbeams for what felt like an eternity, hearing the faint, overlapping echoes coming from the cave. Then the noise had risen to a snarl, and the next moment the two girls had burst out of the cave and rocketed for the surface. With a startled yelp, Thettis took off after them. The others followed, glancing fearfully over their shoulders.

As Pel surfaced, he was half expecting to see the cavers covered in sand and tears again; but this time, they were dry-eyed and silent, shivering from head to tail-flukes and staring blankly at the sea.

"What happened?" Thettis asked as soon as her head broke the surface.

"Nothing," Riakka answered shortly. Mielikki was silent.

Thettis eyed them closely. "What do you mean, nothing?"

Riakka gritted her teeth. "Nothing! We went inside, we looked, we didn't find air, we came out. Nothing!"

Helmi edged closer to Mielikki, but her friend would not meet her eyes. Her heart was still racing with the fear of that black, sharp-toothed hole.

"Boat!" called Dohan suddenly, pointing off to the right. Sure enough, a thunder boat was bashing its way across the waves towards them under a white light.

They breathed and dived all together; by the time it went by overhead, they were safely six fathoms down.

- Are you all right? - Helmi asked Mielikki timidly, on their private channel.

- Tell you later, - she replied curtly, knowing that she never would. She had thought she was brave enough to face anything in the ocean. She had been wrong.

- So what do we do now? - Thettis asked impatiently. - Look for another cave? Or is there more to look at in there? The echoes sounded big. -

Riakka hesitated. Her instinct was to tell them to go on, find another cave and forget that they had ever been near this one. But in all truth, they had not explored half of this one. There was still a chance that there was air in there, somewhere higher up, and if there was…

- We didn't explore it all: it's too big, - she admitted. - There might be air. -

Mielikki groaned.

- All right, - Thettis said briskly. - So we'll try again. But this time, I'll go, with Viliga. You and Mielikki can wait outside. You need to have a rest. -

- What? -

- No! -

Riakka and Mielikki burst into protest at the same moment. It was one thing not to want to go back in, quite another to be told they could not. They argued, quietly at first, then louder, hot indignation washing away the cold fear.

- Shark! - yelled Helmi suddenly. They scattered, turning to blast their sonar at the threat, but there was nothing there.

- There wasn't one, - Helmi admitted nervously. - But there will be if we keep shouting. - She edged closer to Mielikki, awaiting an explosion from the school.

Thettis gave her sister a hard look, then nodded abruptly.

- She's the most sensible mer here, - she said; Helmi sagged in relief.

Thettis went on, - We don't have time to waste. So I think Mielikki and Riakka have earned a rest, and Viliga and I should try our luck instead. Who agrees? -

- Me! - said Viliga, instantly and forcefully.

- Me, - said Dohan.

- I want to go! - Pel said, but they ignored him.

Helmi looked down at her hands, hesitating. Then, - Me, - she said, almost inaudibly.

Mielikki stared. Helmi looked at her beseechingly.

- You've done so much already, - she whispered on the private channel. - Every time you go in there, I'm scared you won't come out. -

Mielikki stared for a moment longer; then her gaze softened. But there was no time for more speech.

- Right. That's four out of seven. The school's decided, - Thettis said calmly. - So, where do we go?

Riakka glared at her, but there was no help for it; not against the vote of the school.

- The tunnel goes in and up. After about ten fathoms, you come to a small cave. There are two more tunnels leading out of it, left and right. We took the left one. After what, a minute? -

- Two minutes, - said Mielikki. - More like two. -

- Two minutes, then... It lifts up, and you come into the biggest cave there's ever been. -

There was a stir of excitement.

- Why don't we all go to see? - Pel asked.

- Not me, - said Helmi firmly.

- There are four tunnels out of it. The one farthest to the left goes nowhere. The second one narrows to nothing. Don't go in there. –

Mielikki shut her eyes briefly, remembering the terror of that narrow gap.

- We got that far, then came back to breathe. -

Thettis nodded. - Good. We'll start where you finished. Come on, Viliga, - and the two turned, accelerated and disappeared into the cave.

As soon as they were gone, the school turned to Mielikki and Riakka.

- What's it really like? Is it really that big? Can we all go in? - Pel's thin face was bright with excitement.

- Yes it is, and no you can't, - Riakka answered shortly. She turned her back on them and swam a little way away, staring out into the depths. Pel made as if to follow her, hesitated and came back.

The others turned to Mielikki.

- What was it like? Come on, be fair! You got to see it, we had to wait out here. Mielikki, be fair! -

Her tail flicked in irritation. The last thing she wanted to do was think about that cave again. There was something unnatural about the sharp-toothed mouth and the sudden blast of sonar. She could still feel the terror of it.

- Big. Dark. And I don't want to talk about it, - she snapped. - Now leave me alone! - And she turned and swam off to join Riakka.

At first, she was too angry to think. Angry that they had bothered her with questions; angry that she had been so afraid; angry at the caves, the divers, the humans; even angry because she knew she had behaved badly in front of the school. But gradually, as she hung there staring at the dancing moonbeams, the tide of her mood began to turn.

It was a very beautiful night. The waves overhead heaved gently, broken up like little windows so that she saw four moons gazing down at her together. The tide had died away. Below on the reef, a handred damselfish had come out to feed, darting this way and that, mouths opening and closing, every one a reflection of all the others. Deeper, an octopus poured itself slowly over the rocks. The sounds of the sea, her beloved sea, were all around her, and for once the humans' racket was far away.

She looked back to the cave mouth. Dohan was hanging head down in the entryway, sending his sonar into the tunnel. Pel and Helmi were watching him, half nervous, half excited. Even this far away, she could hear the musical tones of his calls. He had a beautiful voice.

Riakka was still staring into the darkness, arms folded, shoulders up. Her desire to be left alone was palpable. Mielikki half-moved towards her, then drew back: she knew how the elder girl must feel.

- Mielikki, - said Riakka, without turning around.

- Yes? -

- You did well in the caves. Thank you. - Her tone was flat with barely-controlled anger.

Mielikki did not know how to answer.

- Mielikki. -

- Yes? -

- Do you really think we'll find a cave with air? -

Mielikki shot her a startled glance. The silence lengthened.

- Do you? - repeated Riakka insistently.

Mielikki bit her lip. Now that the question had been voiced, she was afraid to answer it, as if putting her doubts into words would set them on a course they would not be able to turn back from.

- Mielikki? -

- No, - she said, at last. - No, I don't. -

- Nor do I. - A silence. - And the longer we stay this close to shore, the more risks we run. -

As if to emphasize her words, they heard another thunder boat growl in the distance, come closer, bash its way overhead and fade away, leaving a scum of foam and sparkling seafire behind.

- You were right, - Riakka added, still staring into nothing.

- What? -

- Yesterday. When you said we should swim out to sea. You were right. -

Mielikki blinked. That argument seemed to belong to a different world.

- It's too dangerous here, - Riakka went on remorselessly. - Even at night, the netmen are here, and by day... It's like you said: these islands aren't our home any more. -

Something about the way she said it made Mielikki want to make it untrue. Hearing her own deepest fear from the mouth of their leader made it suddenly real.

- But... Maybe we'll find a cave still. One with air. And we'll be able to hide, and come out at night, like before... -

For the first time Riakka turned to look at her, and Mielikki was shocked into silence: her face was ghost-white.

- Like before? When you know what the netmen can do to a cliff? Do you want to sit there every day, and listen out for the first thunder machines, and think to yourself: Is today the day they bring it all down on top of us? -

Mielikki swallowed; but Riakka's anger burned out as quickly as it had flared up. She turned back to look out at the sea, and her voice was tired and sad.

- Even if we do find a cave, we won't be safe there. Not with the netmen on the island. -

There was a long pause. Then they looked at each other again, and somehow Mielikki knew what Riakka was going to say.

- You think we should leave right now, - she

said quietly. - Swim out, and not come back. -

- It's the only way. Near the land is near the netmen. We should go right out to sea, out to the ocean. Follow our parents, and not come back. -

Mielikki nodded. Again, there was silence. They stared out into the moon-streaked blackness, as if trying to see its secrets.

- But Thettis was right. They've left the Sapphire Sea already. We'll never find them. -

- I know. - There was forced optimism in Riakka's voice; it rang as false as a broken bell. - But I was thinking... We know which way they're going: north, to the Diamond Seas. I bet Pel knows the map songs to get us there. Why shouldn't we go north too? Look for them there, out at sea. Far from the netmen. -

Mielikki shook her head. A day ago, she would have been thrilled by this conversation; now, she was terrified, because she knew where it was leading, and she did not want to go. Dreams are wonderful things, until they come true.

- Have you told the others? - she asked, hoping to put off the moment.

- Not yet. I didn't even realize it myself until just now. I think Thettis has the same idea. - Another long silence, and then she went on very quietly, - I'm afraid of telling the others. Viliga will be all right, and Dohan could swim to the North Pole. But what about Pel and Helmi? They're so little, and so scared. Wouldn't it just panic them if I took them out to sea? -

Riakka turned again, and at last Mielikki saw the shell of desperate bravery crack.

- You see, that's the problem. If we stay here, we die. And if we go out to sea, we die. And either way, *I have to decide*. I have to decide. And I can't. -

She turned to stare at the sea again, hands clenching and unclenching as she fought back tears.

Mielikki reached out a hand, then drew back.
I've got to be strong. For her. For me.
For all of us.

- Pel and Helmi... They're tougher than you think. You saw Pel yesterday. -

- He couldn't even get across the current! -

- But he got away from those divers, didn't he? He can do it. –

Riakka looked at her, with the faintest new hope in her voice, like a diver in the very deepest trench of the ocean who suddenly dares to look up to the surface.

- But what about Helmi? Can she cope? -

Mielikki thought back to the conversation she and her friend had had at sunset. Even that seemed a lifetime ago.

- *Trrr...* I think she can. We were talking earlier, just before we swam back here. After we slept. And she said: we managed to sleep out, maybe we don't need a cave at all. -

- Helmi said that? Are you sure? - The hope was stronger now, the diver shrugging off the mud of the abyss and setting her sights on the surface.

- I'm sure. She always used to be scared of the idea of sleeping out. We talked about it a lot. We talked about it the night before last. Poseidon! Just two nights ago... But now she *has* slept out, and it was all right, and she was ready to do it again. I think she can cope. -

Riakka turned and looked at the cave for the first time. Dohan had left the cave mouth and was poking around in the rocks. Pel had swum down to join him. Helmi was hovering anxiously, close to the cave. Riakka's eyes moved from one to the next, as if measuring them, and slowly the hope rose higher in her eyes, the diver moving through mid-water, looking to the light.

Abruptly her face darkened again.

- What if we're too young? We haven't even found our life-names yet. How can we face the ocean already? - she said.

Mielikki bridled. It was the one argument she would never accept.

- We're not too young! We can all learn. Everyone does. We'll find our names on the way. And at least we can do it together. -

- We don't know where our parents are. -

- We'll find them. Everyone else does. Merpeople have been doing this for myriads of years. -

Riakka was silent for a long time, hands still opening and closing. Then, at last, she clenched both fists and breathed out hard, like a diver breaking the surface.

- You're right. Maybe we can do it. Maybe we can. - She looked towards the cave, and the school.

- Come on. Let's get them out of there, and fin back out before the sun comes up. We'll swim to the Lone Rock tonight. Tell them it's so we can find food. And tomorrow night... Out to sea. -

Mielikki swallowed. There was something

she had to say.

- Wait. Riakka? -

- Yes? -

She hesitated. - That night, when you thought we were out on the surface in the daylight... -

- What about it? -

- We were. We finned out to swim with the dolphins. Ukko and his pod sang for us, and we sang for them. By the time we came back it was daylight. Ukko and the pod brought us home. -

There was a long silence.

- I'm sorry, - Mielikki added.

Riakka stared at her, emotions chasing across her face: anger, envy, admiration, and then, most unexpectedly, humor. Suddenly, she laughed out loud.

- Well, better to tell me late than never! Come on, we should go. And if you see Ukko on the way, tell him he can join us, too. -

Together, they swam back to gather the school.

Helmi was still hovering at the mouth of the cave, listening to the faint echoes of clicks from within.

- I think they sound all right, - she said nervously, twisting her fingers together. - They went very quiet once, but then the sound started again. -

Riakka and Mielikki exchanged glances. There was strain in Helmi's voice, the strain of too much danger, too little rest.

- There's a narrow bit just before the big cave.

Their bodies probably blocked the echoes, - Riakka said soothingly.

Helmi nodded, then looked up towards the surface.

- They've been a long time. How much longer are we going to stay here? We shouldn't be here when the sun comes up. -

Again, the two girls exchanged glances. Riakka swallowed.

- Once they come out, if they haven't found air, that's it. We'll head back out to sea, and find somewhere lonely to sleep, - she said, loudly enough for all to hear. Below them, the boys looked up sharply.

- Sleep out at sea again? But I thought we were going to find a cave! - There was bewilderment in Dohan's voice. - It's not safe out there, is it? -

- It *is* safe. - To the amazement of everyone there, including herself, it was Helmi who spoke. Her voice was shaking, but determined. - We've done it once, and we can do it again. I'll even keep watch, if that helps. -

Riakka and Mielikki stared at her; then Mielikki put a hand on her shoulder.

- I'm proud of you, - she whispered on the private channel.

There was a burst of sound from inside the cave: a growl of sonar that struck fear into all their hearts. Helmi shrank back; Mielikki and Riakka flinched. It was the same terrifying echo that they had heard from the saw-toothed entrance. Before they could recover, they heard other sounds: high-pitched alarm calls and the thump of tails against the rock. Suddenly the voices of Thettis and Viliga sounded loud and clear, coming nearer. A second later they swept into sight, burst out of the cave and finned madly for the surface. Mielikki caught a glimpse of staring eyes and terrified faces, and then they were gone in a flurry of leaking bubbles. Slowly, the school followed.

One by one they surfaced. Thettis and Viliga were breathing in great, panicked gasps, their eyes wide and staring. Whatever it was they had seen or heard in the great cave, it had scared them witless.

"What did you find?" asked Riakka urgently. "Was there any air?"

"And what was that noise?" Dohan asked.

"Nothing," Thettis said shortly, answering both questions at once.

"But ... that *noise*?" Dohan insisted. "It sounded like ... like..."

"I said it was nothing!" Thettis snapped. "The echoes are just really loud. That's what you get when a passageway narrows down in front of you."

Riakka nodded understandingly. "We had that too. Mielikki sent a little click at it, and it came back like a shout. It must be something about the rocks in there."

"Oh, is that what made you so scared?" Dohan asked slowly. He sounded disappointed. "Just an echo?"

Riakka swung round on him, but Viliga was faster.

"Just an echo? It nearly took my head off! The cave gets narrower and narrower, and there's a chamber beyond the gap, and when I sent a click into it I thought I'd gone deaf! I've never heard anything like it!"

"It was the same for us," Mielikki confirmed. "The passage got narrower and narrower, and the echoes got louder and louder, and then..." She swallowed. "There was a cave like a ragged-tooth shark, and it ... it *roared*."

They stared at her.

"Well, it's obvious we're not going to be able to live there," Riakka said firmly. "And dawn's not far off."

She pointed to the sky. Sirius had set, and Mars was dipping to the west.

"We should head out to sea before the sun rises. Further out, this time. Get well away from the netmen. That way we'll have a good sleep, and be ready."

"When will we eat?" Dohan asked. He was always hungry.

Riakka shot Mielikki a warning glance. "When we get there. It's too dangerous to come inshore again: we're going to the Lone Rock."

There was a moment of silence; then Viliga laughed sharply.

"Did you get sunstroke yesterday? Half of us can't even swim in the shallows. How are we going to get *there*?" He looked at Pel scornfully; Pel flushed and looked away.

"He can do it! We all can!" Mielikki snapped. Viliga stared at her and folded his arms.

"It's a silty idea," he said flatly; *silt* is a mer vulgarity. "Swim to the Lone Rock, without even eating? We'll never do it!"

"We hadn't slept out before, but we managed that!" Riakka snapped, trying to silence him before the others caught his mood. "Anyway, you've swum to the Rock before. That's where the food is! The sooner we get there, the sooner we can eat!"

She looked around the group, hoping that that would convince them, but even Dohan was looking doubtful. Helmi looked scared.

Riakka looked at Mielikki in mute entreaty. *Help me!* the look said, clearer than any click.

"Well, I think we can do it!" Mielikki said, more stoutly than she felt. "We slept out all right, and we can swim to the Rock, too! I did it without even meaning to!" She hoped they would laugh, but there was silence.

"Of course we can do it!" Riakka said heartily.

Thettis gave them a long, hard look, as if trying to read their intentions. Then:

"I think we can do it. And I'm sure Pel can remember the map songs to get us there, can't he?" she said.

Mielikki's little brother blossomed with pride.

"Of course! Every word! I'll name every rock on the way," he promised.

"That's four of us. It's decided," Thettis said, staring at Viliga.

"No, it isn't!" Viliga snapped. "I don't care if it's four out of seven! You'll get us all killed!"

Dohan stared down at the water, biting his lip. Helmi was twisting her fingers in anxiety. Then she looked up.

"Five. I trust Riakka and Mielikki," she said.

"And Pel. If they say we can do it, then we can. I'm with them."

"Six," rumbled Dohan.

"What?"

"Six. You've kept us alive this long. I'm with you."

Viliga gave them a long, angry glare. All of a sudden he was standing alone against the whole school – a bully left without allies.

"All right," he muttered at last, "We'll swim to the Lone Rock. I don't know why you're making such a fuss about it anyway. *I've* done it before. And I meant to." He looked sidelong at Mielikki.

Riakka and Mielikki exchanged a look of relief.

"Right, let's go," the elder girl said. "We dive down and head north-east. Keep together and keep to a safe depth. We'll swim to the Rock. Then we'll sleep. Tomorrow is another night."

"Remember I get to go on guard this time!" Pel said insistently.

Riakka laughed.

"All right! Just make sure you stay awake. Mielikki, will you watch with him?"

Mielikki nodded, with mixed feelings. She was proud that Pel was being so brave, but if he and she watched together, all the responsibility would be on her. There would be no Riakka to rely on this time.

But at least the decision was taken. They would swim out to sea, and not come back.

As the others breathed and dived, she looked back at the familiar black bulk of the island. Even this late at night, lights still crawled along the coast. Soon it would be morning, and the noise of mutter-cars and thunder machines would fill the air again.

"Mielikki?" It was Helmi, just behind her. Pel was with her.

"Coming," she said quickly.

"Mielikki, we're not coming back, are we?"

"What?"

"Once we head out, we're not coming back, are we? Pel and I, we both think so."

Mielikki looked at them both: her brother and her best friend. How could she hide the truth from them? What would be the point?

"No. We're swimming out to the ocean, to follow our parents. We're never coming back."

They looked at one another; then, as if drawn by a common will, they turned to the island again.

"I'll miss Älykki, if he's still alive," Pel said.

"I'll miss the Cleaning Station," Mielikki said.

"I'll miss the home-cave," Helmi said, and it sounded like she was fighting back tears. "But it's not there anyway, is it? It's time to go, before they catch us."

As if to confirm her words, they saw a fishing boat come wallowing out from the shoreline. The thudding of its engines carried clearly over the still air.

"It's time to go," Pel agreed.

"I'm not ready," Helmi whispered. They put their hands on her shoulders.

"Yes, you are," Mielikki said. "We all are. We've got to be."

They cast one long look back towards their

home, turned, and dived for the open sea.

Behind them, the trawler *Artemis* nodded to the waves, like a hound picking up a scent. Slowly, her bow came round. Then she settled on her course and began to thud her way north-east, towards the fishing grounds of the Lone Rock.

18

The Breaking

How were the merpeople scattered, so that our race drifted apart like ropes when the knot is cut? What strange tides drove Atlas' children into stranger seas?

This is what the songs told us, when the wound still bled...

Atlas and Amphitrite were gone. Andromeda was dead. Perseus was buried in the wreckage of Atlantis, and Atlantis was swallowed by the sea. None can say how many mers died in that cataclysm, driven by Poseidon's wave on to the rocks, or burned by the lava, or broken by the explosion. They say that not one family in the ocean escaped whole that day; but the warships of Perseus were scattered like sand upon the tide.

Yet the daughters of Atlas survived: the Seven Sisters, grand-daughters of Poseidon. The wave did not take them. The fire passed them by. They fled out to sea through wreck and ruin, westwards through the waves; and the songs said they bore the Three Treasures of Atlantis with them, the Trident of gold, and the Scepter of glass, and the Rod of the Black Pearl.

As they swam, they wept and called out; and one by one, other mers came to them, scarred by fire and rock and spear. A few, a few dozen, a few hundred. A ragged handful, all that was left of the greatest people the seas had ever seen; and among them Thettis, most faithful of friends.

There was no way back. The recoiling wave was flooding westwards in a thundering surge, and west they went with it, while the rising sun shone red as blood on the wreckage. The air was filled with the cry of gulls, swooping to feast on the floating dead; the water seemed to boil as sharks rose and snatched at corpses. But none attacked the exiles of Atlantis, for why would any beast fight for living meat when there was enough carrion to last a hundred years?

So they swam west, weeping, a bedraggled band bearing the treasures of the ocean. Day and night they swam. The winds drove them apart. The Sisters led them together again. The sky roared with thunder as Zeus laughed at Atlantis' fall. The sound of their clicking could barely be heard over the fury of the storm. And ever and again, another sonar voice would fall silent, as another mer sank into the abyss.

We will never know how many perished on that desperate, storm-tossed swim; we only know that, of all the people of Atlantis, not one in a thousand made it across the ocean, to the haven of the Blue Reefs.

There, our people had founded a colony among the islands, where turtle-grass swayed in the shallows, and the sands shone white. There the exiles of Atlantis came, hoping for shelter and rest; hoping, perhaps, to found a new kingdom, and so drown their sorrow at the ruin of the old. And Maia, eldest of the sisters, begged for help.

But the leader of the colony, Kallio the Black, frowned at her words, and would not answer them. For a day and a night, he kept them waiting in the deep waters beyond the reef; and when he called them to him at last, he would not meet Maia's eyes.

He said, "Atlantis is fallen, and no power in the ocean can bring it back; and King Atlas who ruled us is dead. The netmen attacked your kingdom; they could attack mine. You must go from here, before they follow you."

"But the netmen are dead!" burst out Taygettë, the second sister, always fiery, always outspoken. "The sea took them!"

"More will come," Kallio said. "Your plight is not our plight. Your fight is not our fight. You must go from here, before the netmen come."

"But you are the blood of Atlantis!" Taygettë cried; and Kallio looked away.

"I must think of my people. Go, before the netmen come."

At that, some of the people of the Blue Reefs were silent, and some were ashamed, and some offered the refugees food. But none would give them shelter, for all were afraid. So sadly, the remnants of Atlantis turned and swam north, through the shining islands and along the jagged coast, to where the seas are as clear as glass and as cold as iron, and the fish and birds teem like clouds.

There, too, Atlas had sent a colony, in the prolific waters of the Iron Seas; and there the exiles hoped to start a new life. When the chieftainess in those waters, Anttila the Red, saw them, she smiled, and spoke fairly, and offered them shelter and peace. But Merope, youngest and wisest of the sisters, saw how her eyes flickered to the Three Treasures, and away, and back again, like the tentacles of an octopus reaching towards its prey.

"You may stay here, and start your life anew," said Anttila, and her smile was as wide as a stonefish's mouth as it sucks in its prey. "And in return, you will give me the treasures you carry, the Trident and the Scepter and the Rod; for Atlantis is gone, and your rule is over, and I am Queen now. For we of the Iron Seas are the eldest colony of Atlantis, and the empire of the ocean is our inheritance."

But before she could take the Three, Merope snatched them up and fled; and the exiles followed her; and perhaps Poseidon was still watching over his grand-daughters, for as they fled, a storm blew up as black as night.

Anttila the Red screamed and cursed and called for the pursuit, but they made their escape down the raging waves, and out to the open ocean.

Now they swam eastwards before the storm, back across Atlas' Ocean; and they were weary beyond exhaustion. But just when their last hope died, Poseidon sent them a current of blood-warm water to carry them east; and that current runs there to this day.

The fish were rich and slow in that current, so that they ate, and their strength returned; and at the very end of summer they came to a land of black rocks and gray clouds, green waters and greener hills. No song had ever spoken of that land; nomer of Atlantis knew its name. It was a place of clinging mists and drifting rain, wild currents and maze-like shores, so they called it the Tangled Sea. And to their amazement, they heard merpeople living there, who sang in a strange tongue.

Then the exiles were afraid, and Asterope, the young and gentle, said, "We do not know these islands or their people. Our father's law never came here. Let us go back to sea, before they find us."

But Taygettë disagreed, saying they had swum across the whole ocean in search of refuge, and they could not turn back now; and most of the exiles were with her. So, in the end, they approached the shore, and came to the strange mers, and saw that they were strange indeed, bigger and thicker in the body and the tail than anymer of Atlantis; and their bodies were covered with tattoos.

The strange mers did not talk with them, but gave them food, and a cave to sleep; and in the morning they led them through choppy seas and whispering rain, to meet their king.

And at length they came to an echoing cave at the root of a mighty rock, where the tide swirled and tumbled like a living thing. And there the king lay on a throne of bare stone, and he was massive and strong, and round his waist he wore a belt of trophies — a shark's tooth, and a kraken's beak, and the blade of a black marlin; and he spoke in the tongue of Atlantis, and his voice was harsh with anger and pain.

And he said, "Atlantis is fallen, but what is Atlantis to me? Atlas is not my king. He was never my king. He was my brother, and he ruled the waters which we should have shared. I am Orion, Poseidon's strongest son, and I slew the White Death and the Red Death and the Black Death, and made these wild seas safe. Now give up those trinkets you carry, for this scepter rules the oceans," and he set his hand on the black blade at his belt.

But the sisters would not give up the Treasures, and for all his anger and grief, Orion the Wild Hunter would not harm them, daughters of his brother; for whatever evil he did in after life, nomer was ever so loyal to the ties of blood. So he had them taken to a cave above the reach of the highest tide, where the rocks rose like the pillars of giants, and the waves broke in mourning tones. And he set guards to watch them, but gently; and he had *food brought, and fire for warmth and comfort; and every day he came and argued with them, seeking to persuade them of his right to the Treasures of Atlantis.*

And so the months went by.

Then there came a night of storm, a black gale driving out of the west; and the moon was new, and it was spring tide. And at the very height of the flood, the waves piled up each on each like a mountain of water, and the cave was flooded, and the guards were swept away; and the Sisters led them out into the wild waters, and away.

And when the storm had calmed, they looked at one another; and Merope said, "The ties that bound our people together are broken, by fear, and greed, and envy. The seas are one kingdom no more, and no place is safe for us, save home. Let us go home."

"But Atlantis is gone!" Asterope said; and she wept.

"Atlantis is gone, but memory lives," Merope replied. "The mountains still stand as markers over our father's grave. The sea still breaks on reef and rock. The fish still swarm silver under the waves. Let us go back there, and start anew, and keep alive the memory of Atlantis, until what was stolen is returned."

"It is true," said Maia quietly, and a look of understanding passed between the eldest and the youngest of the sisters. "Let us go home, and keep ourselves and our memories alive."

So, slowly and sorrowfully, they turned their faces south; and slowly and sorrowfully they bore the Treasures back to the waves they knew. And there amidst the wreckage of their father's island they rested at last, hunting for food, hiding the Treasures from light and sound, and weaving their loss into songs. And across the seas, the clans of the merpeople went their own ways and chose their own kings, Kallio and Anttila and many more; and they made their own laws, and their languages changed, and the ties that bound the oceans were broken indeed. And in time Orion arose, and went to war, to avenge his brother on the children of Zeus. And that was a war that shook the ocean and scarred the face of the land; but that story is for another day.

And still the Seven Sisters held on to their father's treasures, the Trident and the Scepter and the Rod; and they remembered their history, and told their tales, and taught them to a new generation of exiles.

And memory survived in song.

19

Out to Sea

It was late at night. The old moon shone like molten silver, and gusts of seafire billowed from the children's fins as they swam ever further out into the ocean. Far, far below, the sea bed rolled slowly by, faint, dull echoes drifting up from the abyssal plains – Hades' realm.

- I wonder what lives down there, - Pel said, sending a low moan of sonar into the depths. His call came back a long, long time later, faint and blurred. He and Dohan were swimming close together, as they always did on long swims, so that Dohan's bow wave helped him along. A fathom to their right, Helmi and Mielikki were doing the same.

Helmi shuddered.

- I don't want to know! As long as it stays there. Squids and giants and things with lights on their teeth. Give me the shallows! -

Mielikki copied Pel, reaching into the depths with her lowest sonar tone. The first time she did it, there was no echo at all; the second, straining her ears, she heard the faint call drift back off the endless, silty plains. She shut her eyes and called a third time, trying to picture the world below. Somehow it called to her. She longed to dive down there, to break through all the barriers of depth and distance and see

217

with her own eyes the rolling bed of the ocean. She fought the feeling down. This was not the time for exploring.

All of a sudden, her eyes snapped open. In the same moment, Helmi hissed, - Listen! -

- I can't hear anything, - Dohan said quickly.

- Ssh! -

All four slowed down, so the rush of water past their ears was stilled, and listened with all their concentration. For a moment, nothing stirred; then there it was, on the edge of hearing far behind them: the low mutter of an engine.

- That's a boat, - Pel said quietly.

- I know, - said Mielikki, equally softly.

- Is it that one we saw? -

- I don't know, - she said. - It's a long way away. -

- I hope it stays that way, - Helmi said nervously. - Should we warn the others? -

Mielikki thought for a moment. - No, - she decided, uncertainly. - It's a long way. And if it goes away, we don't want to worry them. -

- You don't sound sure. What if it doesn't? - Helmi asked instantly. Mielikki bit her lip and wished that she had sounded more decisive.

- Then we'll hear it and hide from it, - she said, more firmly than she felt. - Come on, let's keep going. -

They swam on. Viliga was a little way ahead of them, arms folded, every movement a declaration of disgruntlement: even his tail-strokes looked sulky. At the front, Riakka and Thettis were deep in conversation.

- I wonder what they're saying, - Helmi whispered to Mielikki.

- Probably wondering how to tell the others that we're not coming back, - Mielikki replied. She had been wondering the same thing herself.

There was an anxious silence. The two girls looked ahead to their companions, outlined in billowing green fire.

- Thettis knows, doesn't she? - Helmi said. Her sister always knew things.

Mielikki nodded. - Dohan and Viliga don't, though. -

Helmi looked thoughtful. - Dohan could swim to the Diamond Sea anyway. He'll be all right, once he knows that Pel's coming with him, - she said.

They looked forward again.

- Viliga, - Mielikki said, voicing their shared thought. - How are we going to tell him? -

Helmi clicked encouragingly. - You'll find a way. -

Mielikki sighed doubtfully. - I hope so. -

Only much later did she realize how strange that conversation was. One week before, "we" would have meant "me, you and Pel." Now, without discussion or dispute, it meant "Riakka, Thettis and me." The shape of the school was shifting. Mielikki was not the oldest, or the cleverest, or the strongest; but she would fight the oceans and the sky to protect the school, fight with every scrap of heart and mind and courage, and the school knew it. Leaders are chosen by their followers, not the other way round.

She did not know it; there was no way she could have known; but Mielikki was beginning to find her name.

They swam on. It was amazing how quickly the journey became boring: swimming out to sea sounds exciting, but what it means is finning for a long, long time through empty, empty water. There was nothing to see behind them, nothing to see below. The gusts of seafire grew monotonous, then distracting, tugging the eye forward when they should have been looking around and down. From the sea bed, the echoes were a dull murmur; from the sea to each side there was no echo at all.

Only, far behind them, the mutter of the boat's engine never quite died away.

After half an hour, Riakka took them up to breathe. The moon was dipping towards the southwest, and in the east the skyrim was growing pale; but overhead, the sky was ablaze with stars. The younger children had never come so far out at night: without the island's lights to dim them, the constellations burned in splendor. Some were named after creatures of the water: Cancer the crab, Pisces the fish, Cetus the Ghostwhale, Hydra the kraken, Delphinus the dolphin, Cygnus the swan. Others told the story of the blood feud of the gods: Atlas and Andromeda, Cassiopeia and Cepheus, Perseus, Orion, the Scorpion, the Seven Sisters. Some had names that no human would have recognized: the Peace-fish, the Eagle-ray, the Wave. And above all of them, a lantern in the darkness, hung the Rudder of the Sky, steering the stars eternally towards the beacon of the Pole.

Riakka took a sight on the Pole Star, ducked under the water and sent her lowest call forwards and downwards. The sea bed was all but featureless, but in one place a mile or two ahead there was a faint echo, as if the abyssal plain had lifted into a gentle mound. Riakka clicked in satisfaction and raised her head.

"Aim to the right of that mound, and we'll be all right," she said, shaking the spray from her hair.

Helmi grinned and looked at Pel.

"Mark the modest mountain
In fathoms too far for counting,"

she quoted. "See, you're not the only one who remembers."

Mielikki laughed. It was amazing how happy she felt, with the stars shining above her. They were out at sea, under the flaring arch of heaven, and the netmen and their danger were far away.

Except...

"Ship!" hissed Thettis suddenly, pointing back the way they had come. They all wrenched around and stared. For a second they saw nothing; then, as the waves heaved by, they saw a distant light wink and disappear.

Mielikki and Helmi exchanged a glance.

"We heard it, behind us," Mielikki said. "A long way behind. It's coming this way."

Thettis looked at her sharply.

"Following us?"

"I don't know," she replied honestly. "But it's

going the same way we are."

The school looked at one another, and back over the glittering black waves. For a long while there was nothing, so long that they began to hope that they might have imagined it; but then the light showed again.

Riakka set her jaw.

"All right, it's coming. We should fin."

They dived.

Now that they knew the ship was there, they could all hear it, a low, threatening rumble thudding like a headache. Somehow, with that sound behind them, the beauty was gone from the night. They swam on, tense, alert, afraid.

- Why can't they leave us alone? - Pel asked Mielikki, the note of strain back in his voice. It was all happening too fast: the collapse of the cliff, the hunt, sleeping out at night, swimming out to the rock, leaving the islands to follow their parents. Four years' worth of adventure had come crashing in on him in a few short hours, and he felt like a merbaby caught in a whirlpool. Mielikki reached out and touched his hand.

- It's a big ocean. They'll never find us, little gillfish - she said reassuringly. She had no idea, then, how terrifyingly effective a human hunt could be.

- They find fish, don't they? -

- Yes, but we're clever. Especially you. They'll never catch us. -

They swam. Riakka stayed shallow, just three fathoms down, and finned fast and straight. Too fast: soon Pel and Helmi were struggling to keep up, even with Mielikki and Dohan helping them.

- Riakka, slow down! - Mielikki called after a while, angry and afraid for them. - There are people with short tails here! -

The big girl stopped and turned at once, and Mielikki could see impatience battling the concern in her face. For once, concern won: there was no point pushing them so hard that they collapsed.

- I'm sorry, - Riakka said after a moment. - I don't like that ship behind us. But the Rock's not far now. -

- I can keep going, - Pel said stoutly, but his face was pale. Helmi said nothing.

Riakka swallowed. - All right. I'll go slower, - she said reluctantly. - Stick close, all of you. I know you're doing your best. It's not far now. Really. –

But she gave Mielikki a glance which said plainly: *I don't know what to do.*

- Let's keep going, - Mielikki replied to that glance, trying to sound reassuring. The thud of the boat behind them felt like a tremor in her heart.

- We can make it. We all can. -

They went up to breathe again, and swam on.

Soon they were all struggling. The going was slow and heavy, as if the sea had turned against them. There were strange currents in the water. Stabbing surges cut across the swell. If they had been used to the ocean, they would have known them for what they were: the first outriders of a monstrous storm, sweeping up from the south. But they did not know. They battled on, deeper and deeper into the night.

Mielikki tried to swallow her fear, but there was too much tension in the dark waters: the boat, the empty depths, Pel, Helmi. Her mind spun, trying to find comfort. To distract herself, she began to watch her companions, studying how they swam, and wondering if she would ever be as good as them.

Dohan swam beautifully, with the beauty of an assassin whale: sweeping motions, swift gestures, the impression of huge power only just kept in check. He had a trick of lifting his head up just as his tail swept down, his hair billowing backwards with the speed of the surge, that she would have given a year of her life to imitate: it was speed and grace and power all caught in one beautiful movement.

Ahead, Thettis and Riakka looked like opposites of one another, one so slender and silver-bright, the other strong-bodied and dark. But they swam as if they were a single mer, their fin-strokes and head-lifts in unison, so that it was like watching a reflection move across an unseen mirror: beauty, poise and grace. All the things she felt she lacked in herself.

She sighed inwardly and turned her eye to Helmi. She was finning steadily onwards, timing her tail-strokes to two heartbeats after Mielikki's to make the most of the bow wave. She looked pale and drawn, but her fin-strokes were still firm and controlled. A sudden rush of protective feeling swept through Mielikki. Helmi had come so far and grown so much in these past two days...

Then she looked across to Pel, and cold shock bumped her heart. Her brother was as white as a manta's belly, and his tail-strokes were quick and ragged, the sure sign of impending exhaustion. A chill hand grabbed Mielikki's heart: *He's not going to make it.*

She cast a panicked glance back over the school. Helmi was concentrating on keeping swimming; Dohan was looking stolidly forwards. Riakka and Thettis were deep in conversation, and Viliga was sulking alone. Nobody else had noticed that Pel was on the edge of collapse.

Desperately, she scanned ahead. Far, far away, on the edge of sonar, a new echo came out of the deep: a long, steep slope rising to an underwater mountain, the Lone Rock. She knew it at once, and her heart gave a lurch: they were getting there. But it was still a long, long swim. Even with help, would Pel make it?

She looked back at her brother. His hands were flapping as if they could help push him along.

Handswimmer.

Ice stabbed Mielikki's heart. That was the last sign of fatigue; only babies and the drowning swim with their arms. His eyes were half-closed, his sonar a whisper. He had not even seen the mountain ahead.

- Look! The Rock! - called Mielikki loudly, deliberately trying to encourage him.

- Steady! - Dohan protested. - You nearly burst my ear! -

Mielikki ignored him; Pel's head had come up, and for a second his sonar took on a more determined sound. But then his head drooped wearily again, and Mielikki could almost hear him thinking: *I can't.* In the same moment, the noise of the engine seemed to grow louder, as if it had heard them weakening.

She gritted her teeth, desperate to find a way before Pel's strength ran out. At home, he could have pulled himself hand over hand along the sea bed; but here the abyss was a thousand fathoms deep. If the boat had not been there, they could have taken him to the surface and supported him in their arms; but not now, with dawn approaching. If he had been smaller, they could have carried him like a baby, but even Pel was not that small...

Suddenly, Mielikki remembered a day from her distant childhood, swimming next to her parents soon after Pel was born, while he splashed with his tiny tail at the moonlight and gurgled with laughter. They had swum far out to sea, and Mielikki had ridden back home, clinging to her father's hair... *His hair!*

Without stopping to think, she reached up and twisted her hair into a rough plait. Then she ducked down, rolled under Dohan and popped up right in front of Pel.

- Pel, take my hair! - she said urgently.

- What? - he asked, bewildered.

She was speaking on the open channel. At once the leaders looked back.

- Mielikki, Pel, are you all right? - Thettis called.

- Take my hair! - Mielikki urged him again. - If you go on like this you're going to drown. Take my hair, I'll pull you. -

Pel stared at her, uncomprehending; then his hand crawled out, slow as a sea-slug, and wrapped around Mielikki's plait.

- Now hang on! - And she gritted her teeth,

and kicked.

She was braced for the shock, but still it felt as if her head had been rammed onto her spine like an urchin crushed on a rock. Agony flared along her back. They had barely moved.

- What are you *doing*? - called Viliga sharply.

Exactly the sort of mullet question he would ask! she thought.

She kicked harder, shoving her head forwards and downwards. This time it hurt less.

- Mielikki, stop it, - Pel protested faintly. - Let's just rest here, you'll wear yourself out. -

- You just hold on, little pup, - Mielikki retorted, calling him what their parents had called him in those far off days, and kicked again. Another fathom forward; at this rate it would take them until winter to get there.

But then Dohan swept down on one side of her, and Riakka was swimming back towards them.

- Are you all right? Pel, I'm sorry, I should have noticed sooner! - Riakka's voice was sharp with anxiety.

Dohan swam closer to Mielikki, so close that their shoulders touched.

- Get on the other side, - he grunted to Riakka.

- Mielikki, hold your arms out. -

- But... -

- Don't get too close! - Viliga called spitefully from ahead; so far ahead that he had not, perhaps, seen the danger. - Or she'll elbow you in the eye. -

Pel opened his mouth, but Dohan was faster. He back-flipped and swam straight at Viliga.

- Mielikki's fine, - the big youth rumbled. - She's a better swimmer than you'll ever be. -

The two boys glowered at each other, but it was Viliga who backed away. Dohan turned his back on him contemptuously.

- Right. Mielikki, swim right next to me. Hold your arms out. Riakka, take the other side. –

Mielikki gave him a grateful look, edged closer, misjudged the strength of her kick and bumped into him.

- Told you! - jeered Viliga.

- Shut up and drown, - Dohan said. – Come on, Mielikki. -

She held her arms out. On one side, Dohan locked his elbow with hers. On the other, Riakka did the same.

- Now, are you ready? Kick! -

Mielikki kicked, and felt an enormous surge of power as Dohan and Riakka, the strongest swimmers in the school, kicked at the same moment. They shot forwards so fast that Pel almost lost his grip.

Thettis swam in below them, using her bow wave to help lift them. They kicked, and kicked again. She could feel their joint strength driving her through the water, faster than she had ever gone before. The sound of the ship faded. Pel shut his eyes and clung on in utter exhaustion, holding onto Mielikki's plait like a tired child with its mother.

They swam on. At first, Mielikki was so worried about Pel that she had thoughts for nothing else. Then, as they ploughed forwards and she felt his hands still locked safe around her plait, she began to lose the edge of panic, and started worrying about bumping into the others. Once she rammed Dohan with an elbow as she rolled to scan the seas around, but he only gave her an encouraging click and kept on swimming. After that she began to relax, and the more she relaxed the easier it became to keep control. There was a real skill to swimming in such tight formation, timing their tail-strokes so that they kicked together, timing their sonar bursts so that they did not shout straight into each other's ears. If it had not been for her fear for Pel and the threat of the ship behind them, it would almost have been a pleasure.

After a while, she realized with surprise that it had become automatic, and she had time to look around. The night was almost over. The bellies of the waves showed the zebra-fish pattern of daybreak, their eastern faces white with the growing light, their western backs midnight-black. Out here in the open waters, the swells were much bigger and wider spaced, but with an ugly cross-current that betrayed the coming storm. The seafire was all burnt out.

Half an hour later, they came up to breathe. The tide of day was rising. The waves rolled blue and brilliant towards Africa. Far below, the Lone Rock heaved up its head. Far to the south, a dark line on the skyrim marked the gathering tempest. They clung together, too weary to talk, but triumphant: they had crossed the first part of the sea.

Far behind them now, out of sight and out of hearing, the *Artemis* ploughed steadily onwards. And far ahead, and to either side, the drift-nets that she had laid two nights before hung down from their lines of buoys, waiting for their prey to swim in.

20

The Hiding

How were the Three Treasures hidden? What made the Sisters sink them beyond sight and sound? This is what the songs told us, when the truth was lost beneath the sea...

It was a ship that made them do it, a black ship that stank of blood and death, sweeping into the waters of Atlantis with a trail of carrion-sharks behind.

For six years the exiles had lived in peace, a mournful and grieving peace amidst the memories of their loss. No humans had dared to come there since Atlantis fell; for Orion had gone to war, and his fury had ravaged the Landlocked Sea.

The exiles knew nothing of that titanic conflict. They had drifted apart among the scattered islets and shattered rocks; for nine-tenths of the fish in the islands had died, and there was not enough food left to support a large community. Only the sharks had thrived. And the exiles took Thettis as their queen, for the Seven Sisters refused all power, saying that they had to guard the Treasures of Atlantis; and the people accepted, for their one concern now was to stay alive.

Far, far out on the ocean currents, so far that the snow-capped tip of the Tombstone Mountain, highest of peaks, was no more than an unmoving gleam amidst the waves, the sisters found a hidden island, known only to the seals. There, in a narrow cave, they kept the Three Treasures, and lived as best they could; and the daughters of Atlas and Amphitrite, who had been born in the greatest palace the seas had ever seen, slept on the gritty sand and the cold rock, and caught what fish they could, and cooked them on a secret fire. Because although Atlantis had fallen, its secrets remained, and they still had the arts of making fire, and diving deep, and preserving songs.

But the netmen came at dawn, a bloody ship over a blood red sea. It anchored in the bay where their cave was hidden, and men rowed ashore in boats: men with spears and knives and clubs, who walked among the seal colonies, and drove the mother seals away, and slaughtered the pups along the shore, so that the blood ran hot into the sea, and the sharks came ravening in.

And in an evil hour, one of the men looked across the bay, and saw the narrow cave where the sisters were watching with horror; and he saw their movement as they ducked back out of sight, and walked towards them with spear raised.

But these were the daughters of Atlas, and they had fought their way across the reefs on the night Atlantis fell. As the man opened his mouth to shout, Taygettë picked up the ebony rod and hurled it with all her strength, and struck him between the eyes. And while his death scream still hung in the air, Maia took up the golden trident, and struck the rocks in anger.

The island shook. The sea heaved. A great wave came roaring out of the dawn, and broke over the ship, and pulled the men into the sea; and the sharks swarmed through the wreckage.

But Merope looked east, where the track of the rising sun blazed a trail from the Landlocked Sea; and in the bloody light it seemed to her that the shadow of every wave was a boat crawling towards them; and the waves were beyond counting.

And she said, "More will come, and the seas will not be enough to hold them or fill their hunger. We cannot turn them back."

The sisters stared at her, and would have argued, Taygettë most of all; but in that hour Merope spoke with the voice of prophecy, which none can turn aside.

"The men will come with blood and death and flame, and there are not enough mers left in the sea to stop them. Andromeda's curse will drive them, as they drive the slaves at their oars. Their own hunger will drive them, and we have no king to drive them back."

"But we have the Trident, and the Scepter, and the Rod," said Asterope. "We have Maia, and Taygettë, and you. You can turn them back."

But Merope shook her head and pointed to the beach of slaughter.

"There will be more men than the grains of sand on that beach, and every one stained with blood. We cannot stop them all. Only the king could do that, and Father is dead. And if we fight, they will overwhelm us, and take the Treasures, and the sea will never be ours again."

"Then what must we do?" asked Maia.

"Fight!" said Taygettë defiantly, lifting the rod from the seal killer's corpse.

"Flee," said Asterope, looking over her shoulder at the dawn, as if the ships were already on the way.

But Merope said, "We will hide the Treasures, deep and dark, so that neither man nor mer knows where they lie. And they will lie safely hidden for years beyond *counting, until one comes to bring them to the light, and take back what was lost."*

"Who will he be? When will he come?" all the sisters asked at once.

Now Merope smiled for a second, sadly, as if she saw more than she would say; but then the smile faded, and the voice of prophecy rolled on.

"One will come. When fire burns on the water and under the water, and thunder rolls in the deep, one will come. They will find the lost song, and enter the secret deeps, and bring the Treasures back to the light.

"And in that hour, Andromeda's Curse will be broken, and our freedom will be given back to us, and the evil that Perseus wrought will be undone."

And now her tears were flowing, and she looked at her sisters with desolation in her face.

"And until that day we must scatter, my sisters, to keep the secrets safe and the memory of Atlantis alive. We must go into exile, and we shall be princesses no more, but priestesses, guiding and teaching our people in all the Seven Seas. We will give them the last gift, which is Memory, so that they will not forget their kinship once we have gone into the abyss."

Then she told them what they must do, and they grieved, and made their grief into a song. And the song was more beautiful and terrible than any that has ever been heard, and it echoed across the islands and over the waves, and came even to the Landlocked Sea; and all those who heard it were bound by its spell, and never had peace in their hearts again unless they were in sight and hearing of the sea.

Then the Seven Sisters carried the Treasures across the oceans, and hid them, to rest through the centuries undisturbed by mer or man. And the place they chose was a Labyrinth so deep and dark that only one who knew the secret of diving deep could reach it; and nomer knew in which ocean the Labyrinth lay.

They sealed the Labyrinth with a lock of fire, so that only one who held the secret of flame could open it.

And they wove a song describing where the Treasures lay; and only a mer who heard that song would find the Gates of the Labyrinth, and know them for what they were.

Then, to keep alive the memory of what they had done, they set an image of the Golden Trident in the fire of the sunset waves; and to this day, humans see it as the sun goes down, and know that its power is beyond their reach.

And they crafted an image of the Glass Scepter, and set it where the full moon lays her track across the waves; and ever since, humans have yearned for the moonlight on the water, and spend their whole lives seeking it.

And last they shaped an image of the Rod of the Black Pearl, and set it in the black troughs of the ocean waves when the storm-winds blow; and ever since, men have looked with fear on the fury of the deep, and dreaded its just revenge.

So the Three Treasures came to their resting place, deep and dark and secret, far beneath the waves; and there they will lie to the end of time. For who now knows the hidden song, or the art of fire, or the secret of diving into the abyss?

And still the netmen search. Still they see the treasures of Atlantis in the track of the waves. Still Andromeda's Curse drives them to further waters and deeper seas, always hungry, always restless; and their nets *reach around the world.*

21

Nets

In the end, Mielikki and Helmi took the first watch. Pel was too tired even to swim: as soon as they reached their resting place, he leaned his head back on the waves, let out a long sigh and fell asleep. Helmi, white to the lips but determined, offered to take his place. Mielikki, knowing how much a rejection by one of the elders would hurt her, accepted before anyone else had the time to react.

She took the first spell under the water, so that Helmi could spend her time on the surface before the sun was too hot. At first her friend's presence was a distraction, because there was so much she ached to talk about: what they had seen, where they were going, how they would eat, how to survive another day. Every time she saw the flicker of Helmi's fins overhead, she wanted to call up to make sure she was all right.

But the blue was all around, shot through with harpoons of sunlight, and she had to keep watch.

Soon a new feeling grew, an uneasiness that spread and deepened until it was like an itch in the back of her mind. Right on the edge of hearing, she thought she could hear the thunder boat, but slow and intermittent, and moving strangely. To start with it was south-west, back the way they had come; then it began to drift slowly westwards. For a while it disappeared; then it seemed to reappear right on the cusp of hearing, but this time it was due north. Something about the noise made Mielikki uneasy. It sounded as if the ship was circling them, just as the dolphins had circled them in their play-hunt.

But humans do not play. When they hunt, mermen die.

Mielikki strained her ears, desperately trying to pinpoint the boat against the background rumble of the ocean. There was something sinister in that slow, predatory movement, as if something were trying to creep nearer, stalking them through the waves...

- Mielikki! -

She jumped and spun around, heart in her mouth. It was Helmi, calling from above, her face flushed and her eyes scared.

- Mielikki, I thought I heard that boat! -

Mielikki looked around into the endless, shifting blue, looked up at the circle of the school, and made her decision. She kicked herself towards the surface, broke water at Helmi's side, and looked around. She even forgot to be scared of bumping into her friend.

The waves were empty, shifting and dancing in the light. The cross-waves had grown stronger even in the little while she was below, a rocking unease in the pattern of the ocean that she did not understand. For a moment, she thought she heard thunder. Overhead, a sharp-winged black-and-white bird shifted and swooped lower. But there was no sign of danger – no sound but the wind.

"I thought I heard it," Helmi whispered. "But it sounded like it was that way." And she pointed to the north.

Mielikki nodded, and looked at her friend. Her face was flushed, her eyes strained. Helmi looked as if she were close to the end of her strength. Something deep inside Mielikki clenched like a fist. It was a cold feeling, hard as floating ice: *I need to be strong for her.*

"Listen," she said quietly. "I thought I heard it too. West, then north. Your ears are better than mine. Why don't you dive now, and see if you can hear it?"

Helmi gave her a look of gratitude and relief. The openness and brightness of the daylight ocean had unnerved her; she was used to the gentler light of the moon, the smaller seas between the islands. She took three deep breaths, filling her lungs with the salt scented air, and dived.

Mielikki turned and watched.

The sun was well clear of the skyrim now. The waves shone a deep, translucent blue. It was much cooler than the day before, and the gusting wind chased snakes of foam across the waves. Due south, the thunder heads were gathering, towering reefs of shining cloud with black, glowering bases. *That'll make listening even harder*, Mielikki thought grimly. She turned in a complete circle, straining her eyes as if she might catch the menacing shape of the ship somewhere on the skyrim; but nothing moved.

After a surprisingly long time, Helmi surfaced. She had stayed down to the very limits of her breath, trying to listen; trying to impress Mielikki. She glanced quickly north-east, as if afraid of what she might see there.

"There's something out there. A thunder boat. I think it's hunting us," she said, lowering her voice as if the netmen might hear her. "I heard it for a minute, north-east this time, then I lost it again. But it sounds like an old one: you know the *karr, karr* noise they make." She imitated the sound of metal bolts rattling in a rusty engine casing. Mielikki blinked: now that Helmi mentioned it, she had heard that sound too.

For a second they looked at one another nervously. Every instinct was to swim away, as fast as possible, but how can you swim away when the thing you are afraid of seems to be all around you? *Surely*, Mielikki thought, *if it comes towards us we'll hear it. There'll be time to wake the others then. We all need sleep. I need sleep. If only it stays away…*

"Come on," she said suddenly, reaching the decision before she was even aware she was thinking of it. "We'll dive together. Not far, just deep enough that the waves don't bother us. But we can listen for it together. Four ears are better than two."

"All right." Helmi looked around at the shining waves, shuddered and drew another deep breath.

But back under the water, it was hard to find the sound again. The wind and the waves seemed to have blotted it out. *Maybe it's gone,* Mielikki thought suddenly with a flare of hope. *Maybe it's left us alone, and we can be safe…* But then Helmi's head swung round and she pointed north of east. Mielikki shook her head and shut her eyes, heart sinking. After a moment she heard it too, the faintest grumble of a boat's engines, and yes, Helmi was right, there was the rattle of age in it. It dropped almost to nothing, rose briefly, then dropped again, like the distant mutter of thunder.

- That's it, - she said quietly. Helmi nodded.

- What's it doing? -

- I don't know, but I don't like it. - She glanced up at the ring of tails above them. - I'll go back up and keep watch. You keep listening here. -

Helmi nodded again, her face scared. Something about that distant, menacing noise grated on her nerves. Mielikki surfaced, winced at the bright light, and returned to her watch. All through the next hour she felt the wind freshen and the movement of the waves grow rougher, the tumbled chaos of a south wind cutting across the westerly swell. The boat's sound came and went, like a whisper in a language she could not understand.

It was still there when Helmi surfaced, and they woke Thettis and Dohan to watch. She took her place in the circle, holding hands with Pel and Helmi, and sank like a stone into sleep. The mutter of the engine haunted her dreams.

When she awoke, it was dusk. The sun had vanished into a black bank of storm clouds, and the waves were like savage hills, crested with foam. She had slept for almost ten hours, and she was refreshed in body, but anxious in mind.

"Is the boat out there?" were her first words on waking; from the looks they gave her, it was clear that it was. They were tossing on the surface, up and down, up and down, sliding on the face of the angry waves. The storm was coming near.

"It's there," Riakka said grimly. She looked as if she had hardly slept. "I heard it now and then, going round to the east. Viliga says it never stopped the whole time he was listening."

Mielikki shot the dark one a look. He was capable of making things up just to spite them; but he was the best player of hide-and-sneak in the school.

"Well, he's got the best ears," she said grudgingly. She was already looking east, and did not notice the sudden look on his face: a startled, wary happiness that made him look much less baleful. "He probably did. But what's it doing?"

"Something dangerous," said Helmi instantly.

"Something we don't understand," Thettis corrected her, and Mielikki had the feeling that this conversation had been going in circles before she woke up.

"Which is probably dangerous," Riakka said. "Anyway, it's a long way off. So first we'll feed, and then..."

"Then?" asked Viliga, suddenly all attention. Mielikki winced. She had been so busy worrying about the threatening noise that she had forgotten the argument ahead.

"Then we'll see what we do next," Thettis said quickly. "Now, who's hungry?"

Fortwé fathoms below the Atlantic waves, the Lone Rock rose majestically out of the abyss. A thousand fathoms from base to crest, and a good sea-mile across at the summit, it looked like a cone of stone dropped carelessly into the sea. It had been the mers' landmark and fishing ground for generations.

It lay where two currents ran together, a cold stream flowing out of the north and a warmer current out from the islands to the south. Where they met, the two currents swirled up a cloud of silt, rich with a thousand years of decay. Plankton fed on that bounty in great clouds, and corals and sponges and fish fed on the plankton, so that the Rock rose like a tree of life out of the dead, dark plains of Hades.

One by one, the children dived, swooping down on the Rock like penguins, snatching left and right among the fish and curving back to the surface. It was exhilarating to dive so fast and deep, thrilling to chase fish flashing between the rocks, exciting to eat on the storm-tossed surface like real grown-ups. Even the sound of the boat seemed to have left them for a moment.

And then between one bite and the next Viliga lifted his head up sharply and said, "It's coming."

Their heads snapped up, listening; but there was no sound but the waves and the wind and the far off threat of thunder.

"Are you sure?" asked Dohan doubtfully.

"If this is one of your shark tricks..." said Riakka dangerously: Viliga had scared them with false shark alerts many times. He flushed, angry at being mistrusted, and still more angry because he knew they were right.

"I'm sure! It's that ship again! Listen for yourselves!"

They shot him suspicious glances, but dipped their heads into the water, and there it was: far away to the south-west, but coming right for them, the slow, sinister thud of the rattling boat that had haunted their dreams, cutting through the storm noise.

- See? I told you! - snapped Viliga, with all the indignation of a liar who has told the truth for once.

- Back to the surface! - Riakka said quickly.

"He's right," she went on as soon as they surfaced. "That ship's out there, and it's coming this way."

"*Silence*!" Even in that moment, they looked at Viliga, shocked: it was the worst curse a mer could make, an invocation of ruin and death. "It's between us and the island. Now what?"

Mielikki and Helmi exchanged a glance. Then, as one, they looked at Riakka.

She took a deep breath.

"We're not going back to the island," she said in a voice that shook slightly. "It's too dangerous, and that boat is coming. We're not going back."

Viliga's eyes widened, then narrowed. He licked his lips, looked around the skyrim. Then he turned and glared at Riakka.

"You planned this, didn't you? You never meant to go back."

"She didn't plan the boat!" Mielikki burst out. "It's coming this way!"

"Shut up, Mielikki," Viliga said levelly, slitted

gaze on Riakka. "It's still miles away. I want to hear Riakka tell the truth."

Riakka met his stare for stare. "The island's too dangerous. We can't stay there," she said flatly. "We realized that yesterday, and if you didn't, you should have. We're going to do what all merpeople do. We're going to swim out, find our parents and not come back."

"But … you said we're going back…" Dohan said, bewildered. All of a sudden there were tears in his voice; Pel moved closer protectively, and put a small hand on his massive shoulder. Dohan started to sob. "We're not going … going *home*?"

"You planned this! You know we're not ready, and you planned this!" They had never seen Viliga so angry. His lean face was pale with fury.

Helmi surprised them all by pushing her way forwards.

"Yes we are ready! We swam out here, didn't we? And we found food! We're ready!"

"You, maybe, but what about *him*? What about Pel? He didn't even make it this far!"

"He made it!" Mielikki snapped, coming to her brother's defense. "Of course he can do it!"

"But … it's home," Dohan sobbed. Pel was patting his shoulder helplessly.

"You shut up!" Viliga snapped at Mielikki.

"No, *you* shut up!"

Panic had grabbed them. They were too tired, too far from home, too scared of the grumbling engine, too shaken by the racing waves. The school was breaking up, tormented by fear and anger. And all the while, the rattling engine came nearer…

"Enough!" screamed Thettis suddenly, and once again she tail-slammed into the middle of the group. The sheer shock of the blow pushed them apart, panting and spluttering.

"We can't go back! We can't stay here! So we've got to go on!" she said brutally, and she was looking at Viliga. "You stay here if you like, but we're going! Come on, Mielikki, Helmi, Pel, we're leaving." And without a further glance she drew a deep breath and dived forward into the waves. After a moment, Pel took Dohan's hand and drew the giant underwater. They could hear him whispering comfort as the two dived.

Riakka and Viliga glared at one another, as angry and afraid as ever.

"I'm going," Riakka said after a moment, but she did not move.

"Lying again," Viliga said spitefully. "I'll get you for this one day, Riakka."

He ducked forwards and dived, almost hitting her with a tail-slap. Riakka lunged after him, and they heard her shouting angrily as she left the surface.

Mielikki and Helmi exchanged glances.

"Out to sea?" whispered Helmi.

"You can do it," Mielikki told her. "We both can. I'll look after you."

Helmi looked at her, bit her lip, swallowed – nodded. Together, they dived.

Two miles ahead, the lightning glinted on a long line of buoys.

They swam angrily, in a tight formation like the tip of a harpoon, pointing northwards, riding the racing waves. It was the straightest route towards their parents, if their parents had indeed swum north... If they had been paying attention, they would have seen the slopes of the Lone Rock drop away beneath them, back to the ooze of the abyss. But they were not paying attention: they were too busy arguing.

The fight began the second they were underwater. Riakka flung herself after Viliga, accusing him of trying to hit her. He turned in his own length and called her a liar. Thettis turned back to support Riakka: the island had become too dangerous, and he should be intelligent enough to realize it.

Behind, the noise of the engine grew...

Mielikki tried to ignore the shouting and focus on her own sonar, but it was no use: with all the noise, she could barely hear her out-going clicks, let alone the returning echoes. All at once she had had enough: she shouted at the elders to shut up and let her scan. It shocked Riakka and Thettis into silence, but only made Viliga angrier – and louder. Then Helmi jumped in to protect Mielikki, and the row started all over again.

Ahead, the buoys heaved hungrily on the swell...

Pel and Dohan looked at one another and grimaced. Then, by unspoken consent, they kicked harder, broke out of the formation and hurried ahead, tired of the shouting, eager only to get away. Mielikki called after them, but they ignored her; it was just part of the shouting. Mielikki accelerated after them. Riakka shouted after her. Helmi tried to follow, realized she was too slow and called desperately to Mielikki to wait.

The swish of drift-nets whispered through the water, lost amidst the shouting...

Suddenly Pel screamed. A split second later Dohan yelled in shock. Their bodies jerked as if they had run into an invisible reef. Mielikki froze, too shocked even to throw her arms out, momentum driving her forwards. Then all at once she slammed into something knife-sharp and grasping that twisted round her neck and flukes, and held her tight.

- Net! - she screamed. - *Net!* -

Helmi, behind her, braked desperately – too late. A second later, the *Artemis'* drift-net shook as she crashed into it headlong. Clammy tendrils bunched round her head, and she was caught in the smothering grasp.

Mielikki panicked. It was like being caught in the sand-fall in the cave, but a hundred times more terrifying: she became a trapped animal, as wild and unthinking as a dolphin on a beach. She thrashed and kicked and flung her body sideways, desperate to break out of the throttling wires. The net heaved and bulged. She could hear Pel and Helmi fighting for their lives, and the sound drove her to fresh efforts; but all her fighting only twisted the lines deeper into her flesh.

Riakka and the elder children flung out their arms, wrenched to a stop in mid-flight and stared, appalled. The "little ones" were twisting and threshing wildly in mid-water, fighting for their lives, and there was nothing to see or hear but the faint flash of moonlight off a shifting filament. Drift-nets are silent and invisible; that is why they are so deadly.

Behind, the engine was drawing closer...

Riakka was the first to break the spell. She let out a scream and hurled herself forward, grappling at the net that held Mielikki. Thettis lunged for her sister, trying to drag apart the lines about her neck. Viliga hung there as if paralyzed, his mouth opening and closing in shock.

The engine noises stopped.

A second later, a new noise began: a crunching and thudding like the beat of a giant drum. Then, with a jerk, the net began to move, heaving them sideways through the water, making a current that forced them even more firmly into its bonds.

The *Artemis* had reached the first of the buoys, and started to reel in her catch.

Pel thrashed desperately against the throttling fibers. His lungs were burning, his eyes glazed over, his hearing almost gone. With a mighty wrench, he tore one arm free, and felt something stab his upper arm. Pain shot through him. He stared at the spot – and saw the haft of Mielikki's knife.

- The knife! - he yelled at the top of his voice, desperately trying to get a hand to it. - Mielikki, the knife! -

Mielikki heard him, and it was as if lightning flashed in her mind.

- Thettis! - she yelled. - Get Pel's knife! Cut him and Helmi out! -

She saw Riakka gape at her, saw her fingers freeze where they grasped; then Thettis flashed past them both, and her hands were on Pel's arm.

- It's stuck in the net! I can't get it! -

- You've got to! Helmi needs you! -

Pel saw Thettis' hands wrench at the hilt; Thettis, whom he wanted to impress more than anyone in the ocean. With the greatest effort he had ever made, he forced his panic down, and made himself hold still.

- Push my elbow down and lift the sheath up, - he gasped through the pain. - That'll make the hilt come free. Then get Helmi out. -

Thettis shot him a single glance, and nodded. Then she put one hand on his elbow and pushed down hard.

Pel gasped as the unyielding wires tore his skin. Thettis yelled triumphantly.

- Got it! -

- Get Helmi! - Pel gasped through the pain. But Thettis' hands were already at work, sawing at the net around him.

- Get Helmi! - he shouted again, angrily. She did not look up from her work.

- I will! Now hold still! -

The drum-beat grew louder. The net was moving faster. Now they could see a faint light growing on the edge of sight: the searchlights of a fishing boat hauling in its catch.

The strands of the net were smooth and hard and resisted the stone blade fiercely. Slashing at them just made them bulge and settle again; sawing was no better.

- Wrap them round the blade! - Pel gasped, craning to see out of the corner of his eye. - Then pull! -

Thettis did not waste time wondering: she twisted one evil, translucent fiber around the blade, gritted her teeth and pulled. The mesh whined, screamed and snapped.

- That's it! That's it! -

She twisted and pulled, twisted and pulled. The meshes parted with a snarl like the anger of leopard seals. All of a sudden Pel felt the choking pressure round his throat relax.

- That's it! - With a great wrench and heave, he twisted his upper body free. At once he bent forwards and grabbed the meshes encircling his tail.

- Quick, Thettis! Between my hands! -

She stared for a moment, then understood. She slid the stone blade between his fingers, where a dozen strands came together.

- Now! -

She cut downwards with all her strength. Pel pulled upwards. The net resisted, resisted, and broke, and he tumbled free.

- Quick! Quick! - Riakka yelled, pointing. The lights were clear to see now, pillars of fire stabbing into the water. In that evil glare, they could see the corpses trapped in the net like flies on sticky paper: tuna, trevally, a manta, two sharks. If they had not been so busy arguing, they would have spotted them long before.

Thettis hurled herself at her sister, and Pel was right behind her.

- You cut, I'll hold! - he snapped, and twisted

his fingers into the net. Thettis nodded, the knife already working; but the mesh was tight around Helmi's face, and the blade cut so slowly, and the lights were very close...

- Yes! - and Helmi broke forwards and tore herself free with a sob.

- Mielikki! Get Mielikki! - Pel exclaimed, in agony for his sister.

- No! Dohan needs air! - Mielikki shot back; and indeed, bright bubbles were streaming up the net above him.

Pel groaned and hesitated, but Thettis was already diving, the blade twisting into the mesh. This time they were lucky: Dohan was only held by one arm, and with the other he could pull the strands tight for cutting. In moments, he was free.

- Give me the knife! - Pel almost snarled. He snatched it from Thettis before she could answer and flung himself on the net, slashing at Mielikki's bonds.

- It won't cut! - he sobbed, panicking for her as he had not panicked for himself. But now Riakka was there on one side of him, and Thettis was on the other, and Mielikki herself was sending him soothing clicks as she used to do when he was very little and scared of the depths, calling him gillfish, little pup, and here were the strands of the net, pulled taut and ready for cutting...

- Yes! Well done, Pel! - And Mielikki was free and hurling herself away from the net and the promise of death.

They were just in time. The lights seemed close enough to touch, and the din of gears and motors shook the surface. There was no time for stealth, with their breath nearly gone: they shot to the surface and dragged in great sobbing lungfuls of air, and stared in horror at the sight that met their eyes.

The ship lay heaving on the towering waves barely fivetwé fathoms away, a behemoth of rusting steel, and the water behind it bubbled and smoked with engine fumes. One side was in darkness, as black as the abyss, but from the other side four lamps blazed down on the wave-tops. Above, lightning stitched the storm clouds. The gale was a scream of wrath.

There were men on the deck, in orange jackets as bright as sea-snakes, and beside them a giant box roared and shuddered as it pulled in the net. All along that side of the ship the waves were churned to foam, and out of the darkness in an endless procession jerked the marker buoys. The longest drift-nets can stretch for miles, and every foot is deadly.

The net rose slowly out of the water, its fibers gleaming like the ghosts of daylight; and corpses fell out of it onto the deck with a soft, wet, deadening thud. It seemed as if all the fish of the open ocean had been trapped and drowned there, tuna, marlin, sharks and mantas, barracuda and jack. On the deck, the men moved back and forth, tossing overboard any fish they did not want. The unwanted corpses splashed and sank like mournful rain.

The merchildren gaped in horror; it was impossible not to stare at that callous, murderous sight. The light was blinding, the sound deafening, the smell sickening. The netmen went on with their work, oblivious to the watchers: with the flare of the searchlights above them, they could see nothing else.

"Come on!" Riakka shouted at last, struggling to be heard over the noise. "Let's get out of here!"

Mielikki shook her head, trying to clear the horror. It was almost too much to take in, terrifying and fascinating together. She heard the others breathe and dive, followed them by instinct, and then they were back under the sheltering waves and watching the terrible net heave past.

Fathom after fathom and mile after mile the procession of death went on: fish and seals, turtles and sharks, seagulls with their feathers bedraggled and gray. It was as if some cruel god had called all the pelagic species together, to be counted, and be killed. And still, from the ship, the slow rain of discarded bodies splashed into the water and arched down into the darkness.

Then Helmi gave a terrible cry and pointed along the net.

- Look! Oh, Mielikki, look! -

Mielikki looked, and a harpoon of ice ran through her. There, hanging head down in the net, was the body of a dolphin. His flanks were scarred with age, his fins broad and powerful, his dead mouth still locked in that mocking smile. Ukko, the leader of the pod, would lead his people no further.

Mielikki gaped, too stunned even to cry out, and watched the horror unfold. After Ukko came a female, and another young male, then three youngsters together, all twisted in the nets and drowned as they tried to rescue one another. Another corpse, and then another, and still the net dragged by.

- Ukko! - She heard a hoarse voice scream the name, and did not realize that it was her own. There was no thought, no plan. Pel was beside her. Without a word she reached out and snatched the knife, and then she was lunging forwards and grappling with the net around the dolphin's corpse.

- Mielikki! -

- Come back! -

- No! - she screamed, hacking away at the net. - They're not having him! -

- Get away from there! - Riakka yelled.

- *No!* -

The knife whined on the fibers. Ukko must have fought like a thresher shark: the net was wrapped around him like a shroud. She could feel it heaving her through the water, but she was too distraught to care. All she knew was that she must rescue Ukko's body. The humans would not have him. They would not!

- Get off there! - a harsh voice yelled. Hands pulled at her shoulders. She shoved them off with a great thrust of her tail and kept on cutting. Nothing existed, nothing mattered except her hands and the knife and the dolphin who had been her friend.

- She's mad! -

- Get her off there! -

- Mielikki, get *back*! -

Now the net was straining upwards, the air popping in her ears. Mielikki set her teeth and cut faster, oblivious to the shouts around her, oblivious to the hands pulling at her. He was almost free now, the great body hanging loose, only one pectoral fin still entangled in the net.

- Mielikki! -

- *No!* -

All of a sudden her head broke the water. The roar of engines filled her ears. The net was rising above her, dragging Ukko's body with it. With a wild scream she lashed out, clutching at that last flipper. She was halfway out of the water. Her friends' hands were dragging her back. The knife flashed in the searchlights and hacked into the net. And then hands grabbed her tail and pulled her downwards, and the last strand parted, and knife and mermaid and dolphin crashed back into the water.

And the netmen saw.

22

The First Convocation

Who called the first Convocation? Who brought the seven clans back together, so that the memory of Atlantis was kept afloat?

It was Merope who called it; Merope, youngest and wisest of the Seven Sisters; Merope, in whom the power of prophecy rose like the spring tide.

They had hidden the Three Treasures in a place dark and deep, and sung a farewell song. When all was done, Merope said to them, "There is one more thing to do. We have hidden the Treasures, and only one who can dive deep and make fire will be able to bring them back to the light, and lift Andromeda's Curse."

"Those were the secrets of the stewards. And all the stewards are dead," said Maia. Merope nodded.

"We are the last mers to know those secrets, and we must scatter them, for safety. We shall swim across the oceans, from clan to clan; and we will leave one secret in each ocean, to wait until Curse-breaker comes."

"But the Curse-breaker will have to swim round the world to find them!" Taygettë protested. "How will he know the way?"

"They will swim through all the oceans, and learn to love all the oceans," Merope said. "We will leave a song to guide them. A map song, that charts every reef and channel and island in the world, stored as we alone know how to store it. And we ourselves will separate, and live

among the clans, teaching every one of them the tale of the Treasures and the Search; for we do not know in which sea the Curse-breaker will come."

"So must we part for ever?" asked Asterope, and there were tears in her voice. But Merope shook her head.

"No. We shall be stewards to the clans, the last stewards of Atlantis; we shall guide them, and teach them our songs and our wisdom. We will keep alive the remembrance of our kinship, so that the seven clans do not forget it, nor fall to fighting as the netmen do. And every year, we will lead them to the Diamond Seas, to renew the bonds of love; and so history and hope will be kept alive, until the Treasures come out of the sea."

They swam together to the wreckage of Atlantis, and looked down to say farewell. And as they looked, they saw a current, deep and fierce like a light in the darkness, that swept west through the abyss far beyond the reach of day; and they dived down, and let it carry them, speeding across the ocean as if Poseidon's hand were guiding them.

So they came to the Blue Reefs; and Kallio the Black, who had been king of that place, was gone, dragged to his death by a great white squid, so that the people called it Poseidon's Wrath. His son who came after him, Kelttin, feared the sisters, and thought they had come to drive him from his throne. But they calmed his fears, telling him they would not challenge his rule; and the fairest of them, Keläenno, loved the blue water off the long deep reefs, and chose to stay there, and became a priestess, and in time became his queen.

Then the six looked down into the depths; and behold! Another deep current ran there, far out of the sight of Zeus; and they rode it north, and came with unheard of speed to the Iron Seas, where Queen Anttila was dead, *slain by a Ghostwhale that was white from tip to tail; and the people called it Poseidon's Vengeance. The new queen was wiser and less greedy, and welcomed them, and called them her kin; and they stayed there a little while. And Alcyone, the fourth sister, loved the surge of the teeming waters, and chose to stay there; and she kissed her sisters farewell.*

Then Maia led the remaining sisters northwards past mountains of floating ice, and bays as wide as seas. There were merpeople there, and some said they were mers of Atlantis, and some said they were mers of Orion, but all said that they lived in peace. And when they learned that Atlas' daughters had come, they were amazed, for they thought all Poseidon's kindred had died on the night Atlantis fell.

Then some say the Sisters taught those mers the secret of fire; but they did not say where lay the Gates that the fire would unlock. And others say that the mers already knew it, having learned it from Orion; and nomer knows the truth. They made the Sisters welcome, but would not let them live there, lest the rivalry of Orion for Atlas be reawakened; and so the five swam on.

Then Asterope, who had wept so much, seemed to find new strength. She led them onwards, into the rockbound channels of the Jaws of Winter and through the gathering ice; and on a day of frost-bright light, they left the rocks behind, and saw the shining expanse of Poseidon's Deep.

But the light betrayed them. All of a sudden, a storm swept down upon them; and that was Zeus at work, eager to end Poseidon's line. Then Asterope dived deep, deeper than anymer had gone before; and her sisters followed her. Once more they found a secret current, and

259

followed it through the darkness, until they felt the abyss fall away beneath them, and looked down into a chasm ten times deeper than any sea they knew. And there were merpeople on the islands around it.

They were few, and poor, and leaderless, for Zeus' storm had swept whole reefs away. But they were the kin of Atlantis, one of the Seven Clans, and they greeted the sisters with honor. And Asterope the gentle looked on them with pity, and chose to stay, and help heal their hurts and rebuild their homes, for she could not rebuild her own. And she taught the twin queens of that place the secret of deep diving, so that they could go down into the abyss and come back unscathed. But the sisters made no mention of where the Treasures were hidden.

Then the last four sisters went on, Maia and Taygettë and Elektra and Merope; and Poseidon's current held true, and swept them on over the curve of the watery world, into a new ocean as warm as the sun, where snakes swam and turtles walked and birds flew for a year without coming to rest. And after countless days and nights they came to an island, the Island of the Last Song, alone in a waste of sea; and there were mers there, the last of all the colonies of Atlantis.

They lived so far away that they had not heard the news of Atlas' death; and they had thought the sound of the eruption that destroyed the island was no more than thunder beyond the skyrim. They wept to hear the sisters' tale, and grieved for their loss, and offered them sanctuary. And Elektra, who loved the silence of the open ocean, chose to stay; and she taught the mers of that island the song that held the secret of the Labyrinth.

Then Maia and Taygettë and Merope swam on, back down the miles towards home. But when they came to the Flat Rock Cape and would have turned north for home, Taygettë looked at her sisters and said, "We have seen the oceans, and they have lit in me a fire which will not be quenched. I cannot go home until I have seen them all. My way lies there, beyond the sunset," and she pointed to the burning track that led into the west.

And her sisters knew that her fierce heart would not be persuaded; and so they kissed her, and blessed her, and let her go. And the songs say that Taygettë swam on alone, west and south through seas of opal, even to the edge of the southern ice; and the wonders she saw and the battles she fought were beyond all counting.

And at last she came to the Black Crag Head at the very tip of the Coast of Great Rivers; and there were merpeople there, the southernmost colony of Atlantis. And there, at last, she stayed, for she loved the roar and crash and heave of the stormy breakers, and the mountains burst into a fire which matched her fiery heart.

But Merope and Maia swam on north without her, weary now and bereft. And they passed through the White Shark Roads, and swam north with the red coast on their right. In time, the red gave way to green forests, and rivers thick with mud, and marshes where the birds swarmed thicker than glassfish on a reef. And there, to their wonder, they found a strange race of merpeople, hidden in the mud and marshes at the river's mouth; a people who were short and dark, with great bulging eyes, but their voices were the sweetest the sisters had ever heard. And Maia, who loved singing above all else, felt her heart grow light within her, and realized that she had found her home; and she stayed there with the marshmers, to turn the sea to music.

Then last of all Merope swam on alone, back to the

ruin of Atlantis, and the narrow cave, and the beaches of the seals; but the beaches were empty, and the seals gone. Then she set to work, and made in secret a vessel all of gold, and into it she sang the map songs of all the oceans of the world. And in time, other mers came to her, hearing that their princess had returned; and they sat with her and learned her songs, never knowing that they were both history and map. And Thettis, the wise queen, came to her, and would have made her queen again.

But Merope said, "You are queen by right, and the right queen. Nomer could lead our people as you have done. Lead them now, and I will teach them, and together we will keep hope alive. Only, when spring comes, let us lead them together to the Diamond Seas, for our sisters will be waiting." And Thettis bowed, as to a queen.

So when spring came, Merope called, and Thettis came to her, and together they led their people out to sea, north and ever northwards, through the Sapphire Sea, and the Emerald Sea, and the Sea of Jet. And when they came to the Diamond Sea, the sisters and their clans were there, so for a little space there was music and love and laughter beneath the ever turning sun, and their hearts were eased. And when the night began to thicken in the air and the ice to thicken on the water, they parted and swam south, each to their own place; and each clan guarded the secret it had been given.

And so the years rolled on like waves to a beach. And ever the humans spread and grew, and fought and killed and multiplied; and ever Andromeda's Curse galled them like a harpoon in a wound, so that they had no rest. The more they took, the more they desired; and the sea groaned under their ships. And ever the merpeople dwindled like foam before the wind, so that one by one *their caves grew empty, and their voices fell silent, and their songs rang faint above the surf.*

But still, year on year, the battered bands swam north to the Diamond Seas, and sang their songs, and told their tales, and kept the memory of Atlantis alive. And still from generation to generation the secrets were passed down in whispers, of hidden treasures and hidden knowledge; and the little beacon of hope kept flickering, like seafire within a wave.

And every sunset the waves flamed red and gold, and the image of the golden trident lay across the sea; and every moonrise the black water glittered white, and the image of the glass scepter pointed to the sky; and everywhere the storm clouds rolled and darkened, the image of the black rod swam beneath the waves.

And far apart, in Atlas' Ocean, and Poseidon's Deep, and the Sun-Warmed Sea, the three secrets lay hidden, whispered from generation to generation. And deep in the Labyrinth, the Treasures slumbered.

And the oceans waited.

23
Stormdancer

As the water closed over her head, Mielikki took a death grip on Ukko's dead fin and arched her body forwards. Hands clutched at her. She kicked out, knocking something solid aside, and then she was plummeting downwards as his weight dragged her towards the abyss. Once again Ukko's cold skin was against her arm; once more they were diving together; but this time he would not curve back up to the sunlight. She heard the school shouting behind her, but their voices were far away. The fathoms flashed past, twain, thrain, fortwé, past the reach of netmen and nets, and still she went on down...

At fortwé fathoms she looked one last time, and saw in the glare of her sonar the dark eye and enigmatic smile. Ukko looked as if he were laughing at a joke she could not see. Mielikki leaned forwards, and for the first and last time kissed that cold, scarred forehead.

- Go in peace, - she whispered, and let him go.

At once her own dive slowed, and the great gray body dropped below her. In a second he was out of sight, lost in the blackness of the night-time deeps, but still her sonar followed him, falling, always falling, deeper and deeper into the abyss. Grief stung her eyes and burned in her throat. Ukko had gone on his last dive, and nothing in the world seemed to matter any more.

But the world does not wait for grieving…

- Mielikki! -

- Get out of there! -

- What in Poseidon's name are you *doing*? -

They were there, deep in the water but still high above her, finning desperately towards the north; and higher still, the water was churning white as the ship bellowed and threshed and tried to turn and chase them.

Sound and sense came back with a crash: she realized she was hovering fortwé fathoms down, the knife still clenched in her fist, and right overhead the drift-net with its load of death was jerking back and forth, as if angry that its prey had escaped. Above, the lights were lashing back and forth, probing the sea.

Terror choked her. What had she *done*? She angled upwards and kicked violently, surging away from the seductive depths, while the school waved and screamed and cursed her.

- You idiot! -

- Are you mad? -

- What have you done, silence take you? -

- They saw you! -

Viliga surged down to meet her, a bruise mottling half his face.

- You're crazy! You could have broken my jaw! -

Behind him, Riakka stooped like a fishing eagle.

- They saw you! They saw you! You little fool,

they *saw* you! -

Mielikki flinched from their anger; even Pel looked appalled by what she had done. Only Helmi did not look angry: her eyes were full of terror.

- We've got to get out of here! - Helmi called, panic cracking in her voice. - That ship is coming! -

The ship was churning the water white, heaving and wallowing round.

- Of course it is! They saw her! - Riakka screamed. - Swim! Swim for your lives! -

There was no more time for shouting then, no more time for anything but a desperate, flat-out race. At least Mielikki's dive had taken them under the net: the sea to the north was clear, and they raced away as if every shark ever born was on their tails. At such a speed, a lungful of air could last only minutes: they angled shallower, burst out of the waves, snatched a breath and raced on. Somewhere in her mind, Mielikki marveled at the speed they were going: she had never swum so fast before.

- We're going the wrong way! - Pel gasped suddenly; he was already fathoms behind the rest.

- What? - snapped Riakka.

- Wrong way! We need to head more to the west! -

- With those nets out there? That's insane! -

They crashed out of another wave and gasped a desperate breath.

"But how will we find the parents?" he yelled. The last word was half lost in spray as the wave swept down on them.

- They'll be… heading north too! We'll … find them! - Thettis gasped, spitting out foam.

- How? -

- We'll find them! Now shut up and swim! -

The thunder boat bellowed and churned like a living thing. Men ran to and fro on the decks, pointing and shouting. Engines roared. The rusty bow swung north, then jerked east, as though it could not decide which way to turn. The drift-net flailed through the water. The buoys leaped and jerked. Waves broke white around it. Lightning crackled. Voices clashed. Men argued, face to face.

The school was barely a mile away, finning desperately to the north...

A figure stormed onto the deck, taller and broader than the rest, in venomous yellow: the captain of the *Artemis*, the man who had laid the nets. His roar of rage drowned the shouting. His fists separated the arguing men. The sheer force of his anger drove them back to their places. Then he was shouting orders, his massive arms gesturing frantically.

The school was a mile and a half away, but exhaustion was dragging them back...

Steel blades flashed in the searchlights. The net shuddered. All of a sudden it broke free, and slide back into the waves. The engine roared triumphantly. The ship backed water, eased away from the net and swung its bow towards the north.

Two miles away, the school broke the surface and dragged air into burning lungs...

Spray crashed across the ship's bow. It rocked and heaved crazily, searchlights stabbing back at the lightning. The thunder of the engines rose to a scream. The sea boiled white behind it.

- Can't! - gasped Pel weakly, holding his side in pain. - Can't go on! -

Riakka threw a glance over her shoulder and kept on swimming.

- Riakka! - Mielikki yelled, swinging in beside Pel. - Slow down! -

- Shut up! You've caused enough trouble already! - was the furious reply. - Keep swimming, or it'll catch us! -

Mielikki flinched: she had never heard Riakka so angry, or so scared.

"Lights!" yelled Dohan, snatching a glance backwards as they broke the surface.

Mielikki snapped a look over her shoulder as she flew: there, between one crest and the next, blades of light seared the darkness as the *Artemis* smashed her way up a wave.

"They're catching us! They're going to get us! This is all your fault!" Viliga raged.

Mielikki looked around desperately, but there was nowhere to hide, nowhere to run, just the wild, vast, stormy ocean.

"Just swim!" Thettis shouted, plunging ahead.

- I ... can't, - Pel panted, and suddenly it was as if something broke inside him, and he rolled belly-up to the waves. Beside him, Helmi was flailing with her arms in the last gasp of exhaustion. They had come too far, too fast, for too long; they had nothing left to go on with.

The storm roared around them, hungry for the kill.

Mielikki looked at her friend and her brother,

and all of a sudden her heart turned to fire-coral within her: hard, angry, aflame.

They're killing us without even seeing us. They smashed our home, now they're hunting us.

Lightning flashed, right overhead.

I broke the secret. I was seen.

Thunder cracked the sky in two.

It's my job to fix it.

She looked south, eyes ablaze.

What if they catch me? a terrified part of her wailed.

Then they catch me, the answer came. *They're not having the others.*

She set her jaw.

"Pel!" she called, and there was a new tone in her voice, a whip-crack of command that made every head jerk round. "Can you remember the map songs?"

They stared at her stupidly, hearing the ship's motors hammering nearer. Its lights were burning over the waves.

"The songs! Pel, what comes after the Lone Rock in the songs?"

He stared at her, eyes glazed, but something inside his head was still working. His voice came out hoarse and cracked.

"The plain, then the trench, then the Dry Reefs…"

"Right! Swim that way! Take Helmi with you, and swim to the Dry Reefs! I'll meet you there!"

The idea burned her, so clear that she felt no need to explain it: surely they could see? But the school were looking at her in bewilderment and fear.

"Don't you see?" she burst out. "I'll swim back, let them see me, and lead them back south! You go north! When I get away, I'll come to the Dry Reefs and meet you!"

"Mielikki!" Pel gaped in horror.

"No!" Helmi screamed.

She ignored them and spoke directly to Riakka, shouting over the gale. "We can't outswim that boat! Pel and Helmi are too tired! You've got to lead them. And I'm the best swimmer apart from you. I'll lead them away!"

For a second that seemed to last a year, Riakka and Thettis looked at one another, and the exhausted school, and the blazing lights behind.

"Come *on*!" Mielikki urged them desperately. "There isn't time!"

Riakka clenched her fists. "Better to lose one than lose all of us," she said brutally. "You got us into this: you get us out of it. You're on your own. Dohan, Viliga, lead us north. Mielikki, go!"

It was not so much a command as a curse. It cut straight through Mielikki's determination and left her feeling scared, cold and very much alone. She looked at her friends. Helmi's eyes were terrified, Pel's beseeching; the rest would not meet her gaze.

"Go!" shouted Riakka angrily.

"Sorry," she whispered to her brother and her friend. None of the others heard her.

She turned and dived back towards the lights. Behind her, she heard the swish of their tails. Despite herself, she looked back over her shoulder. They were already gone.

For a second, she felt as if darkness had

swallowed her too. She was on her own, lost in the midst of Atlas' Ocean, with danger ahead and on every side. She had broken the secret. She had been seen. She had thrown away three myriad years of secrecy.

But how could I do anything else? she screamed in silence at the storm. *How could I have left Ukko in the net?*

A wave broke over her head. Foam pressed her downwards. Fear stabbed her. She stared into the depths, and thought her heart would burst.

Poseidon, what do I do?

The wave rolled on. She surfaced, gasping. The wind tore through her hair.

And Poseidon answered.

Again the lightning flashed. The thunder boomed like an earthquake. She shook the spray from her eyes, and for a frozen heartbeat, she could see.

She was in the trough between two breakers. All along it, the water was streaked with foam. The clouds boiled. Spray lashed skywards as though sky and sea had gone to war.

And in the middle of that hell of wild water, a little bird fluttered along the wave.

It was barely bigger than her hand, black as soot save for the white patches on its wings and rump. It looked as vulnerable as a leaf in a gale. Yet it hung there with its long legs paddling the front of the monstrous wave, as calm and carefree as if the tempest was its home. It was a Stormdancer, what the netmen called a storm petrel, and its appearance was so shocking in that mad night that Mielikki stared.

Then the lightning winked out and the heartbeat of wonder was gone.

A Stormdancer, she thought numbly. *Dancing on the waves.*

Dancing on the waves...

It was as if a voice spoke out of the sea to her.

Dance for them, Stormdancer!

Hard fire blossomed in her heart. Her fists clenched. The noise of the boat was like a wound.

"I'll dance for you," she snarled.

She turned and sped towards the boat.

Behind her, the school battled their way northwards. Riakka was half-carrying Helmi; Thettis was supporting Pel. Every ear was turned to follow the engines, every heart hammering with fear. They had been furious with Mielikki until she turned back; now their anger had sunk down to join Ukko in the abyss. Helmi was not the only one with tears in her eyes.

Raging, the storm drove them on.

Mielikki surfaced. Close to, the fishing boat was a terrifying black shape armed with spears of light. It crabbed up over a wave and foamed down the far side. For half a heartbeat, she stopped, appalled at the size and noise of it; but it was far too late to turn back. She set her teeth, felt a wave heave up behind her, waited for the moment as she had once waited when she played catch with Ukko...

Dance for them, Stormdancer ...

... and jumped.

Right through the beam of a searchlight she leapt: a burning, golden dart. At once there was a roar of voices, and the ship staggered and lurched. Mielikki landed, sliced through a wave, swerved to her right and jumped again.

It was terrifying how quickly the lights whipped round: they were like stingray tails, lashing towards her. She hit the water. It flared silver around her. By reflex she went deeper, burrowing into the waves like a scared eel. The engines howled as the ship swung round to follow her. Some tiny part of her mind noted the sound with a flare of triumph: she had drawn it away from the school. But the rest was awash with terror. She cast one flying glance behind her, saw the lights stabbing into the water, turned on her head and dived straight downwards, clawing for safer depths.

All at once there came a sound, a shrill, shrieking "EE-EE-EE-EE-EE!" so loud it almost burst her eardrums. She screamed and clapped her hands to her head, corkscrewing out of control. The sound was like a merman's navigating sonar, but a hundred times louder.

They've got sonar!

The realization struck her like Zeus' lightning bolt.

They've seen me!

Her mind froze in horror.

I'll never get away!

We'll see about that! a furious voice inside her snapped back.

Her body took over. She twisted sideways and dived still deeper, desperately hoping to get away from that appalling noise.

She was twelve fathoms down when it hit her again, a scream that shook every bone in her body. The ship came roaring after her, tethered to her with an invisible line. In desperation, she twisted further to the right. It lumbered after her, battling the waves.

It can't turn as fast as me! she thought with a blaze of hope.

But again the scream came, filling the sea with lightning. The boat straightened up behind her, slamming directly into the waves. She kicked harder, speeding ahead, but it was accelerating again. She could feel it like a second heartbeat. It was gaining … it was gaining…

All of a sudden it was right overhead. She looked up in horror as the long black shape shot by, blasting out foam. Again, its sonar screamed. She swerved to the left by instinct – and watched in amazement as it crashed straight on without reaching down to take her.

Then she was behind it, and gaping with disbelief. The ship was past! It had driven right over her head, and had not caught her! Mielikki knew nothing of netmen: she had not realized that a ship alone cannot catch anything, without nets, or harpoons, or dynamite. She did not know that the netmen had set off after her blindly, desperate to catch the first mermaid to be seen in human history. All they had was the remains of a drift-net, hacked through by their own knives – and a drift-net trailed behind a boat at full speed is more likely to catch in its propellers and wrench them clean off than it is to catch a mermaid.

Mielikki knew none of that: she only knew that she was still alive, that the boat had had the perfect chance to catch her, and missed it. The knowledge ran through her like a breaking wave: *I'm still alive!*

All at once, she laughed, and her fear dropped away into the abyss, and in its place was a wild excitement, too great to contain.

- Can't catch me! - she yelled up through the storm, and laughed to hear the thunder boat roar.

She shot to the surface with a great whoosh of air, saw the boat plunge into a turn ahead of her, and hurled herself after it to keep it from the school.

Once more she came up close to it, once more she leapt, and this time she shouted as she flew, a deep-throated battle shout that even a netman could hear. It was the war-cry of Atlantis that nomer in those waters had used for three thousand years; a name like a spear in the heart of the human race, until the Curse was lifted.

"Andromeda!"

The lights swung towards her. The ship lurched round. The propellers churned the water. She ignored them, and jumped straight across the searchlight beam.

She heard the sonar peal as she hit the water; but all of a sudden she felt she could ignore it, as she could ignore Viliga's taunts. It could not hurt her just by shouting, she knew that now, and at this rate she could keep it chasing her for hours. The storm was still rising, the wind a scream every time she surfaced, great foam-piled breakers sweeping out of the night and crumbling as they came. She pointed herself straight at a thundering crest and kicked for the south, away from the school. The boat turned and thundered after her, smashing headlong into the waves, slewing crazily from side to side as it pursued her.

Mielikki jumped and glanced back. She saw the blinding fingers of the searchlight reach for her, and swam as she had never swum before. She had always been strong; too strong for the sheltered waters of the island, too strong for her half-grown mind to tame. She had never learned to control her strength fully; she had never needed to learn. There had always been barriers: her youth, her fear, her doubts about herself. Now she was out in the fury of the open ocean, and she had to break through those barriers, or die.

Between one leap and the next, her body clenched itself and turned to a thing of speed and fury. Fire coursed through her veins. New strength and speed flowered within her. The ship's screams and her own battle shout were the birth cry of a new mermaid, strong, swift, unstoppable. As she hit the water, she arched her back and jumped again, soaring over the collapsing wave like a spear, a sailfish, a Stormdancer; and again, and again, faster than she had ever swum before, faster than anymer in Atlantis had ever swum, and only a marlin could have caught her as she fled down the waves.

Again the sonar shook the sea. Again she

swerved, a blinding right-angle turn to the right, westwards, so that the ship was forced to turn side-on the gale, rolling in her wake. She shot to the surface, smashed through a wave, snatched a breath as she flew, felt the searchlight flicker over her and plunged back down into the sheltering water.

Leap, dive, swerve... Leap, dive, swerve... The bellow of engines and the yell of sonar were part of the sea, part of herself. The boat was a black shape blundering behind her. Her lungs and muscles burned with effort, but still more with the excitement of battle. The netmen were as much an enemy as any shark, and Mielikki tormented them as only a mermaid could, diving, swerving, dancing, bursting out of the sea right ahead of the ship, letting it hurtle up behind her and swerving to right or left or straight down at the last moment, leaving it floundering.

All at once there was a splash just beside her; she ducked by reflex, and saw a long metal shape plunge past her. Another followed, and another, so close it almost grazed her tail. She risked a glance behind: yellow-dressed netmen lined the ship's rails, brandishing bits of metal and wood and hurling them in her wake. Behind them, a flash of lightning split the sky, and the ship stood out black and ghastly against black and ghastly clouds.

Mielikki dived. A second later an iron bar splashed sideways-on across the wave she had just left. She stood on her head and clawed for depth, but it must have been a lucky throw: the next two bars flew wild. Again the sonar screamed, again the ship veered in pursuit. In a snatched second Mielikki sent her own sonar ahead, a wide, long-range fan of sound, and almost shouted in excitement as she heard the echoes come back off the pinnacles of the Lone Rock. *Deep water. Coral and crags. A place to hide!*

If I can reach it...

She accelerated, kicking for the safety of the Rock with every ounce of power she had. Again she sent a stream of clicks ahead, faster and narrower to light her way – and the blood froze in her veins. A mile ahead of her, right between her and the Rock, a dolphin hung upside down in the water, motionless.

For a second, she froze in bewilderment; it was so unexpected, so unreal, that she could not grasp or understand it. Then the fishing-boat gave another sonar scream, and in its glare she saw it clearly, lit as if by lightning: the drowned body of an immature dolphin, and around it the wispy half echoes and glints of a drift-net.

She stared, mouth open in shock, so stunned she almost forgot to swim; then all of a sudden, horror flared. Somehow the ship must have left its net behind, back where they had first swum into it. It had chased them north, and she had led it south again – right back into its nets.

There was no time to think. Abruptly, two metal bars slammed into the water above her. The roar of the boat crashed back in upon her. She looked at the black hull, the Rock, the corpse, and a desperate plan formed in her mind between one lightning flash and the next.

First, she had to see. She stood on her tail and raced for the surface, breaking out of the waves in a vertical jump that took her two fathoms clear of the water. In the second of flight she stared to the south. The ship's searchlights glinted off the line of buoys snaking through the water – glints bright enough for mermaid eyes to see, but not the weak eyes of men... Then she splashed down headfirst.

Next, she had to be seen. She swooped upwards and jumped again, leaping through the lights. The boat swerved and came thundering after her, leaving a great creamy slew of bubbles down the back of the breakers. Mielikki threw one glance at the hull towering above her, and kicked for her life. The ship was right on top of her. She could feel its bow wave driving her on. The buoys were racing towards her. Above, the crewmen clustered on the rails and heaved up an armful of net, ready to throw...

In the very nick of time, Mielikki gathered herself and jumped. The searchlights flared around her. The line of buoys flashed past underneath her. The thrown net missed her tail by a handspan.

And the *Artemis*, surging forward at full power, bored straight on – into its own net.

For a moment, Mielikki thought that she was caught. As she hit the water and clawed desperately deeper, she heard the scrape of mesh on steel, the knocking of buoys against the hull, the engine's triumphant roar. Then there was a tumult of voices yelling, gears crashing, metal groaning and snapping, and mile upon mile of discarded drift-net wrapped itself around the drive-shaft, piled up bulging along the metal, and wrenched the propeller off.

The engine screamed. Mielikki flinched. Despite herself, she looked back, and saw the black hull come skidding sideways, lurching as if driven by some malignant spirit.

She watched in awe. She had no idea of the damage a net can do. She had only wanted to entangle the ship, and stop it long enough to escape.

But now every vestige of control was gone. The bow tossed wildly. The netmen were running around in panic. The nets jerked like a kraken's arms. The noise of its engine was a death cry.

Beneath the black hull rose something blacker still: a wave like a mountain, impossibly tall, as dark as the wave that had sunk Atlantis. Spindrift flew from its crest. Foam poured down its face.

Now the ship was leaning on its side, white water pouring over its deck. Higher the wave climbed, and higher still. For a freakish second the searchlights bored straight into it, as if they were trying to hold off death. The netmen froze.

Then the crest crumbled, and toppled forwards.

And the ocean slammed down on the fishing boat like Poseidon's revenge.

Lightning flashed. Metal screamed. A black shape went rolling through the water. The gale roared in triumph.

The *Artemis* was gone.

Mielikki stared. It was too much to comprehend. One minute the ship had been there, bellowing its bloodlust. The next, the sea had taken it. She shook her head, stunned and shaking in every limb. The next wave lifted under her, rushed past and swept on. Still she stared, uncomprehending.

The net almost killed her then: mile after mile

of treacherous webs, snagged on the dead ship's hull. From left and right, the buoys came racing towards her, hissing with hunger. By some last malice of Zeus', the wreck corkscrewed as it sank, and the buoys twitched viciously sideways and lashed at Mielikki from behind.

At the last moment she heard the ravenous slurp. She spun round, and they were barely a fathom away, bearing down on her. She back-paddled desperately, flailing with hands and tail, and perhaps Poseidon truly was watching over her, for at that moment a new wave rose and thrust her backwards. The net shrugged in fury and plunged beneath her. The topmost rope scraped her tail, and then it was gone down into the darkness. And far, far below, the netmen struggled in the nets that they had laid; struggled among the corpses of fish and dolphins, and died.

Mielikki took a deep breath. With shaking hands, she pushed the hair back from her face. The ship was gone, the men, the nets. The nightmare was over. The hunt was done. She could find the school. They could go home … no, not home, because they had no home left. They could go on, and find their parents, and seek a new home on the deep ocean, where netmen never came.

Stormdancer, the gale roared around her.

"Stormdancer, " she whispered back.

Slowly, she turned towards the north. Slowly, she began to swim. The gale still blew, the breakers still heaved, but it was as if they could not touch her. She had come into her own.

Mielikki, the Stormdancer, had found her

name.

She gathered speed. As lightning flashed, she looked up at the sky. In a break of the clouds she saw the stars racing past, the Seven Sisters looking down on her. She smiled and nodded to them, a silent tribute. Then she looked down, across the backs of the thundering waves, and headed for the north.

Somewhere out there, the school must be waiting for her. Somewhere, there would be safety and rest. But for now, there was the storm, and the swim, and the fury of the ocean.

The last mer of Atlantis had swum out to sea.

Merspeech: a short glossary

Not all merwords translate easily into human speech. This list explains the words which ten-fingered land-dwellers may find strange.

Assassin whale: killer whale.

Benthic: living in or on the sea bed. Free-swimming creatures make fun of benthic ones.

Convocation: the annual gathering of mers of Atlantis in the Diamond Sea.

Crash hull: a short, fast, noisy motor-boat or jet-ski. Usually seen close to shore.

Demersal: living just above the sea bed. Often used as a curse word.

Diamond Sea: the Arctic Ocean.

Fathom: with your arms outstretched, the distance from fingertip to fingertip across your chest. A mer fathom is slightly shorter than a human one, and measures one and a half human yards.

Fin's breadth: for mers of Atlantis, half a fathom. (The Oldmers have a different measurement, but that is a story for another day.)

Floater: a mer who is too fat to sink, especially a merchild. "Floater" is an insult.

Fortwé: four dozen. Mers count and calculate in twelves. The sequence continues fivetwé, sixtwé, and so on.

Ghostwhale: narwhal. Mers call them "Ghostwales" for the way they blend into the dappled gray waters of the Diamond Sea. Their human name means "corpse-whale," because of their coloring.

Handred: twelve dozen.

Handswimmer: a mer who is too weak to swim with their tail alone, and uses their hands to stay afloat. "Handswimmer" is an insult.

Mutter-car: any small motor vehicle on land.

Myriad: the mer equivalent of the human "thousand," but totalling twelve handreds, or 1,728. The word is often used more loosely, to indicate any large number.

Pelagic: living in open water. Also used to mean "wonderful."

Sapphire Sea: all the oceans which lie between the Equator and the Tropics.

Sea-mile: a myriad fathoms, travelled across the surface. It is fractionally longer than a human nautical mile.

Silence: metaphor for "death." It is the most shocking curse word a mer can use.

Spy-bird: Arctic tern.

Stormdancer: storm petrel.

Striped shark: tiger shark.

Thrain: three dozen.

Thunder boat: any large motorised ship. So called for the rumble of their motors, which carries for miles underwater.

Thunder machine: any large motor vehicle on land.

Trrr: the sound of indecision. A human would say "er..."

Twain: two dozen.

Twe-one: thirteen. The next number in the sequence is twe-two, and so on upwards to twain.

Tweleven: twenty-three.
White-belly: great white shark.